# Crocodile Tears

## PRICKLE ISLAND ZOO
### BOOK FOUR

ALI K. MULFORD

ISBN: 978-1-923184-18-3 (ebook)

ISBN: 978-1-923184-20-6 (Paperback)

Cover: Yummy Book Covers

Map: Holly Dunn Designs

# Crocodile Tears

## Ali K. Mulford

*Dedicated to the toucan who traumatized a film crew*

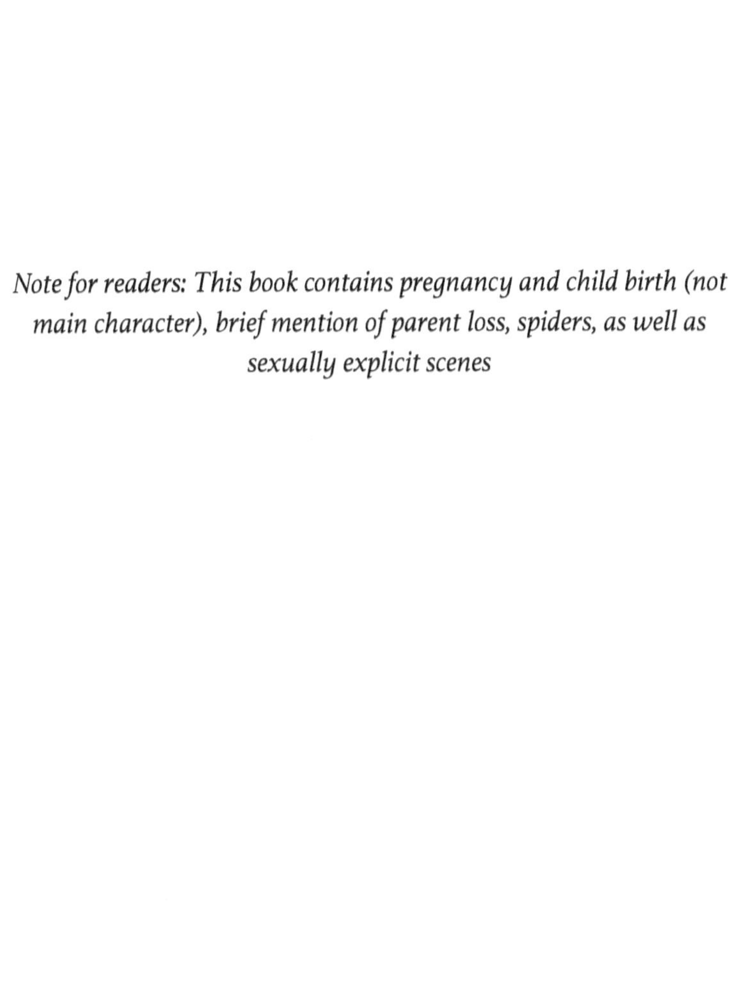

*Note for readers: This book contains pregnancy and child birth (not main character), brief mention of parent loss, spiders, as well as sexually explicit scenes*

PRICKLE ISLAND ZOO
KEY
TOILETS
FOOD
SHOPPING
FREE WIFI
GIFT SHOP + ENTRY
ENTRY
VET HOSPITAL
CAFÉ
PLAYGROUND
REPTILE HOUSE
THE PECKISH PEACOCK
SAVANNAH
AVIARY
BABOONS

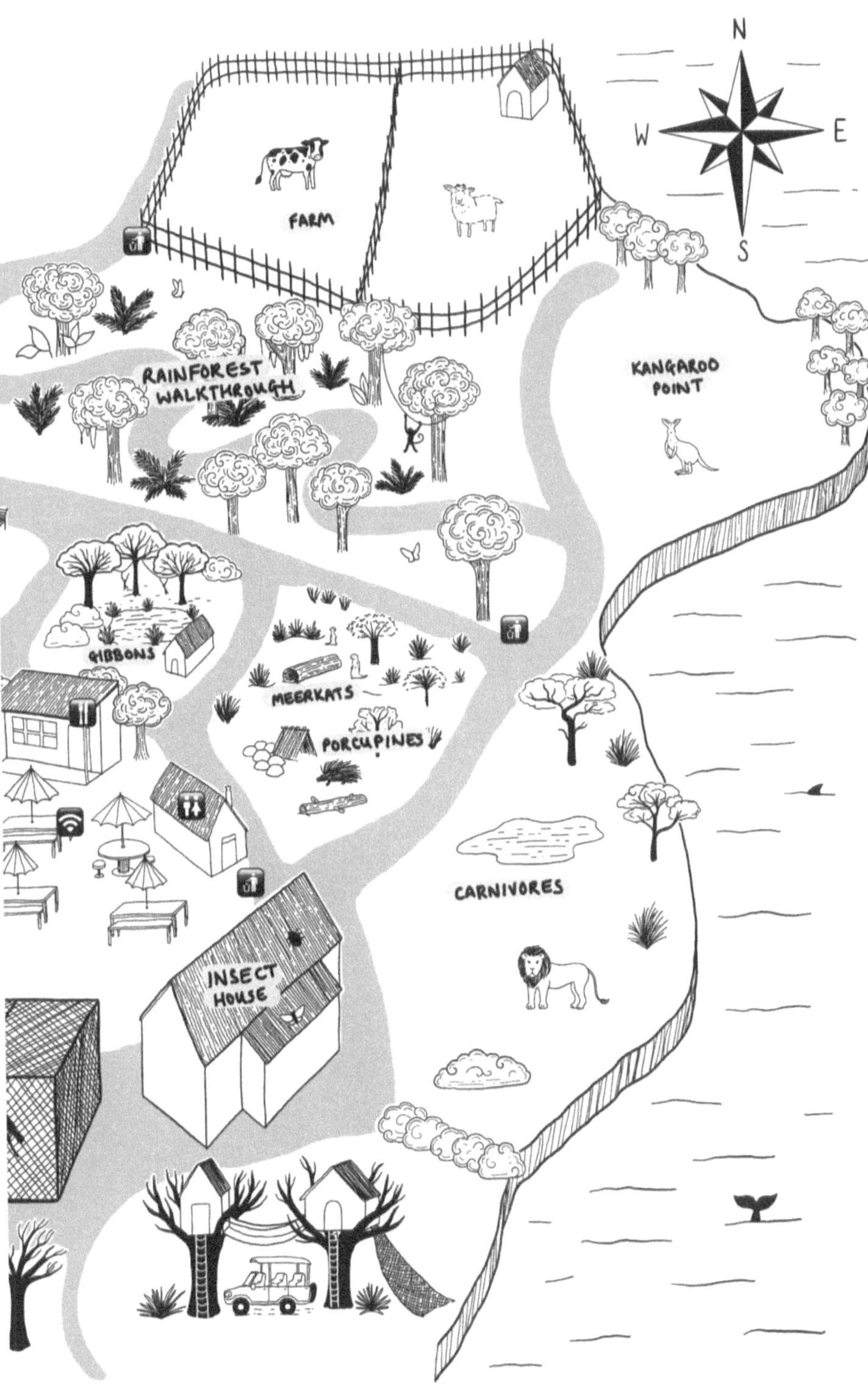

N
W
E
S
FARM
RAINFOREST WALKTHROUGH
KANGAROO POINT
GIBBONS
MEERKATS
PORCUPINES
CARNIVORES
INSECT HOUSE

# MEET THE ZOO TEAM

Evelyn Lachlan (she/her) CEO of Prickle Island Zoo

Hawk Lachlan (he/him) Carnivore Keeper

Lark Lachlan (she/her) (Moved to New Zealand)

Finch Lachlan (she/her) Head Veterinarian

Dove Lachlan (she/her) Birds and Primates

Heron Lachlan (they/them) Hoofstock Keeper

Crane Lachlan (he/him) Reptiles and Inverts

Wren Lachlan (she/they) Birds and Rainforest

Hannah Murphey (she/her) Farm animals

Frankie Benedetti (she/her) Head Chef

Aya (she/her) Food Prep Manager

Mateo (he/him) Gift Shop Manager

# Chapter One

Dove

I never thought I'd want to murder someone for sending me a fruit basket, but movie star Deacon Harrow might make me change my mind.

"If you stare at that thing any harder it might explode," Mom said as she cradled her favorite koala-shaped mug.

"If he thinks he will win my forgiveness with a fruit basket, he's even more delusional than I thought," I grumbled, angrily refilling my coffee cup.

"It's not addressed to you. It's for *me*," Mom chided. "A thank you for letting us use the zoo as a filming location for his new movie. Our little zoo is about to be one step from stardom! We should make a sign that people can take selfies with that has Deacon's face." She swatted the air in front of me to catch my attention as I pointedly ignored her enthusiasm. "You know, I heard Ivy Blanc is going to be his co-star. I hope we'll get to meet her!"

I narrowed my gaze at my starry-eyed mother. "Listen to yourself. So easily wooed by a Hollywood starlet coming to the zoo."

"*You* were the one who orchestrated this whole thing," Mom pointed out. "The production money *saved* the zoo. If you hadn't barged into Mrs. Westworth's office with that contract when you did, this place would probably be a golf course by now, hon. I'd have thought you'd be gloating about it instead of complaining."

"I don't want credit anymore," I muttered, folding my arms tightly across my chest. "I don't regret finding a solution to our problems, but I wish that solution hadn't involved insufferable, arrogant, toxic, movie star bastard Deacon Harrow."

"That's a lot of adjectives for a fruit basket, sweetie," Mom said. "A fruit basket that was addressed to *me*, mind you."

Despite what my mother said, I knew it was really an olive branch that I was meant to see. Deacon Harrow might be a movie star now, but I'd known him when he'd just been dorky little Deacon, and this was *clearly* his cowardly way of trying to win my forgiveness. He could never handle the cold shoulder with me, even when we'd been kids. Fifteen years might've passed since the last time I'd seen him in the flesh, but I knew an apology fruit basket when I saw one.

"It's not even signed by him," I snapped, plucking the note and flashing the curly, cursive letters to Mom. "Some assistant probably wrote it for him. There are *love hearts* over the 'I's."

"Lots of gift shops write the notes for people who order online." Mom shrugged. Her breezy nonchalance made my muscles tighten with barely-restrained anger. "I think it was very sweet."

"Sweet? Whose side are you on?" I balked.

"There are sides now?" Mom asked, amused. I swore all of my siblings had learned their provocation tactics from the master herself. She'd been present at the creation of the buttons she was now so aptly pushing.

"Hell yeah, there are sides," I demanded with a point of my finger. "You, Evelyn Lachlan, are a noted zoologist and conservationist, and he, *Deacon Harrow*"—I gagged on his name for dramatics—"is the face of an energy drink company that just made the critically endangered Almadran skink go extinct in the wild. You *cannot* call him sweet or you're siding with the species killer."

"I can't believe I'm saying this, but I'm siding with Dove on this one, Mom," Wren called from the couch. She sat so slumped down, working on her knitting, that only the tiniest top of her honey-brown hair could be seen.

Already in her Prickle Island Zoo khakis, my youngest sister worked away on her latest craft project. She was one of my few siblings who would rather chime in to established drama than create her own, of which I was most grateful in this moment.

"There really aren't sides, honey," Mom called. "What Zap Energy did was wrong, but how much are celebrities even involved in the products they endorse? Deacon might be tied up in contracts he can't pull out of even if he wants to. We don't have the full picture."

"He has Taylor Swift level money, Mom," I hissed. "He doesn't need a brand deal, and he certainly has the legal teams to get him out of it if he wanted to. Instead, he just buries his head in the sand and says nothing. One Instagram post from him could probably raise enough money to start a skink breeding program, and he stays silent because he's a selfish, piece-of-crap celebrity."

"Well, that selfish celebrity inadvertently saved our family zoo so I can't completely hate him," Mom said gently. "And he was such a good kid. I can't believe the same guy would do something like that." She clicked her tongue, mouth pinching in disappointment. "Shame what fame does to a person."

"Shame," I echoed bitterly.

I fumed over to the kitchen island, grabbing the fruit basket and getting two steps to the trash can before thinking better of it. I really couldn't handle the needless food waste, even if it would've felt *really* good to throw it out. I'd feed it to the baboons and then leave a basket of the leftover scraps in Deacon's trailer with my own thank you note . . . maybe even add in some feces for good measure just so he fully comprehended how I felt. That would be far pettier and far more satisfying . . . and far more of a *me* thing to do.

"It's good to have you back home, Dove," Mom said with a surprisingly earnest smile. "The mornings have been eerily quiet since the twins moved out. I'm glad for a little angst again."

*Angst.* Great. Out of my seven siblings, when had I become branded as the angsty one?

At twenty-seven, I had only lived away from home for one blissful year before my younger siblings, Heron and Crane, had ruined it by moving into the renovated monkey enclosure that my eldest brother had turned into housing down the hill from our childhood home. I'd decided that any freedom I'd gained from moving a hundred yards away had been ruined by the twin tornadoes moving in. So, I'd Uno reverse carded my way back home to the twins' vacated bedroom and was enjoying the relative peace of just Mom, Wren, Mom's elderly collie pit bull mix, Phoebe, and me.

"What are you going to do when I move out again?" I teased. "I can give you Yellow. She sounds just like me and has plenty of *angst* to spare."

The sulphur-crested cockatoo had been in my care since she'd been a chick, and even though she was happily integrated into a flock now, she still had all of the Dove-isms down.

Mom waved away my suggestion. "Soon the house will be filled with grandbabies!"

"Just one grandbaby," Wren corrected. "And that grandbaby will be living in the cottage at the top of the zoo with its parents."

"I'm sure Hawk and Hannah wouldn't mind if the baby had a couple sleepovers with me so they could get a full night's rest," Mom said, practically bouncing with excitement.

"You'd think you'd be tired after decades of rearing orphaned baby animals," I snarked.

Mom beamed. "It just means I'm well practiced."

"This is a human, not a baby monkey we're talking about," Wren reminded us.

"Close enough," Mom and I said at once, and she laughed.

"And I've had seven humans of my own too," she reminded us, as if we could ever forget.

Prickle Island Zoo was officially on "baby watch" this spring. And it wasn't baby giraffes, or kangaroo joeys, or marmosets we were on high alert for this year. This time, it was my eldest brother's, Hawk's, partner, Hannah, who was about to pop.

We had eighteen different contingency plans for when she went into labor. I was incredibly grateful that the baby was coming outside of the busiest season. The zoo was closed outside the summer months, except for school groups and private events—a new initiative I had launched in the recent years—and for the next three weeks, we were about to be the filming location for Deacon Harrow's latest project. Still, even with a movie filming on site, the workload would be small enough that we could cover Hawk and Hannah's shifts. And

Lark and her husband, Logan, were coming over for the summer to cover for Hawk and Hannah with the new baby.

It was going to be an amazing summer. All of us together at the zoo again, plus my new, little nephew.

"That baby's feet aren't going to touch the floor for the first two years of its life," Wren joked.

"If ever," I added.

"Eventually there will be more babies to hold," Mom said wistfully. "Maybe even yours."

"Well, time to get to work," Wren said, practically leaping off the couch.

I grabbed the radio off my hip. "Roger. Go ahead."

Mom rolled her eyes. "Very slick. Your radio's still off, Dove."

I was already halfway out the door. "Sorry, Mom, got a radio call," I shouted from the doorway as Wren and I darted out.

You'd think having her three eldest children successfully shacked up would have made my mother a little more lenient on the four of us still unpaired, but no. Evelyn Lachlan was forever on the hunt for the rest of her children. She put Mrs. Bennet to shame.

As we hastened down the path to the prep kitchens, Wren said, "What in the world?"

I spotted the crowd gathered at the back gates. Five girls in their late teens stood in a tight group, peering in through the chain-link fence. They squealed when we turned the corner, but their exuberance was short-lived when they realized we were just staff members and not whoever they were searching for.

"Are they . . . fans?" Wren asked, looking at a gaggle of teen girls pressed against the gate.

"Deacon! I love you!" one shouted, and the others tittered.

I spied one exuberant girl who held a fluorescent green poster covered in cut-out images of Deacon. I ground my teeth as I was confronted by the sight of him. His coiffed flaxen hair, his deep blue eyes, his ever-present layer of stubble, his cheeky, lopsided grin as if he always had a secret . . .

"Ugh!"

*So he had a Shonda Rimes level glow up between the ages of 12 and 27, so freaking what? He was still a terrible human being.*

"Marry me, Deacon!" another girl squealed.

I rolled my eyes.

Of course they were here to catch a glimpse of a movie star —and grade A asswipe—Deacon Harrow. How had they even known he was coming here?

"He's not here for another few days," I shouted. "But if you come back in the summer, you can say you walked through the same zoo as Deacon Harrow."

The group's shoulders all collectively drooped as Wren murmured, "Always trying to sell another ticket."

"Always trying to keep this place afloat," I corrected.

"Which is how the zoo became a movie set," my little sister replied.

I shrugged. "I guess I'd sell my soul to the devil to keep our dad's dream alive."

"Oof," Wren said with a light laugh. "This guy couldn't have always been that bad if you two were friends as kids."

"Yeah," I said, feeling a weary, little ache in my chest. "People change, I guess." The sweet and nerdy boy I'd once known was gone. *Deacon Harrow* was a brand now—an actor, a pretender, and I should've known better than to call him after fifteen years, but desperate times had called for desperate measures.

I looked to see the gaggle of girls still hadn't disappeared. "He's not here!" I shouted again. "And even if he was, you should pick better people to worship. Deacon Harrow is a piece of—"

"Okay," Wren said, grabbing me by the arm and steering me

back toward the kitchens. "How are you going to survive the next three weeks of this?"

"Easy," I said, walking ahead of my sister. "Stay far away from the crew and avoid Deacon Harrow at all costs."

"And if you *do* bump into him?" Wren asked. "Think you can manage not to murder him?"

I gave my sister a sideways glance. "I make no promises."

# Chapter Two

Deacon

I smiled out at the ocean as the breeze cut through my clothes, not because I wanted to, but rather because the ferry was passing by our sailboat and one too many cell phones were pointed in my direction.

Maybe they were just taking photos of the view of the island, or maybe they were about to sell my photo to a tabloid . . . or most likely both. And if I frowned for even a *second*, I knew I'd wake up to some headline about "bad boy Deacon Harrow is looking sad after his latest breakup with supermodel Kate Schofield."

Little did they know that the nineteen-year-old British supermodel and I had never been dating. We'd been set up by our publicists for a couple opportunistic photo ops together while I'd been on a press tour in London. And soon I'd be *yet again* labeled a "playboy and heartbreaker" to keep my name in the press while filming this new romantic comedy.

And then my rom-com co-star, Ivy Blanc, and I would start our greatest acting gig yet: not the movie itself, but navigating the media storm afterwards to make everyone think we were madly in love and get more butts in theater seats.

Contracts had already been signed, my personal life leveraged for lots of money, sold to the highest bidder. I was no longer a singular person, I was a *business*, and there were a lot of people vested in keeping Deacon Harrow LLC running.

As the ferry passed and the prying eyes pulled out of view, my posture eased and I stared down at the choppy water. "Clear."

"All good." My agent—Zeke—army-crawled out from under the white leather bench as if it were perfectly normal to hide from paparazzi so they could get a better shot of his client. "Why the sad face, D-man?"

"Not sad, just not smiling," I replied, rubbing my sore jaw.

"This isn't about the whole Zap thing, is it?"

"No," I said tightly. "Although that's not necessarily helping my mood."

Zeke shook me by the shoulders, pulling the neckline of my polo shirt askew. "Loopy is already all over the Zap stuff, brother."

"His name is Luca," I said. "You'd think after six years, you'd know my assistant's name."

"It's a nickname, D-Money," Zeke chided. "Anyway, he's got a conservation organization in LA that is going to make you their new poster boy, and they're going to send some money over to the turtles—"

"Skinks—"

"Whatever," he said as he frantically texted someone. If I

had a nickel for every time I'd seen that man without a phone in his hands, I'd have ten cents. The only person worse than Zeke might be my publicist, Cody. "It'll all be old news, my man. We had this whole Kate breakup in our back pocket for just such an occasion. She even pretended to cry walking out of Nobu the other day, so we are golden. I should send her a fruit basket."

*Great.* The media thought I was the sort of guy who made beautiful, young models cry. And what was even more concerning was that that was somehow *helpful* to my public image.

I gripped the railing tighter, even as I nodded along to Zeke's debriefing. It wasn't worth fighting him on this. I wasn't my own person anymore. I was just a cog in a bigger machine, and too many booby traps were laid out before me for me to deviate from our plans.

"Listen, save the sad puppy schtick for the cameras, m'kay?" Zeke said. "We've only got two days to par-tay before I've got to catch the red eye back to LA. Your team is already at the house getting ready, we've flown in a chef who used to work for Henry Cavill, *and* your trainer is letting you have two cheat days in a row so we can have some real fun. Now, if only this island had a strip club, right?"

I looked at Zeke and let out a long-suffering sigh. He spoke like an amalgamation of eight different kinds of douchebag, but he was the best in the business so I tried to ignore it.

I'd managed to secure the Holloway Estate for my team since it was the off-season on Prickle Island. My father had been the head butler for the rich family, and apparently they were "tickled" by the success of one of their former employees' sons. I was paying an extortionate amount to stay in their home now, but I had money to blow and it was a personal vendetta of mine to stay there.

The image of the giant, sprawling estate was still branded into my mind. I'd told myself every single day over my childhood summers that one day I'd live there. And even if it was only for three weeks, I was going to make that dream a reality.

Of course, those summers I'd spent almost no time at our little cottage in the corner of the Holloway Estate and every waking moment at Prickle Island Zoo. It had been the first time I'd felt like a celebrity—getting to waltz through the front entry and skip the lines, being waved through by the front desk people. I'd been so proud that *I* was personal friends with the family who ran the zoo.

Even though my older brother and younger sister had spent summers on Prickle Island too, they hadn't thought romping around the island with a bunch of feral zoo children was as much fun as I had. I wondered how many of the Lachlan kids still lived and worked at the zoo. I wondered the most about one particular person who'd called me out of the blue two years ago like a ghost from my past.

"I really thought we should've taken the chopper—what's the point of having a helipad if you don't use it, you know? But you're right, man. The boat is the best way to see the island," Zeke said as Prickle Island came into view. "You remember much about this place?"

"Not much," I lied.

The summers between the ages of nine and twelve had been the best of my life. Fifteen years had passed by and still the memories were perfectly preserved in my mind. Well, not all of them, just the ones that involved one stubborn girl with taped-together glasses and permanent space buns that had made me wonder if her hair just grew in that shape.

The fondness of the memory warped as I remembered our last exchange.

*"Never talk to me again."*

That was the last thing she'd said to me. Dove Lachlan had called me out of the blue after over a decade of radio silence, asking me if I had any need of the zoo for swanky events or for a movie I was working on. I could hear the panic in her voice, knew she must've been desperate to even call me, and I'd instantly said yes. We'd called back and forth a few times working out the logistics—something I normally would've passed on to my team, but I'd just wanted an excuse to walk down memory lane with her. But then all of the Zap stuff had come out, and when I'd tried to call her to explain, she'd texted me "never talk to me again" and that had been it.

She'd deleted all her socials and disappeared after that text, and I wondered if it was because she didn't want to see me splashed all over her feeds, wondered if it made her stomach sour to look at me now. I had plenty of people who hated me, plenty more who thought I was a talentless hack, but I'd learned to develop a thick skin and not care what they thought. But there was one person apart from my family who knew all the holes in my armor.

My stomach dropped just thinking about it. I needed things between us to be set right, needed to prove to myself that I wasn't the guy she thought I was. The thought nettled me. In a life that was anything but normal, one where thousands of keyboard warriors professed their hate for me every day, I needed my childhood best friend to still think of me as a human and not a brand.

And now I'd be staying on her island, filming at her zoo for three weeks—something that I had thought would be a fun reconnection with an old friend, but now I knew would be an awkward reminder that I was no longer that kid who'd loved hearing her bird fun facts and binge-watching *Lord of the Rings*.

If I tried hard enough, I could probably manage to avoid seeing Dove altogether. My assistant, Luca, was incredibly skilled at shielding me from people I didn't want to see.

But I already knew I'd be seeking her out. This was a vendetta I couldn't let go. I set myself a challenge right then and there as the springtime sun shone down on Prickle Island: I would get Dove Lachlan to accept my apology and be my friend again before the three weeks were up, so help me God.

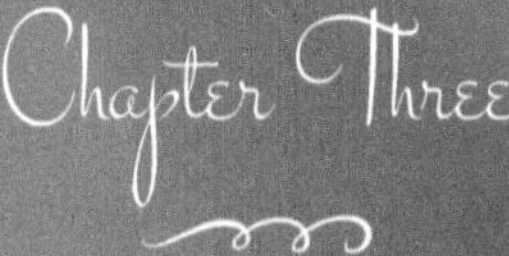

# Chapter Three

Dove

I had once considered myself a member of many nerdy fandoms . . . but seeing the horde of fangirls outside the zoo gates was making me rethink what it meant to be a "superfan."

"Of all the places," I muttered as I held Eddie the toucan for his blood draw. "How did they even get here?"

Finch released a huff as she grabbed a fresh pair of rubber gloves. "Petey said they've added another ferry slot to the spring timetable to handle them all."

"Seriously?" I grumbled. "One of the many benefits of living at a private zoo on a tiny island is that we don't get unwanted visitors—including crazed fans and paparazzi. Increasing the ferry trips is only encouraging them."

"Not their fault." Finch's lab jacket bunched at the neck as she shrugged. "They're just keeping up with demand."

Prickle Island was a sanctuary for the rich elite who flocked here in the summer months—the remote location giving them more anonymity than the Hamptons while still being a stone's throw from New York City. But apparently for mega-stars like Deacon Harrow, there was no such thing as privacy, even on a remote island.

Deacon's die-hard fans existed on a whole other level. Word had gotten out that the zoo was about to become a shooting location for his latest film and they'd popped up at our gates like locusts coming out of hibernation.

I gave a disapproving shake of my head as I heard the chorus of squeals in the distance. "All their squealing is going to disturb our patient."

Finch shot me an incredulous look, a smug smile on her face. "Disturb him more than that?" She shouted to be heard as she tipped her head to the five yellow-headed Amazon parrots in a quarantine aviary squawking so loudly that my ear drums might rupture.

"The squealing set them off! Parrots are allergic to fangirling," I said but couldn't even hear myself over the piercing racket.

"Ooh, this guy has really got your claws out, Dovey." Finch laughed as the parrots died down again. I shot her an angry look that only seemed to egg her on. "Hey, I invented that death stare. It's powers are useless against me. Besides, you know I'm Team Lachlan, always. It's just fun to see you frazzled." She placed a sticker label around the test tube in her hand. "Do you want me to ask Petey if he can set up some barricades in the parking lot? We've only got two and a half more weeks of this and then they'll be gone. Seems like a lot of work for a couple weeks."

"Yeah," I gritted out. "It's fine."

There were only twenty or so frantic fans outside the front gates, hoping to catch a peek of Deacon. Luckily, the crew was filming in the rainforest walkthrough, which meant that they couldn't be viewed from outside the zoo premises. The towering barbed-wire fences, cameras, and electrified gates were designed to keep the animals in, but they were also excellent at keeping unwanted visitors *out*. Still, that didn't seem to deter them from congregating at the gates every morning.

*Prickle Island Zoo just might be the most secure filming location there was. Marvel's got nothing on us.*

The only problem with the current production location was that the rainforest walkthrough was part of *my* route, which meant I had to work around them if I didn't want to bump into demon incarnate, Deacon Harrow.

I'd done the first feedings before dawn to avoid the film crews, a few of the birds giving me curious looks as they were still nestled on their perches, unwilling to start their day before sunrise. It was like Christmas morning for them when they awoke to a platter of fresh cut fruit already waiting for them, no need to squawk their demands for breakfast like usual. Each afternoon, I'd waited until the crew had packed up for the day as the sun was beginning to set to do a final clean of the enclosures—which also greatly perturbed my sleeping flocks. Birds were just so sassy—the true divas of the zoo.

But my plans were working. I hadn't seen the slightest peek of Deacon, to my great satisfaction. I was determined that he would come and go without me ever having the displeasure of encountering him. In our last exchange, I'd told him I never wanted to talk to him again, and I intended to keep that promise.

As the racket of parrots flared and died once more, I asked, "Are you sure you and Frankie aren't having kids anytime soon?"

Finch practically fumbled the blood vial out of her hands as she returned Eddie to his perch.

"That was one hell of a segue there, Olive Branch," she said, removing her rubber gloves and chucking them in the trash beside the sink. I glowered at the latest nickname. Just because my name was Dove, didn't mean there was anything peaceful about me. "Why do I have a feeling this has something to do with the presence of *People* magazine's hottest man?"

"The category was the hottest action star, not man of the year," I muttered.

My older sister's eyebrows lifted. "I won't comment on the fact that you knew that." Finch's smile widened. "So why the sudden talk of me having babies?"

"I was just wondering," I said defensively. "Mom is being more meddlesome than usual, and I think a few more grandbabies might help her butt out of my nonexistent love life."

I grew more frustrated with myself with every sentence out of my mouth. I knew it was nonsensical. It wasn't my intention to sound so hostile, but everything just kept coming out wrong and it was all Deacon Harrow's fault.

"Goldilocks and I haven't even had our one-year anniversary yet, so maybe give us a couple of years? I've got plans for her. A ring, a wedding, a honeymoon that involves a lot of frozen margaritas . . . *then* we can talk about kids, okay?"

I pursed my lips and stared at the ceiling. "Of all the family members I thought would end up being a hopeless romantic . . ."

"You are seriously spiraling here. What is going on with you?" Finch took out her penlight and started checking my pupils. I swatted her hand away as she tried to lift my eyelids. "You're supposed to be the least ruffle-able one of us and right now you're kind of wigging out."

"I'm not wigging out!" I shouted, throwing my hands in the air. "And yes, I realize that the delivery of that statement isn't helping!"

"What happened with you and Deacon anyway? You were cute, little summertime pals once. You two were the *gangliest* of gangly kids. You used to pick matching color bands for your braces for crying out loud, and then suddenly you started hating the guy?" I was about to open my mouth to speak when Finch beat me to it. "And don't say the skink thing. That's recent. What happened fifteen years ago? I swear you went into like a three-year depression after you and Deacon stopped talking."

I felt my shoulders tense up around my ears as I tightly folded my arms. "I was thirteen and our dad had just died." I gaped at Finch.

"Oh, don't use the dad card on me," she replied. "He passed a long time after you turned into a little fucking storm cloud."

"It was just puberty, forget it."

"Yeah, definitely just puberty," Finch quipped. "Puberty that perfectly aligned with your best friend leaving at the end of the summer, never to return. Your best friend who became a model and then a rockstar and then a movie star," she added pointedly. "Definitely had *nothing* to do with that."

"He wasn't my *best friend*." I balked at her sugar-coated sentiments. "He was just another summer friend."

My siblings and I were good at making close attachments to people over the summer, when the population of Prickle Island swelled. And we were equally practiced at moving on from those friendships at the end of the summer. But Deacon had never felt like just another "summer friend" to me. Something about that age, that time of life, it had all felt extra heightened.

"Well, you're acting like you're going through puberty all over again now that there's a certain movie star somewhere currently on the premises," Finch said, "and you're actively trying to avoid him."

"I am not trying to avoid him," I scoffed.

Finch arched her brow. "Oh really? You just decided to get an early start on the day this week for shits and giggles, hm?"

"Mm-hmm."

Her eyes filled with wicked mischief and my gut clenched. "Okay, well, perfect. Then you wouldn't mind going to get Guava for me? I need to do a suture check on her tail."

My mouth fell open. "How *dare* you."

Finch grinned smugly. "That's what I thought, Lovey Dove."

Guava the iguana's enclosure was directly behind where they were filming. There was no way I could get in and out without being spotted by at least a few production assistants and possibly even Deacon himself.

"Look," Finch said. "The Zap thing was bad, like catastrophically bad, but I really don't think he—"

"Please don't make excuses for the famous multimillionaire," I growled.

Finch held up her hands. "Seriously, *what* happened between you two?"

"Besides him using his clout to make a species extinct?" I exclaimed. "That's not enough of a reason for you?"

Finch eyed me, and I could tell she was trying to assess whether it was wise to poke the bear. I'd seen her take less consideration when deciding whether or not to tackle a crocodile.

"Alright." She lifted her hands in surrender. "You win. Keep your prepubescent secrets to yourself."

"Thank you," I said, grateful she finally decided to leave it alone.

"But shoving these things down never ends well," Finch called after me, and I rolled my eyes.

Of course she had to curse me with that ill omen as I walked out the door. I wasn't shoving anything down. I was just actively avoiding my old friend turned movie star turned enemy like a completely normal, well-adjusted person.

# Chapter Four

Dove

I rubbed my weary eyes and headed down toward the old monkey house to steal one of the twins' Red Bulls.

*At least it isn't as bad as baby-bird season,* I told myself for the hundredth time today. There was sleep deprivation, and then there was baby-bird-season sleep deprivation. In only a few more weeks, I'd need a full-on IV drip of coffee to cope with however many chicks needed hand-rearing this year. At least we had two new vet tech interns coming to keep up with the workload. After Finch's complete implosion last year, Mom had put her foot down and brought in more help. Maybe we'd **even** get through the season without anyone hallucinating cats on the ceiling . . . . That would be a win.

I swung my arms as I walked, humming a tune to myself to try and kickstart my energy back into gear.

*Eighteen days. Just eighteen more days and the Deacon-sized shadow over the zoo will vanish.*

My radio chirped on my hip. "Reptiles to birds."

I picked it up. "Birds, go ahead."

"What time do you want to leave for that school visit tomorrow?"

Shit. I'd completely forgotten. I'd been so focused on Deacon, I hadn't checked my calendar in days. "Uhh, ten?"

"Roger," Crane replied. "I'll be bringing Darren and Velma so don't bring Yellow."

"Roger."

Crane's bearded dragon hated my sulphur-crested cockatoo, so the two of them could never be scheduled on the same school visits together. I'd probably bring Sunflower, our three-year-old sun conure. She enjoyed the chaos of children the most.

The zoo had been steadily growing our funding over the last few years, especially with the added income from the school trips and off-season events. We actually had enough money now to hire some more staff members, which opened up a new path for me to finally do something else . . . although I wasn't exactly sure what that would be yet.

I enjoyed fundraising and event planning, and I was starting to take over more of Mom's grant submissions and paperwork. Maybe I could move to the city and work for a big NGO, carry on my father's legacy of saving wildlife on a larger scale than what one zoo could do alone.

But not yet . . . I still wanted the zoo to be well and truly sorted before I left. The zoo was owned by our family now, but that was only step one. We were earning more than we had in previous years, and that was step two. But I needed to make sure we could *keep* earning that amount with enough of a buffer for a few slow years before I was willing to move on entirely.

With my mind on my blurry future, I stumbled blearily down the back pathway past the gardens and almost barreled headfirst into a tall blonde zookeeper.

*Zookeeper?*

I paused and did a double take, rubbing the sleep from my eyes.

"Hey," the lanky blonde said to me without looking up from her phone. She had an eerily symmetrical face, blindingly white teeth, and shining white-blonde hair that looked thicker than a horse's mane.

"Hey." I dragged out the word, more than a little confused. Had Mom hired Zookeeper Barbie without telling me? "Sorry, I thought you were . . . a . . . a staff member for a second."

She peeked up from her phone just long enough to laugh. "Cool," was all she said and wandered away.

As she sauntered off in an odd combination of work khakis and Ugg boots, I realized I knew her. That was *Ivy Blanc*—an up-and-coming actress and two-time *Sports Illustrated* swimsuit cover model. She wore the same style of khakis as mine, except without the porcupine logo—though her body looked *decidedly* different in them than mine did. She was easily 5'10" with big boobs, a tiny waist, and a perfectly sculpted ass—which I was *definitely not* checking out.

As she walked off, I noticed the back of her shirt was held tight with clips to give her even more of an hourglass figure. The Ugg boots I couldn't explain, apart from maybe they were only shooting her from the waist up? If she was trying to look like a zookeeper, maybe someone should tell her that the footwear was entirely impractical.

I frowned down at the white splash of bird poop on my work boots. Great, the hottest woman in the world just saw my shit-stained shoes. I pinched my leg, wondering if I'd accidentally fallen asleep in Finch's office and this was all some insane dream. I'd just bumped into Ivy Blanc at my family zoo and she was dressed like me . . . well, like when hot girls dressed up in Halloween costumes version of me, but still . . .

"What the hell?" I finally said aloud, reality catching up with me.

I grabbed my radio and pushed the button, waiting for the beep. "Uh, is anyone going to tell me why I just ran into Ivy Blanc and why she's walking around the zoo in our work uniform?"

"You got to talk to Ivy Blanc?" Crane replied right away, all too eager.

"What does she smell like?" Heron jumped in over him. "Did you smell her?"

Hawk instantly cut in, "Don't answer that." He let out a long breath over the radio—something he always scolded us for. "They modeled her uniform after ours so that if we walk into the background shots of any enclosures, the footage is still usable. It's why you had to sign that release form."

What release form had I signed? In the mountain of Mom's paperwork that had landed across her desk, had I accidentally agreed to be a background extra in a freaking movie? Had I been so caught up in avoiding anything about Deacon that I'd missed the memo entirely?

I stared down at my boots as if the answers might be scrawled across them before bringing the radio to my mouth again. "And *why* does she need a zookeeper uniform?"

"Did you not read the safety briefing I sent through last week?" Hawk asked, his voice already perturbed, as if he knew the answer.

"Busted." Crane snickered.

Now that he mentioned it, I *had* seen the subject of a few emails that had included Deacon's name and had admittedly decided to move them directly into the trash.

"They're filming a rom-com set in a zoo, Dove," Heron said. "She's playing a zookeeper."

I choked on my own breath, spluttering and coughing. *How* had I not gathered that from the few phone exchanges I'd had with Deacon? When I'd contacted him about using the zoo as a filming location, he'd said he was producing and starring in a new film, but I would've remembered if he'd said the movie was about an actual zookeeper! Why hadn't he told me that when he'd sent me the original contracts?

"Right, yeah," I muttered into the radio. "I was just surprised to see her behind the scenes. Isn't that a hazard?"

"We've designated the parking lot behind the composter as a smoking zone for the crew," Mom said.

"Did none of you read my report?" Hawk grumbled.

"He spent a lot of time on it, guys," Hannah chimed in. "Not cool."

I pinched the bridge of my nose. "I'll reread it tonight," I acquiesced.

"There will be a quiz at dinner," Hawk scolded. "Got it?"

I rolled my eyes. "Roger."

I kept walking, storming faster now. I didn't know why it made me so angry that Deacon hadn't told me he was filming a zookeeper movie. That was so out of character for him. I thought they were just going to use the exotic animals and bamboo hedges for a *Rambo* reboot or something. Deacon's brand was action hero, not gushy romantic comedy. *Why* was he producing a project that was so out of character for him? Was this his way of getting payback at me for ignoring him? *I wouldn't put it past him.* Maybe he'd changed the film to be about a zoo just to spite me.

*Yep.* I decided the piece of shit was doing this specifically to torture me, mocking my job, my home, with his stupid movie and his handsome face as some sadistic game.

I balled my hands into fists as I spied the gaggle of girls waiting at the gates.

"Agh!" Something in me snapped and I stormed down the

hill toward them. "What is wrong with you?" I yelled, unleashing my frustration on them from the other side of the chain-link. They all just smiled and kept looking past me as if I didn't even exist.

They didn't even seem upset that I was raging at them. They were like zombies, so desperate for a glimpse that they would let a hurricane roll right overhead if it meant catching a peek. They held their phones to the fence, staring, unblinking, desperation in their tight gazes.

"Deacon Harrow is a vile piece of crap who doesn't do any good in the world. He's just a hot guy who does unwatchable action himbo movies." I erupted, waving my hands in front of their cameras to try to get their attention. "He has all the money and fame in the world and does *nothing* with it. He is the face of a company that has made the Almadran skinks go *extinct* and he hasn't even issued an apology! He could be doing so much good with his platform, but he doesn't care. All he wants are these sick parasocial relationships that you're all feeding into. This is a cult, and he is your leader. Wake up! You all need to find someone better to worship than that worthless waste of space. He—"

"Vet Team to birds," Finch's voice echoed from the radio at my hip.

"Fuck my life," I muttered as I turned to see Finch's head in the window of the vet hospital. She was most definitely standing on a gurney to spy on me. I picked up my radio. "Birds, go ahead."

"Step *away* from the super fans, Lovey Dovey," Finch said, hooking her thumb to the side.

I rolled my eyes as I started trudging back up the hill. I saluted Finch as I held the radio to my mouth. "They didn't even listen to me anyway."

"Good," she said. "The last thing you need is to be on the wrong side of the Harrow Heads."

I pretended to gag. Harrow Heads. Gross.

I clenched and unclenched my hands. "It's only eighteen days," I whispered to myself. "You can handle anything for eighteen days. Then you will never have to think about him again."

And I really wished in that moment that I could make myself believe the lie, but the truth was Deacon Harrow had lived rent free in my head for a long, *long* time.

# Chapter Five

Deacon

Our director, Gavin, walked over with a pinched expression like he'd just bitten into a lemon—not the sort of expression you wanted to see when you were trying to film a lighthearted romantic comedy. Ivy and I had already run the scene six times and we *still* couldn't get it.

"Deacon, it's great. We just need a little *more* . . ." Gavin twirled his hands skyward, as if I should somehow know the interpretation of that gesture. "Ivy, come talk to me," he added, slinging his arm around Ivy and walking her down the rain-forest pathway and out of earshot.

A mob of assistants and makeup artists chased after them, touching up her makeup as they walked. Luca ran halfway to me, holding out my green juice, when I gave him a little half-wave to let him know I was good. My personal chef was trying to kill me with all of these drinks that tasted like fresh cut grass. Luca went back to typing away on his phone in the shade of the tent set up over a grassy patch of picnic tables.

I blew out a long breath and stretched. This was probably going to take awhile.

Ivy had just found out her very real—not PR—girlfriend was cheating on her, and while I was empathetic, she was massively holding up production with her inability to hold it together. This was part of the job—putting our personal lives aside to get the shot. But Ivy was new to the acting world, and I was beginning to wonder if she regretted her agent nudging her away from modeling and into this acting thing. At this rate, we were losing daylight and might not even get a very simple shot.

"This whole movie is going to be an utter disaster," I muttered to myself. It was a statement that was quickly becoming my personal mantra, but I'd known that it was a disaster from the start and had chosen to do it anyway.

I put my hands on my hips and stared up at the two gibbons swinging through the trees in the distance. This place had changed a lot since I'd been a kid: new exhibits, new animals, everything freshly painted, and a killer restaurant that was providing us with some of the best food service I'd ever eaten in my life.

Luca had gotten the zoo gossip from the eldest brother's very pregnant girlfriend, Hannah. She'd spilled *all* of the current animal and Lachlan family drama to him when he'd asked if he could pet their miniature cow—a cow which was apparently named Colin and Hannah had very strong feelings about it.

My assistant was good at a lot of things, and subtly snooping for me was certainly one of them.

The TLDR of the Lachlan clan was all but one of the Lachlan kids still lived on-site, some with their respective spouses. Hawk had built himself a cottage behind the lion exhibit. Finch had an apartment above the vet hospital, which she shared with her zoo chef girlfriend, Frankie. Even the old monkey house that I remembered from childhood was now a makeshift human house where the Lachlan twins lived . . . which was crazy since they were still six-year-old miscreants in my brain.

"Speak of the devil." I spied one of them walking through the chain-link toward the penguin exhibit and took a stab at which one it was. "Heron!" I called.

The keeper stopped, spun in a confused circle, and then pointed to their chest. "I'm . . . Crane."

"Oh, right, sorry," I said, jogging over with an awkward wave.

"Heron is the hippie-looking, non-binary one with the gauge earrings and long hair," Crane said. "They look like they're a stoner, but they're not. They've just got those chill, tie-dye vibes," he added. "Anyway . . ."

I could tell by his shifty eyes that he was nervous and eager to disentangle himself from this conversation.

I was used to clocking it. Most people who were nervous to meet me either became overly friendly or notedly cold to prove that they weren't affected by celebrity. But I had a feeling these particular shifty eyes had less to do with me and more to do with a certain zookeeper sibling of his.

"Heron and I are very easy to tell apart," Crane added as if remembering himself. *There was that coldness.* "Anyway, I'll leave you to it."

"Wait," I called after him, and he turned back to me again. "It's good to see you. Uh, it's been a long time," I offered. "I don't know if you remember me. I was—"

"I mean, barely. I was a little kid," Crane said, swinging his bucket with mindless irritation. "I think I remember more Mom talking about you than actually you, you know?" He kept looking around awkwardly like he might be caught.

I let out a sigh. "Did Dove tell you not to talk to me?"

His mouth tightened. "No. She didn't," he said. "She doesn't need to tell me anything. Her enemies are my enemies."

"Enemies? That's certainly a strong word," I retorted. "I see the Lachlan family loyalty is still ironclad."

"In this particular instance, it's conservationist loyalty so . . . " Crane saluted me as he started walking backwards. "I wish I could say it was good seeing you, Deacon. Talk to me when you want to start an Almadran skink breeding program."

*Damn. Way to twist the knife deeper.*

I remembered Luca saying that Crane was now the head reptiles keeper, so I supposed that tracked. Of course he was pissed at me about the skinks. The Lachlans seemed to be the only ones who even remembered the Zap incident. The rest of the world had moved on to juicier and less scientific gossip.

I didn't know why they were trying to hold me personally responsible. *I* wasn't the one clear-cutting the island to dump factory waste on it. Just because I'd been contracted to sell the product, and just because sales had sky-rocketed since my endorsements, thereby needing more unethically built factories, didn't mean I should get any of this misplaced hate.

*Nope. Their anger is definitely misplaced.*

I wanted to tell Crane, "Blame Zap for being bad at running a business, not me for being good at selling it." But he was already walking away, and it felt weak to shout after someone to get the last word.

"Should've tried with an easier sibling," I murmured to myself as Crane disappeared behind a bamboo hedge. "Of course I'm at the top of reptile guy's shit list. I need to find the carnivores one."

It was a surprisingly strange feeling to have someone be so blunt to my face. Neither wooed nor repelled by my status, Crane just simply didn't like me, which was both refreshing and pretty awful too.

My publicist, Cody, suddenly appeared through the bored

and waiting crew while Ivy and Gavin were still talking in frantic, hushed voices. I furrowed my brow at Cody's harried expression. I thought he was working from the Holloway Estate today. He had his phone clutched in his hand, notifications making it buzz every second.

"Don't worry," he said, panting and ruddy-cheeked. "I'm already getting it under control."

My pulse quickened. That was never a good way to start a sentence.

"Get what under control?" I managed to see the TMZ video on his phone before he locked it. My heart leapt into my throat as I spied the face on the screen—the wire-rim glasses, the purple-dipped hair, the khakis with a porcupine over the breast pocket. "Is that ... Dove Lachlan?"

# Chapter Six

Dove

One of the many things zookeepers and our animals had in common was our absolute devotion to good food. And the flaky custard cream tart in my hand was no exception. I rocked back and forth like an excited little love bird as I took another hasty bite.

"You are a freaking genie." My words were muffled by the mouthful of sugary custard as I spoke. "This tart is laced with something, isn't it? I think I might be high. Food isn't supposed to be this good."

"While I appreciate all the sex faces," Frankie said with a laugh. "It's just a normal tart."

Hannah moaned. "There's nothing normal about this pillowy slice of sugary heaven."

Frankie waved the comment away, as if we weren't being 100% serious. "It's just a little something I whipped up."

"You know, I love Hawk and all," Hannah said through giant chipmunk cheeks. "But I think you might be my favorite person in the entire world right now."

Frankie smiled wider. "Hits the spot, doesn't it?"

"Not many pregnant women can describe their cravings and have a decorated chef *just whip it up* for them." Hannah grabbed another tart off the tray.

"So I'm guessing this should be one to add to the new catering menu?" Frankie asked, bouncing on her toes.

"Hell yeah, you should." My voice was a little too exuberant as I licked my fingers. "So long as you make double the amount you need every time you bake them. Once the twins taste this, you're going to have to be on high alert for tart theft."

I was forever grateful that Hannah and I were Frankie's chosen food testers for all her new recipes. Heron and Crane always volunteered, but Hannah and I had more helpful feedback than the constantly ravenous twins.

Currently, Frankie was in absolute heaven with the film crew around and a bunch of new mouths to feed. She was really pulling out the big guns, and already two different crew members had professed their undying love for her. I wouldn't be surprised if Finch put a ring on Frankie's finger by the end of the week, just to keep all of Frankie's newfound admirers at bay.

Finch said she'd barely seen her girlfriend the last few weeks. Frankie had been so busy in the kitchen and had already updated the summer catering service menu *twelve times* based off her results.

Hannah's eyes rolled back as she grabbed a chocolate tart and took the first orgasmic bite. "Holy shit, these are good." She propped the tray that held a selection of tarts on her swollen belly.

Hannah had reached the point of pregnancy where there was absolutely no comfortable way to sit or sleep or move, and Frankie and I had made it our mission to distract her as much as possible. Although, Frankie's method of cooking for Hannah was far more effective than me trying to show her all the director's cut *Lord of the Rings* movies.

I couldn't believe one of my best friends was about to have a baby. I couldn't believe I was about to be an aunt. It felt like just yesterday that Hannah had tornado-ed her way into our lives, and now she was going to be bringing a new member of our family into the world. None of it felt real. But I knew the moment I held that baby, it would be.

Hawk had turned into a broodier father than any bird I'd ever worked with. He even put the village weaver to shame with his hardcore nesting and constantly checking on Hannah. It was kind of adorable. Every little kick, he thought the baby was coming and wanted to make the mad dash to the boat. It would be a two-hour trip to the hospital by boat and car, and he was determined to get there with heaps of time to spare.

"Two weeks," Frankie said, rubbing Hannah's shoulders.

"Two weeks," Hannah echoed.

"Or a couple more," I said and instantly regretted it when Hannah gave me a death stare. Due dates were more suggestions than definitive timelines, especially for first-time moms who tended to carry longer. But I wasn't about to be snapped in two by an angry mama bear, so I just meekly echoed, "Two weeks."

"Tomorrow I'll make you mud pies if you tell me what you're going to name him," Frankie suggested.

Hannah zipped her lips. "Not telling until he's out of the oven," she said, rubbing her stomach. "And you'll make me mud pies anyway because you have a new recipe and you're dying to try it."

Frankie chuckled. "You know me too well."

Frankie had slotted straight into our family dynamic just as easily as Hannah had. My older siblings' partners had become some of my closest friends. I loved my siblings, sure, but Finch and Lark had always been super close and I'd never had the same relationship with them. Now that Lark had moved away, we were actually closer, but still, Frankie and Hannah knew me in a way my siblings didn't. I was grateful they were a part of my life. I'd probably have left the zoo years ago if they hadn't been a part of it. Even with them here, I still day-dreamed about when I would officially fly the nest.

The phone in the Peckish Peacock rang, and we all looked at it like it was haunted. Who would be calling us when the zoo was closed for the off-season?

Frankie tentatively picked it up. "Hello?" Her eyes widened and she looked at me. "Okay . . . . Do you want to talk to her? Okay. Okay. Uh-huh. Bye." She hung up the phone. "Your mom needs to talk to you in her office."

I held a hand to my chest. "Jeez, you scared me for a second." I stood. "Why didn't she just radio me?"

Frankie shrugged. "I don't know. Maybe because of the filming? She was cryptically vague about it."

"Weird," I said, not thinking much of it. "It better not be a new requisition because my roster of animals is filled," I added. "Especially with baby-bird season on the horizon. Unless she wants to acquire blue-footed boobies, in which case I'd make an exception."

"You just want an excuse to say boobies every day," Hannah teased.

"Are you sure you're not a lesbian?" Frankie asked.

"Alas," I said with a mocking sigh. "I sit under a different part of the rainbow."

"We needed the demisexual representation to round us out," Hannah said, rubbing her belly. "This family is like queer *Pokémon*. We've gotta catch 'em all."

With a laugh, I waved as Hannah and Frankie went back to their taste testing and I headed off. It was a short walk from the Peckish Peacock to the prep kitchens where Mom's office was located.

As I entered, the sounds of Aya's radio echoing through the cavernous space greeted me. I presumed one of my siblings must've turned it on in her absence. The kitchens had been eerily quiet while she was off on vacation. I guessed Heron was the culprit judging by the chopped up fruit in a bucket labeled "tamarins."

I hummed along to the Mumford and Sons track as I jogged up the stairs to Mom's office door.

But when I opened it, the song on my lips abruptly halted. It wasn't my mother sitting behind the desk.

My stomach plummeted into my boots. There, leaning back in Mom's office chair with his Hollywood-muscled arms crossed tightly across his chest, was Deacon motherfucking Harrow.

## Chapter Seven

Deacon

It was Dove Lachlan who had first taught me that a group of tigers was called an ambush—an anecdote she probably wouldn't appreciate right now, judging by the look on her face.

An ambush attack was not my ideal way of reuniting with Dove, but I had to admit her shocked expression was still satisfying. She was not an easy person to startle. I'd once seen a cheetah charge her and she'd managed to keep her face looking like she was waiting in line at the DMV. But today, I saw the sudden flare of panic in Dove's eyes before she quickly schooled her expression back to her normal bored and slightly grumpy visage.

Dove's piercing stare slid from me to Cody, who stood leaning against the wall behind me. Judging from her tightening expression, I was certain he had a scathing look on his face that rivaled Dove's own.

*Careful, Cody*, I thought to myself. *There's not a powerhouse lawyer or studio executive in the world that could rival this woman's intimidation techniques.*

That wasn't the only thought that flashed through my mind when I saw her, though. An unexpected one popped to the forefront: I hadn't thought it was possible for her to be more beautiful than her social media photos.

She'd deleted all of them during the skink incident, and I missed checking to see if she'd posted any new photos of herself with her animals. I'd kept tabs on her over the years from my fake Insta or "Finsta" account as people called it. *Maybe she knew and that's why she deleted her socials…*

"What do *you* want?" Her voice was tight, her expression sharp enough to slice me in two.

Fuck. I'd rather have fallen into the lion enclosure than hear the bitterness in that question coming from her lips.

I thought I'd be more prepared for this reunion, but the impact of her standing in front of me was making my hands shake. I kept them tightly clasped under the desk as Dove folded her arms and popped out her hip.

At that telltale movement, a wry smile curled my lips.

There were still flashes of the girl I'd known—in her popped hip, in her stubborn frown, in her indomitable spirit that could stare down an apex predator and not be cowed. But she was arresting in a different way now too, beautiful, sexy even. Her hair was dipped in a deep, vibrant purple—her favorite color. I knew from her Insta that she'd been dying her hair like that for years. Her glasses were new though—rose-gold wire trim, highlighting her big brown eyes—eyes that were currently staring daggers into me.

I cleared my throat and lifted my chin. "It's good to see you, Rogue. It's been a while."

"*Don't* call me that," she bit out.

I shrugged, pretending to be indifferent. It took every ounce of acting training to keep my face in a casual neutral.

What had I been thinking? That she would call me my old nickname in return and we'd go back to fifteen years ago, when we'd been muddling our way through our first Dungeons & Dragons campaign like the fantasy-obsessed tweens we'd been? No. Time had irrevocably changed us, and I knew from the look on her face there was no going back.

"Some of us have real jobs, Deacon," she growled, her voice lower and more rasping than last I'd heard it. My muscles tensed hearing that perfect bedroom voice, one that was meant to be intimidating but instead carried sultry notes. *Focus, Deacon*, I thought as she asked, "What do you want from me?"

*To go back to when you didn't hate me*, I wanted to say. To go back to when she and I had been best friends for three brief and beautiful summers. But I knew being a hopeless nostalgic would get me nowhere with Dove.

"What do we want from you?" Cody scoffed, his restraint finally snapping. He slammed his phone down on the desk and slid it across toward Dove. "Care to explain this?"

Dove's eyes widened in surprise as she was confronted with a video of herself ranting behind a chain-link fence to a group of my fans. Normally, being called a "worthless waste of space" was par for the course. Everyone felt they were entitled to loudly share their opinions on celebrities, probably thinking we'd never hear it. But I hadn't expected Dove of all people to be filled with such vitriol. Maybe my skin wasn't as thick as I'd thought, or maybe Dove had always been my Achilles heel.

Cody's voice was cold and cutting. "After all that he's done for you—"

"Cody." I held up a hand, worried he might say too much. "Give us a minute."

The vein in Cody's neck popped out, and I could see he

wanted to rage at Dove. I gave him a look that told him enough. *Bad idea, buddy.* So instead, he took a controlled breath taught to him by his court-appointed anger management counselor.

"One minute," he said, holding up a finger. "One! And then we talk damage control."

He waited until I nodded in agreement to exit, shutting the door loudly behind him. His footsteps boomed down the stairs until Dove and I were left in awkward silence. Suddenly, the room felt incredibly small. I could tell she was mortified by the video but too stubborn to admit it to me. She was a private, curmudgeonly, introverted person—the opposite to me in every way.

I thought she might apologize or come up with an explanation for the video *or* simply shout at me some more, but instead she asked, "What have you done for me?"

"Hm?"

"Your finance bro lackey over there just said 'after all you've done for me'." She tipped her head to the door that Cody had just disappeared from. "Was he talking about you filming here or something else that you've done for me?"

"Don't worry about it," I replied, knowing that comment would get a rise out of her again. As Dove's eyes flared, I smiled wider. "We've got bigger concerns."

She let out a sarcastic huff. "*You've* got bigger concerns." She waved a patronizing hand at me. "I'm fine."

God, I missed the way she could put me in my place. *Maybe I am a sadist.* It was a weird thing to miss, but no one in my circles dared to talk to me this way anymore. Dove never sugarcoated anything.

"We can't ignore this issue," I pressed.

"Tell that to the Almadran skinks!" she erupted, throwing her hands up in the air in exasperation.

I'd known she and I would have our reckoning one day about the skinks, but I hadn't thought she'd be quite so enraged about it. "I'm sorry about the skinks, okay? That was all Zap though. I had nothing to do with it."

Her mouth fell open and she glared at me. Clearly, that hadn't been a sufficient apology.

"You have all the money in the world and still couldn't buy a good idea to save your freaking life, Deacon. Why don't you *do* something about this? Anything!"

"Ouch," I said, pretending her words wounded me. I placed my hand to my chest, feeling the comforting outline of the coin hanging on a necklace beneath my shirt. She'd have to try harder than that though. "I'll have you know, we're going to donate to a very well-known LA-based organization."

"Very well known? Which one?"

"I can't remember," I admitted.

"LA based?" She was talking so loudly now that some would argue it bordered on shouting. "You really are an idiot."

My brow furrowed. "What?"

"What does LA know about tropical rainforests? Or the Almadran Archipelago for that matter?" She put her hands on her hips and raised her eyebrows at me, waiting for my answer. When I didn't give it, she exploded. "Exactly! You need to be working with the locals. You need feet on the ground. Ugh!" She pinched the bridge of her nose in an action I distinctly remembered her mother doing, but I knew if I said that out loud, she would probably cut my balls off. I wouldn't put it past her. She had a veterinarian sister who would probably help her. "I shouldn't have to explain this to you. You should *care* without being told to. You should care that you made a whole species extinct."

"Technically, it was the company—"

"And *you* are the face of that company, you fucking child," she spat. I lifted my eyebrows, impressed. *Damn.* She had always been tough, but now she was downright vicious. "All those teenage douchebags buy your energy drinks because it's *your face* on the can, you total waste of air. Why are you smiling?"

"Still a wicked little tiefling, I see."

"Don't talk D&D to me," she hissed. "I don't remember anything. I haven't played since we were twelve."

"But you still watch people play online."

"*How* do you know that?" She waved her hand as if cutting off her own impending rant. "You know what? I don't even want to know."

She rubbed her palm with the thumb of her other hand. It was such a brief movement before she dropped her hands, but I caught it. I wondered if that scar was still there. I wondered if she was touching it at the memory or if I was just reading into nothing.

"Can we call Cody back and talk game plans now?" I asked, trying to remain patient.

"Absolutely not."

"Why not?"

"You really live in your own delusional little world now, don't you? Have you even been listening to me?"

"Are we still talking about the skinks?" I asked with a yawn. I'd been up since 4 am and was desperate for more coffee. "They were native to one little island and no one even knew they existed until a couple decades ago. No one will miss them."

"I hate you!" She was definitely shouting now. "You could've done something about this with your infinite power and clout and wealth, but instead you're too busy fucking nineteen-year-old models."

I rocked back like I'd been hit. "I thought you didn't have socials anymore?" I gritted out, clenching my jaw.

"Yeah, well, the radio is on in the prep kitchens and some-times even I can't avoid it."

We stared at each other in a silent standoff.

*So this is what she really thinks of me.* I hadn't fully compre-hended the depth of her contempt until now. *She hates me.*

I thought Dove might be able to see the real Deacon under-neath it all, but more and more, I was beginning to wonder if he even existed. I was perfectly okay with hating myself, but I couldn't have her hate me, not Dove. She was the only non-relative who had been close to me before the fame. I couldn't forever ruin the one relationship that kept me a human and not a business.

My throat bobbed as I swallowed back the ugly realization. "I'm sorry, Dove. Truly."

Her shoulders bunched around her ears. "Even if I believed that apology, which I don't, I don't care," she said and turned to the door. "Make this situation right if you want me to forgive you."

She knew perfectly how to cut me open and pour salt in my wounds. I'd rather her rage than her cold indifference, but if she thought she could get away from me this easily, she was wrong. I *would* regain her approval. She could try to dodge me all she wanted, but I wasn't going to give up.

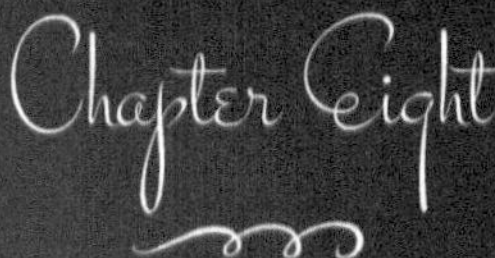

# Chapter Eight

Deacon

Cody walked back into the room, his eyes shuffling to Dove's retreating form and back to me three times before he blustered, "Where is she going? Why are you letting her walk away?"

"Letting her?" I asked incredulously as the sound of Dove's footsteps faded away. "Would you rather I handcuff her to the table?"

"You're Deacon Harrow," he pushed, waving me up and down. "Women don't walk away from you."

I pointed to the open doorway. "That one always does."

"But—we—need to talk logistics and . . ."

"Don't panic," I assured him. "I have a plan."

I could tell by the look on his face he didn't think much of my opinion before I even spoke it aloud. "Does this plan involve you getting a photo of the two of you smiling at each other so I can spin this some kind of way? All the Kate breakup stuff is spiraling out on TikTok after that zookeeper's rant." He waved at the door, and I knew he was saying "that zookeeper" because he still couldn't remember her name. "They're not calling you a heartbreaker anymore—they're calling you toxic. This might take you out of the running for Batman, Deacon. Batman!"

"It won't," I said calmly.

It was odd watching someone freak out over my career more than I ever had. I didn't want to be the next Batman anyway. Action movies were hard work but fun, especially fantasy-based ones where I got to play out every character from my favorite books on screen, but I didn't want to be known forever as the buff guy who was good at fight choreography either.

It was one of the many reasons why I'd green-lit this little indie romantic comedy, so that people could see a different side of me. My music had always been the raw and real me, the lyrics speaking in ways I couldn't, and I wished my acting could inspire the same reactions and not just "whoa, bro, that was cool!"

"Earth to Deacon!" Cody snapped his fingers in the air between us, and I realized I'd zoned him out. "Smiling pictures, yes?"

"Pictures, yes. I don't know if I can promise smiling," I hedged.

"What if she sells another story on you?" Cody threw his hands up. "She could be rolling in the dough once she realizes how much money she'd make off you." Cody took out his phone. "I need to call one of my guys. We're losing control of the narrative."

"Put the phone down." I narrowed my eyes at him.

Cody preferred to massage a situation into behaving for him, but he could be cutthroat when he needed to be, and I didn't want him attacking Dove just to make me look better, especially when she was right—*harsh* but right.

"Dove won't sell stories to the press," I assured him.

"We need her to sign an NDA immediately," Cody urged. "And the rest of her family. I can't believe they haven't all signed one already. I should've seen it coming. You two have history. This whole movie idea should've been a giant fucking red flag."

Luca jogged up the stairs with my coffee, skirting into the room like a ghost and plunking it in my hand. He had a real knack for reading the room and right now Cody was giving off some serious chaos energy.

"You have half an hour before you need to be in hair and makeup," Luca murmured, already stepping away before I held up a hand, and he paused.

"Luca, what's the name of that seafood restaurant Cody wanted Ivy and me to go to?"

Luca looked between me and Cody. "Seafarer's Table?"

"That's the one," I said. "Can you please make a reservation for two for lunch there tomorrow?"

"You're finally playing ball with the Ivy thing? Great," Cody said, relieved. Leave it to him to pull the plug on one fake relationship only to throw me into another. "I'll call her team and try to spin the whole toxic thing into a bad-boy thing and maybe they'll still be willing to—"

"Not for Ivy and me," I corrected him. "For Dove and me."

"Deacon." Cody rubbed his forehead. "Look, I know you and this girl were friends as kids, but I'm not so sure you can handle this one. How are you going to convince her to have an off-island lunch with you when you can't even convince her to have a ten-minute meeting at her place of work with you?"

I picked up the landline on Evelyn's desk. Cody and Luca both watched me with curious expressions. The phone was so old it looked like it had been sourced by the props department for the set of a 90s film.

"What are you doing?" Cody asked.

I lifted the cold plastic of the receiver to my ear. "Calling in reinforcements."

"Who?"

"Evelyn Lachlan," I replied, pushing the home button that I assumed would ring Evelyn's house up the hill—a house that still carried some of my greatest childhood memories. "I want her to be first to hear the good news."

Cody looked like his head might explode. "What good news?"

"I'm starting a conservation charity," I said smugly.

Cody didn't move for several seconds before he stepped forward and snatched my coffee cup from the desk. "Luca, we're going to need some more coffee please."

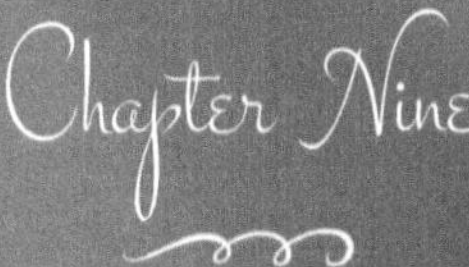

# Chapter Nine

Dove

The entire boat ride to the shoreline, I muttered curses under my breath until Heron finally called, "Anything you want to share with the class there, Dove?"

I glared at my younger sibling as they manned the rudder. We'd borrowed Petey's motorboat for the trip into town. It was slower and choppier than the ferry, but the ferry only ran twice a day in the off-season . . . well, three times a day, while Deacon pretty boy Harrow was in town.

Petey's boat was a barely held together, rusty catastrophe filled with broken tools and snack wrappers. As I took in the sight, I started to consider whether our family had the budget to rent our own for Hannah's emergency labor transit instead of borrowing this one.

As of now, they were planning on catching the ferry over

three days before Hannah's due date and renting a hotel until the baby arrived, which I was starting to think was the more sensible plan. Hawk's anxiety would probably explode if Hannah went into labor at the zoo. Plus, a little hotel baby-moon would be nice for them.

I angrily started plucking up granola bar wrappers and putting them into a plastic bag as the cool springtime wind whipped at my face. The sun this morning had tricked me into thinking it was summer, but the boat ride made my teeth chatter as the cold air lashed into me.

"I should've worn a windbreaker," I said, my voice getting lost on the wind. "This is so ridiculous. I have work to do. Samantha has started plucking her feathers again and I think I might need to move her in with Jeremy even though she hates Jeremy because he loves her and she's better with him even if she doesn't want to—"

"What? Are you talking about plucking your eyebrows?" I could barely hear Heron over the whipping wind. "Your eyebrows are fine."

"What?"

"Huh?"

"Nothing! Never mind!" I screeched right at a lull in the breeze, and Heron's cheeks dimpled in a knowing smile.

"I can't tell if this lunch is freaking you out because he's a movie star or because you hate him," Heron said with a whistle.

"Definitely the latter." I hated him more than Samantha hated Jeremy. And in the world of eclectus parrots, that was a whole hell of a lot.

"What?" Heron shouted to be heard over the engine as we picked up speed to get through the choppy water.

"Mom has really outdone herself this time," I shouted back. "Making me meet up with Deacon in town no less. Like I'm not busy enough already!" We pulled into the bay, slowing until we could talk without shouting as we wound our way through moored yachts bobbing in the marina. "You know someone is going to take our photo, and then he'll be able to pretend that I don't hate his guts. This is manipulation."

"You don't hate his guts," Heron countered. I eyed them incredulously. "Oh, we're not at that realization yet? Got it," they added with a mocking laugh.

"What was Mom thinking? It's like she doesn't know me at all."

"Yeah. I get that." Heron's expression soured, and I knew what they were thinking. "It's gotten worse with all the grand-baby talk. She doesn't know us as well as she thinks she does."

Heron's statement was actually a somewhat comforting reminder to pull my head out of my own ass. I wasn't the only Lachlan sibling going through things right now.

"Just tell her," I implored. "I mean, you obviously don't have to, but . . . I think you should. It's clearly weighing you down, and you know she'd be supportive."

"She's a hopeless romantic. She won't understand."

Something had shifted in Heron over the last year. They'd matured beyond Crane's childish antics, and the two of us had started to surprisingly grow closer. They'd become a friendly confidante for me, and I'd been the first person they'd come out to as asexual last year. They'd known that I was demisexual, so I had probably been the safest person to tell.

On a promiscuity scale of Heron to Finch, I was much closer to the Heron side, but I still liked the idea of physically being with someone. My attempts at one-night stands had made me realize I wasn't sexually attracted to people unless there was established feelings already there . . . which made my relationship options pretty slim in the hookup culture of dating apps.

"She *will* understand. Our entire family is queer in different ways," I added encouragingly. "Well . . . except for maybe Crane. But seriously, no one would judge you for being ace."

"Our mother is literally trying to set you up with a movie star so you can have a bunch of little movie star babies," they countered.

"She is *not* trying to set me up with him!" I balked. "She's trying to make me apologize to him for calling him a worthless piece of crap on the internet . . . among other things."

"Oh, she's definitely shipping you two," Heron said with a laugh. "And she's also definitely not ready to accept that I'm never going to have a partner or children."

"Why no partner though? I thought you wanted to be with someone, just not the spicy stuff." I furrowed my brow. "Aren't you panromantic?"

They rolled their eyes at me. "And how many fellow panromantic asexuals am I going to meet on our little island, hm?"

"God, I feel you there," I grumbled, swiping the strands of windswept hair out of my eyes. "How am I supposed to find anyone to date long enough to even catch feelings for them? Maybe you and I should just move to the city together. I'm sure there'd be people for us if the population of our hometown was bigger than 50."

"I like living at the zoo. Cities seem like a sensory over-whelm nightmare." They shrugged. "I've just accepted it's not going to happen for me. I'm going to be the fun auncle and that will be that."

"You're twenty-two," I lamented. "You can't give up on love already."

"You have," they pointed out.

"I'm twenty-seven years old," I countered, putting on my *Pride & Prejudice* voice. "I'm the one in fun aunt territory."

"We can be fun aunties and auncles together," Heron replied. "The rest of our siblings will have enough kids to keep Mom busy for the foreseeable future."

"I really, *really* hope so," I muttered. "And Mom is *not* setting me up on a date with Deacon Harrow," I added, unable to let it go. "That's the most ridiculous thing you've ever said. She's helping him avoid a PR crisis in exchange for him to continue filming at the zoo."

"Oof," Heron said. "He threatened to pull filming from the zoo?"

"I have no idea." I shrugged. "I'm just guessing based on how adamant she was I come today. I wouldn't put it past him though."

"Damn," they said. "He used to be such a nice guy."

"Did he?" I asked. "I can't remember anymore."

We both knew that was a lie, but Heron, being one of the most emotionally intelligent of my siblings, decided to leave it alone.

The boat pulled into the harbor, and when I got to the wharf, I saw Deacon's assistant, Luca, waiting on the end.

"I'm to escort you to your lunch," he called as I climbed the stairs up the wharf.

I looked at him like he had two heads. "*Escort* me?"

His smile softened. "Deacon would come himself but his reps insisted that it would draw a crowd. He has a reservation for you two at Seafarer's Table."

I frowned at Luca's work attire—a tan blazer with a black T-shirt underneath, slacks, and shined black loafers. I looked between his perfectly pressed clothes and then down to my work uniform. "Seafarer's Table? I was told we were having lunch at the pier for a photo op. As in the pier that is all food trucks, not fine dining?"

Luca shot a quick but noticeable look at my clothes that had my cheeks burning. He gave me a half-smile, half-grimace.

"This would've been great information to know before I came in wearing khakis covered in mud and bird shit," I groused. "I thought we were just getting burgers or something. Who has *lunch* at Seafarer's Table?"

Luca cringed. "I'm so sorry. I should've been more clear in my communication with—"

"It's not your fault. It's Deacon's." I blinked at his overly repentant expression. "I know you probably have to apologize for Deacon all the time, but you don't need to do that with me, okay? In fact, I insist." Luca gave me a tight smile but nodded. "I should've asked for clarification on the dress code. Normally, lunch at the pier in this town means pizza, burgers, or fish and chips."

I waved to Heron as they tore off into the midday sun. They were going to run some errands around town while I had my lunch, and then we were going to ride home together. My mom's fridge had a running list of things we needed from town and it was the job of whoever was running into town next to grab it and do a supply run. Crane needed some WD40, Wren needed embroidery thread, Finch needed a specific brand of protein water, and Hannah had requested a giant bag of chocolate-covered pretzels.

My phone let out an ear-piercing *ding!* but it was only a photo Hawk sent to the family chat of our tiger with her tongue sticking out. Hannah's due date was so close now that I had my phone notifications set to extra loud and obnoxious so I didn't miss anything. I kept getting butterflies in my stomach all throughout the day, getting excited all over again for my friend. I knew Hannah was more than ready to serve this baby an eviction notice.

Luca inclined his head, and I started following after him. I shuffled my boots a little extra when we reached the gravel road, hoping it would rub most of the muck off them before I entered the elegant restaurant.

I swung my arms as I walked. "Let's get this photo op over with."

"This isn't just for an amicable pic," Luca said. "Deacon wanted to have lunch with you to ask you something."

"Ask me to publicly apologize I'm guessing," I replied, staring at my still mud-splattered boots as we wandered the waterfront. "Or issue a retraction or whatever it is you people do."

"Something else."

That piqued my interest. What else could Deacon possibly want from me? "Could I get a clue?"

Luca had a cute, boyish smile when he deigned to show it. "Nope."

"Can I buy a vowel?"

"Nuh-uh."

"Ugh, you're seriously not going to tell me, are you?" I pouted my bottom lip.

"Oh honey, that does *not* work on me," he said with a laugh. "Do you know how many pouting divas I have to deal with on a day-to-day basis?"

"Fine," I gritted out, catching up to him. I eyed him up and down. "You know, I think you might be the only person on Deacon's team that isn't a total douche nozzle."

Luca nodded as we reached the front door of Seafarer's Table. "I completely agree."

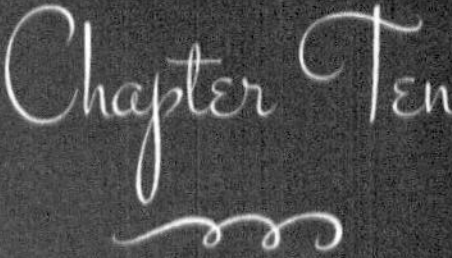

# Chapter Ten

Deacon

Cody had put us at a table right by the bay windows, perfectly framed for him to take a photo through. I spied him sitting in his car, busy typing on his phone while we waited for Dove to arrive.

Uncharacteristic nerves coiled in my stomach as I wondered if she'd stand me up. Even with Evelyn's help convincing her to come, I wouldn't put it past the purple-haired storm cloud. She thought I was a womanizing millionaire content to sell my soul to the highest bidder and leave a path of ecosystem destruction in my wake like some villain off of *Captain Planet*. But I wasn't really that guy, was I?

It hit me like a punch to the gut: *maybe I was.* I hadn't done anything to make myself worthy of her forgiveness . . . not yet at least. I hoped this lunch would change things.

Looking anxiously out the window, I prayed no paparazzi would show up. I hoped we'd make it through lunch with just the not-so-subtle photos the other diners were taking. One woman to my left tried to prop her phone in her bag and point it at me. I gave her a friendly but curt wave and she put it away.

I normally didn't like dining on display like this, but Cody wanted to snap a pic through the windows to make it look less staged. *Et voilà,* we would have the photo that would save my ass.

Luca walked in, flashing an apologetic look at me that told me enough about the state of mind that Dove was in. She blustered in after him, hands balled at her sides, her purple-dipped hair swinging adorably around her shoulders as she stomped over to me.

I stood, placing my linen napkin on the table and adjusting my skinny tie. "Dressed up just for me?" I taunted.

"Argh!" She scrunched her face in frustration. Something about me always seemed to have Dove's temper on a hair trigger. "You know what? I've changed my mind."

She was about to turn away when I caught her by the elbow. "Wait," I pleaded, trying to keep my voice low and not make a scene. "I've already ordered the Lobster Thermidor and the saffron risotto, and if you don't sit and eat with me, they'll throw it all away."

Her eyes widened through her wire-rim glasses in momentary surprise before she scowled at me again. "Curse you for using my hatred of food waste against me."

"They also have a salted caramel cheesecake on the menu," I added, knowing that would seal the deal.

"Fine," she bit out. "One meal. And just because I really want that cheesecake."

I smiled and pulled her chair out for her. "I know you."

She grumpily sat and strangled her napkin like it was the

current substitute for my neck. "You don't know anything about me."

I let out a contemplative hum. "We both know that's not true."

"You knew a nerdy, little twelve-year-old," she said, adjusting her glasses. "Now I'm a nerdy, larger twenty-seven-year-old who has no time for celebrity bullshit."

"I was there when you and I were awkward tweens trying to figure out who we wanted to be in the world," I said. "Maybe I don't know you now. But I know who you wanted to be once."

Dove grabbed the already poured glass of wine on the table and drank the whole thing back in one giant *glug*. But when she lowered her glass from her lips, she found I was already holding the bottle, ready to refill it again. If she was trying to prove I didn't know her at all, she was failing. We'd once shared everything with each other—our dreams, our fears. She'd been there at the inception of Deacon Harrow, and I'd been there at the dawn of the curmudgeon who sat before me now.

"Thank you for agreeing to meet with me," I said, nodding to Luca. He wandered off to tell the servers we were ready for our first course. Still within range if I needed him, he perched at the bar, waiting for his own lunch.

"I didn't really have a choice," Dove replied tightly, staring daggers around the room at anyone who dared to look at us. She was certainly more effective at making people put their phones away than I was. "But my mother seemed convinced that this was a good idea. I still have no idea *why* because she said it was for you to tell me, whatever the hell that means. Great job scheming with my mom behind my back by the way."

"I wasn't scheming," I countered—*I definitely was*. "I just had some questions for her."

"What questions?" she asked, picking up a breadstick and angrily biting off the end. Leave it to Dove Lachlan to make eating lunch an act of aggression.

I took a sip of sparkling water from my Champagne flute. "Questions about my new charity."

The masticated breadstick flew from her mouth onto the plate, and I looked around to see how many patrons had noticed. Two by my count. At least she didn't inhale the chunk of food and make me have to Heimlich her in front of everyone. Although, a part of me thought that would make for a great headline.

"Your new *what*?"

"I've founded a new conservation charity," I said warmly. "Feel free to congratulate me."

"As of when?"

"As of yesterday." My smile broadened. "It's going to help fund breeding and reintroduction programs for critically endangered wildlife, starting with the Almadran skink."

"I . . . you . . . what?" was all she could manage to say. I could see the cogs in her brain grinding together as she tried to catch up.

"We will be working with local charities and helping assist them in their conservation efforts through grants and funding. We're trying to put the money in the areas that matter most and with established local organizations that know better than us what to do with said funds."

"Wow." She blinked, slowly nodding as she came back down to earth. "That's actually a good idea."

"It was yours," I replied. "I'm just trying to implement it, but I'll be honest, I would be terrible at running a nonprofit. I can barely run my own life."

"No shit," she said with a huff.

"Which is why I'm appointing an interim director until I can find a permanent one to run the charity."

"Oh," she mused with another approving nod. "That's also a good idea. I'm impressed." She looked perplexed, as if she couldn't believe she'd just said that aloud. "What are you naming it?"

"Lucky Role Conservation Trust," I said, and I was rewarded with a genuine smile from her. "I don't know if you remember, but it was actually you that inspired the stage name—"

"I remember," she cut in, her face softening in a way I hadn't seen since we'd been young.

I watched it in her eyes as she thought back to those days. We used to always joke that everything in our D&D campaign was the name of our future band. First, it had been Misty Step, then it had been Mage Hand, and when we'd realized that most people would have no clue what we were talking about, we'd decided on Lucky Role. So when I'd started my singing career, I'd adopted the pseudonym as an homage to those days.

*She remembered.*

The moment had been unimportant—just two tweens talking about gaming. I hadn't expected Dove would've held onto the memories as tightly as I had.

I lifted my glass of wine, and, confused, Dove lifted hers and cheers-ed me.

"To Lucky Role Conservation Trust," I said.

"To Lucky Role Conservation Trust," she echoed, still not quite getting it. "Could you explain to me why it was imperative for you to tell me this over lunch?"

"I thought I'd treat my new interim director to a celebratory meal," I replied, watching the realization dawn on her face. "Congratulations, Dove."

I'd anticipated the fact that she'd completely release her glass and had already grabbed the stem before it crashed onto the pristine white linen. It made me look like I had supernatural reflexes, but really I just knew Dove Lachlan better than I knew myself.

"You've appointed *me* as the interim director of your new charity?" she asked, her words slow as if dissecting each one.

I tipped a pretend hat to her. "That I did."

"Without asking me."

My smile tightened, but I was determined to remain aloof. "If I'd asked, you would've said no."

"Deacon."

"Dove," I countered in the same scolding tone. "You are the perfect person for the job. You already knew exactly what this charity should be before it even existed. You will lead us in the right direction until we can find permanent leadership."

The food arrived, granting us a momentary reprieve from the tense conversation. Dove's Lobster Thermidor looked so good that she instantly dove in, pausing our argument, to my great relief.

We ate for a minute in companionable silence, and I gave her a moment to mull over everything I'd just said. I glanced out the window, and Cody was standing across the road, swiping a dramatic hand across his face in an instruction to smile like the most insufferable stage mom. I fought back the urge to roll my eyes and smiled at Dove while she was too busy eating to notice. I loved that she devoured her meal, not giving one flying fuck about being demure and delicate, not performing for anyone, least of all me.

When she finally spoke, she asked, "How long?" and I was very relieved it wasn't "absolutely not, you insane weirdo." There'd been a 50/50 chance of that.

I sighed in relief. Moving my risotto around with my fork in contemplation, I mulled it over before answering. *Maybe this will work out after all.*

"Only a few weeks until we can organize some interviews," I assured her. "But I didn't want to wait to get started."

"Because you're trying to cover your ass." She spoke through a mouthful of food, and even though she clearly had more to say, she took another bite before speaking again.

I didn't blame her. The food here was amazing, and I'd

eaten at Michelin star restaurants all around the world. Maybe it wasn't entirely the food though. Maybe it was the company. Despite her overt anger toward me, twelve-year-old Dove and Deacon would've been high-fiving each other in disbelief that we got to eat in a restaurant like this.

My inner child smiled even as I wore a casually bored expression in an attempt to neutralize Dove's ire. So far it seemed to be working.

"The girl in the viral video being your *interim director* is damage control," Dove pointed out.

"I've already donated a large chunk of money into the trust for specific allocation to the skink breeding program," I said, blotting my lips. "Here's your chance to spend all my money on something you deem *worthy*."

"Tempting." She tossed her head back and forth. "But I don't want to be your scapegoat. You only want to make the situation *look* better. You don't actually care about fixing anything."

That was a wallop of an accusation. Worse, she was right. For a long time, I'd only wanted to deflect the blame onto someone else. It was still my first instinct. I cared so much about being perceived as a good guy that I allowed bad things to happen without taking any action. But ever since Dove's video, it was like a hurricane of reckoning had stormed into my consciousness.

Dove reached for another breadstick, and I covered her wrist with my hand before she could retract it. I swept a thumb over her warm skin and waited until her deep brown eyes met mine to speak.

"Despite what you think, I actually care about making this right," I admitted. "Now more than ever. You made me see how selfish I was being and I'm trying to fix it. Please, help me? When it comes to this, I don't trust anyone more than I trust you."

She seemed pleasantly surprised by that statement, and I felt momentarily victorious in cracking an inch through her icy exterior.

"Well, I mean, I would be an excellent interim director," she said with an uncomfortable laugh, as if she weren't quite boastful enough to admit it. "I was born into conservation work. This is the kind of opportunity my parents dreamed about. My dad always wished he could've made an impact on this kind of scale, but we never had the funds."

"Exactly," I encouraged. "And you can make that dream a reality."

"With your money," she added smugly. She retracted her hand from my touch to nibble on her breadstick. "Me holding your purse strings? I kind of like the sound of that. So what now?"

"Cody will handle all of the press releases and announcements." I nodded out the window to where Cody stood with a baseball cap and sunglasses, snapping photos of us on his phone. "It would help us both out if you smiled at me just once."

"Absolutely not."

"You know, I knew I was pushing it." I gave her a wink.

Dove waved through the window as three more cars pulled up onto the sidewalk. "Are *they* part of your entourage too?"

Before they even got out of their cars, I knew that they were paps. Uncaring that they were illegally parking, nothing else mattered but getting close enough to snag the perfect shot. I didn't know how they did it. There was nowhere in the world I could randomly appear that wouldn't be swarmed with cameras after an hour.

"Actually, let's have lunch in the private room."

I flagged down Luca to tell the staff to move our table. If the paps got a shot of us, Cody wouldn't be able to control the narrative the same way. I wanted the news to be about the conservation trust and not about the angry, viral zookeeper.

"Ooh, fancy pants with the private room," Dove jeered, doing little jazz hands as she stood, holding her plate of lobster.

"The servers can bring the plates," I said, rising.

"You will take this plate from my cold dead hands," she countered, biting the air between us and making me guffaw. "As your interim director, I order you to bring yours too."

I couldn't hide the laughter in my voice as I said, "That's not how this works."

Dove shrugged. "Fine. Let your food get cold." She sauntered off, swirling another forkful of pasta as she moved deeper into the restaurant.

I laughed as I watched her go, hope blooming in my chest as I wondered if maybe we might actually have a chance of being friends again.

*Well, I'll be damned. This just might work.*

I picked up my plate and followed her.

# Chapter Eleven

Dove

My neck hurt from craning it at the frescoed ceilings of the Holloway Estate. "I can't believe he's staying in this creepy place," I murmured to myself. Floating through the giant space, my limbs felt too light. I shuddered as the hairs at the back of my neck lifted. "This place is giving serious *Saltburn* vibes."

The decor looked like something more akin to the Vatican than the nautical Prickle Island style I was used to. I'd never seen so many cherubs and gilded filigree in my life. I swore somewhere in the place was a sliding bookshelf that led to a secret dungeon.

Luca appeared through one of the many side doors down the long hallway. "Ms. Lachlan," he said with a smile.

"Just Dove," I corrected him.

Luca nodded and gestured for me to follow. "Deacon is just

finishing his workout. He'll be with you shortly. Can I get you a coffee or tea?"

"I'm good, thanks," I said tightly.

I side-eyed the portrait on the wall to my right. The painted old lady's eyes followed me as I moved. If she stared any longer, it felt like I might stumble into an alternate dimension. I wiped my clammy hands on my shorts and hurried after Luca.

This was the sort of place Deacon and I had joked about living in as kids, but I'd never thought either of us meant it. Even if it was just a rental, it was like a walking fever dream.

*Why did we want to live in this eerie place again?*

Luca waved me into an ornate sitting room and left to go find Deacon, I presumed. My only company was two giant marble greyhounds sitting on either side of the fireplace like horror movie sentinels.

To avoid the stares of their hollow white eyes, I took my notebook out of my bag and started jotting down more notes for the Lucky Role Conservation Trust. We needed to get some of the high-level stuff out of the way before we could get into the minutia: mission statements, goals, commitments, branding, etc.

I spent twenty minutes writing detailed notes before I checked my watch and realized how much time had passed.

"Seriously," I muttered aloud. I still had so much work to do, and sitting around in a random fancy—and frightening—sitting room was a complete waste of my time.

Having had enough, I shoved my notebook back in my bag and made a beeline for the stairs, finding loud pop music blaring from down the stairwell. I couldn't believe he was still working out.

"Deacon!" I shouted, stomping up the creaking, old steps. "We have a meeting now." I rushed down the oil-painting lined hallway and to the open door at the end of the hall. "You seriously need to hurry up because I haven't got all the time in the world to sit around and wait for you to do sit-ups or whatever the hell it is—"

My words ended on a choked gag as I turned the corner to find Deacon panting and glistening, a towel slung over the back of his neck, a tight black tank top revealing chiseled arms and the sides of his cut obliques. His face was ruddy with exertion as he tousled his wet hair off his face.

"Sorry," he said, blotting his forehead with a towel. "Ricardo made me do a super set today."

"I . . . uh . . ." *Quickly, Dove, put some freaking words together!* I held up a hand, covering Deacon's torso so my brain could think. "Where are your clothes?"

"I'm wearing them?" He let out a hoarse laugh that was so ungodly sexy, and I hated him even more for it. "Am I distracting you?" Deacon asked tauntingly. How dare he look *and sound* so hot.

"You are annoying me, is what you're doing," I grumbled.

"Sure," he said, grabbing another towel off the seat of the rowing machine and blotting his face. My eyes trailed the ever-present leather necklace that dipped into the low neckline of his tank, the outline of some round talisman underneath. He'd probably gotten it on some LA yoga retreat or some other pseudo-spiritual bullshit.

My eyes roved his body as if they were magnetized to him. This man was the definition of bulging muscles. His arms were so defined that it looked like his personal trainer had sculpted each one from stone.

*If anyone deserves a fruit basket, it's Ricardo . . . .*

I cleared my throat and looked up to the ceiling.

"We were supposed to have a meeting now," I said. "The trust? The new leaf you've apparently turned over, remember?"

"I remember," he said, giving his skin one more sweep of the towel before tossing it in the hamper in the corner. This was the bougiest gym I'd ever seen in my whole life. Who worked out in a room with sconces and floral wallpaper?

"This is how you come dressed to a meeting?" I asked, waving at his soaked tank top clinging to his eight-pack abs.

"And that is how *you* come dressed to a meeting?" Deacon countered, waving at my khaki uniform.

"This is part of my job!" I seethed.

"And working out is part of mine," he said with a dimpled smile, as if he knew just how much of a rise he was getting out of me.

"Fine! Look, I only have ten more minutes before I have to be back," I said. "Here is some paperwork for you to look over." I dropped it on the rack of dumbbells. "I expect you to have answers to the questions on page three by tomorrow."

"I trust you to answer those questions without me," he said.

"Nuh-uh. No. We are not doing this." I folded my arms tightly across my chest.

"Doing what?"

"You've dragged me into this charity now, and I won't be attached to some fluffy, ineffectual nonsense with your face on it," I snapped. "You want me? You got me. Now I expect you to actively participate in this charity, so help me God. You will pay attention, and you will *care* because I care, understood?"

He stared at me for several seconds before saying, "Understood." He shook his head. "And I thought it was just going to be Ricardo kicking my ass today."

I maintained eye contact with Deacon like my life depended on it. *Do not check him out again, Dove. You are a stronger woman than that. Think of the skinks!*

A woman walked in carrying a giant glass of grass-green liquid. "Your smoothie, Mr. Harrow."

"Thank you, Divya," Deacon said, taking the drink.

"Can I get anything for your *friend*?" she asked, looking between us as if trying to ascertain who I was. I wondered how many "friends" Deacon invited round. *That doesn't matter, Dove. Stop thinking about his love life and his abs, his sweet, sweet, glorious abs.*

"I'm not his friend," I said tightly, my voice thick as I struggled with the hot, sweaty presence of one of the sexiest men in the world. Apparently, my hormones didn't care that he was a pompous asshole. Still, I managed to keep a steely tone as I said, "I'm the interim director of what is going to be a very successful charity."

Deacon's cheeks dimpled again. "Divya, could you please make Ms. Lachlan one of your famous lavender matcha lattes?"

"Of course," Divya said, giving a little bob of her head before leaving.

I glared at Deacon. "I—"

"It's purple. You'll love it," he said with a wink. Before I could rage at him some more, he added, "Cody wants us to get some footage of us with an animal to use for the trust announcement. Do you have any ideas?"

"Oh, so you want to be a part of this if it involves your face on a screen?"

He sighed. "It will bring positive attention to the charity, which will mean more donations and awareness, which will mean a more successful organization, which is something you and I both want, so yes." He waved me up and down. "I thought you'd understand how this goes. It's part of the deal. Look at the Madigans."

"You did not just bring up the Madigans to me."

Deacon retreated a step, which was wise because I was ready to go full ape shit on him. "You still have beef with them after all these years?"

"They are our family's sworn enemies," I snarled. "And forgive me if I don't want to slap my face on yoga pants and toilet brushes to raise money for conservation and pretend to be a reality TV celebrity."

I balled my hands into fists. It was really low bringing up the Madigan family to me. *Madigan Mountain* was a hit reality TV show set at their family's zoo in Australia. They were like the trashy knockoff brand of the Irwin family.

"Why exactly do you hate them again? I could never really remember," Deacon said with a chuckle, as if our family feud were just some joke. "Your dad was best friends with their dad or something and they had a falling out before any of you were born, right?"

"Besides the fact they stole all of Dad's ideas and then went on to have eight kids all named after animals just to fuck with us?" I could feel the blush burning across my cheeks. "Or when after Dad died, they tried to make our family into a spin-off reality show but keep all the money and rights for themselves? *Or* when they tried buy the zoo out from under us, including hiring Hannah under false pretenses as a spy?"

"They did what?"

"That's a story for another time," I said, folding my arms tightly.

"No Madigan talk, got it, sorry." Deacon took another sip of his juice and set it down on the table by the window. "I didn't mean to compare you to them. We just need something filmable for the announcement."

"Fine," I muttered. "I'll have a think about it. Eddie might be good for that."

"Eddie?"

"The toucan," I said. "He's currently at the vet hospital, and you could release him back into his enclosure tomorrow. Get a slo-mo of him flying off from your hands and all that. Very inspirational."

Deacon's cheeks dimpled. "Great, I'm free tomorrow at 11 if that works for you?"

"It does." I took a step back. "I'll see you then." I took another step without looking, my foot colliding with the corner of the treadmill, and Deacon shot forward, grabbing my elbow to steady me.

"Whoa there," he said with a laugh, his face a hair's breadth from my own.

I wrenched my elbow away like it was on fire. I absolutely could not have him touching me right now. Despite my feelings toward him, I was only human, and seeing his obliques made me want to run my fingers over them like playing a guiro.

"Tomorrow," I said, unable to meet his gaze. I turned just as Divya walked back in carrying a purple-and-green concoction. I accepted it with thanks and took a sip, the flavors exploding on my tongue. I tried to contain an indecent groan. "Damn you."

Deacon laughed. "Delicious, right?"

I refused to acknowledge his smugness. "Tomorrow at 11," I said again. "Be on time for once." I eyed him up and down one last time, unable to contain myself. "And wear a shirt."

# Chapter Twelve

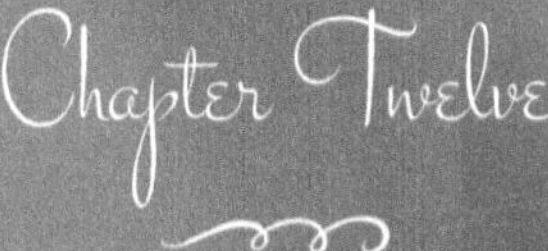

Dove

When I turned the corner holding Eddie's carrier, I stopped short when I saw Deacon leaning against the fence post, looking away from me as his publicist nattered in his ear.

Curse him. Couldn't he just look ugly sometime? Why must he constantly look ready for the cover of *Vogue*? There was nothing this man could wear, nothing he could do, no silly faces that he could pull that would make him look less swoon-worthy.

"Stupid genetics," I muttered to myself as I started walking toward him, hoping I might be able to skirt past without him taking notice. *Yep, nothing to see here, just a purple-haired zookeeper carrying a toucan in a crate.*

I walked faster, and Deacon breezily turned my way and gave me a little wave. The memory of him grabbing my elbow in the gym flashed through my mind. The way his eyes had scanned my face, how, for a split second, he'd been close enough that I could just lift on tiptoes and kiss him . . .

*I refuse to notice those freaking cheekbones, and lips, and jawline, and broody bedroom eyes. What the hell is wrong with me? I never care about hot men!*

Hackles raised, I lifted Eddie's carrier higher and approached. "Let's get this over with then."

Deacon looked me over, his mild expression darkening as he noted the way I scowled at him. If he thought one amicable lunch and flustered gym encounter would make me tolerate all his nonsense, he had another thing coming. I couldn't believe I was agreeing to do a fluff piece about one of our animals to help repair *his* image. And poor Eddie the toucan was caught in the crossfire.

*Think of the skinks, Dove. Think of the breeding program.*

Deacon jogged ahead of Cody to keep up with me. "I see the little storm cloud is back over your head," he said playfully, swatting the air above me.

"Don't touch me," I snapped.

He swirled his fingers over my head again. "I wasn't touching you."

"Don't touch the air around me."

"You don't want me to touch the *air*?"

"Ugh," I groaned. "You are worse than all of my siblings combined."

"So you're saying I feel like family now?" Deacon waggled his eyebrows.

I tried to walk faster, but it was no use. The man was 6'3" with legs sculpted by the same personal trainer that worked with Hugh Jackman for goodness' sake. His superhero-worthy calves could run circles around me.

"This is the most insane thing I've ever said yes to," I muttered. "Why are we doing this again?"

Deacon shrugged. "I just do what Cody tells me."

"Great to see you still think for yourself."

"I know when to defer to people with more knowledge and skills than me about something," he corrected. "Which is why I have appointed *you* as the interim director of my charity, which, you have to agree, was a smart move."

"You're trying to flatter me so I go through with this buffoonery, aren't you?"

"Yep."

We turned the corner to the aviary, and I passed the carrier to Deacon as I unclipped the carabiner of keys from my belt. Cody huffed and puffed behind us as he caught up. "I didn't realize we were doing cardio first."

I ignored Cody and pointed to the carrier in Deacon's hand. "Don't shake that."

Deacon chortled, giving me a look of disbelief. "I'm not a toddler."

I flashed him a mocking smile. "Then stop acting like one."

"I'm sorry I sprung all of this on you. I know it's a lot." He cocked his head at me. "But the best way to show people I'm getting hands-on with this is to do something hands-on. We want them to know we're taking the conservation trust seriously, don't we?"

"Your strategic use of the word 'we' is noted," I said flatly.

"We need to make a show of it. Politic a bit. I need to kiss some babies, you know?"

"So call that British model you were dating."

He clenched his jaw and a golf-ball-sized muscle popped out because of course it did. At least it was satisfying getting under his skin.

"Whoa," Cody said, waving his hands between us. "I'm calling an audible here. Let's just focus up, okay, team?"

Deacon ignored him and leaned in toward me, his temper flaring. "Kate and I never dated. We barely even met."

I whirled on him as I unlocked the door, holding the airlock gate ajar with my boot. "What?"

Deacon let out a mirthless laugh as if disappointed in me. "It was all publicity. The photos we took in one day with a bunch of outfit changes. They were fed to the media over months to make it look—"

"Uh, uh, uh," Cody said, slicing a hand between us. "Those are Harrow team secrets. Cone of silence, m'kay? Unless you want her to sign an NDA, something I would highly recommend at this point."

"So this is what it takes to be your real self around people?" I scoffed. "Contracts, legally gagging them into keeping your secrets. Do you really not trust anyone anymore?"

"Don't answer that," Cody said, taking out his phone. "Right, *director*," he added pointedly at me. "You ready to launch your new charity? Shall we get this show on the road or what?"

I let out a bracing breath and ushered Deacon and Cody into the aviary. "Careful where you step," I instructed as I latched the door behind us. "And if you don't want bird poop in your hair, don't stand directly under any perches."

"The things I do for you," Cody said to Deacon as he clapped him on the back.

We moved to the center of the aviary, and I put Eddie's carrier down on a tree stump. I could feel the terrible grinding of my logic and my emotions, stuck between several rocks and even more hard places.

This temporary director role would've been an absolute gift if it had come from anyone else. It would be great for my CV. I didn't plan on working at Prickle Island Zoo for the rest of my life, but if I'd only had one job since I'd been fifteen, who else would ever employ me? Especially when that employer was my mother.

Plus, when else would I have *millions of dollars* of conservation money to allocate as I saw fit? This was a really big deal despite how much I hated that it had been given to me by Deacon. And I still wanted to do a good job, wanted to make a difference, and maybe doing a deal with the devil to get there would be worth it.

*Great, now I'm sounding like the Madigans.*

But no matter how much I loathed Deacon, I couldn't bring myself to run this thing into the ground just to spite him. The charity deserved a chance, and I wanted to build it into something at least semi stable before I passed the baton off to whoever the permanent director would be.

"Okay," I said, dusting a hand down my cargo shorts. "I am going to get him out and pass him to you." I tipped my head to Deacon. "Then all you have to do is throw him up in the air and he'll fly off to a perch and it'll be some majestic bullshit when you play it in slo-mo or whatever it is you plan to do, got it?"

Deacon's cheeks dimpled. "Got it."

I went to open the carrier door, but Cody said, "Wait." He swirled his hands as he got his phone out and pointed the camera at us. "This way. Better lighting."

I had a million petty retorts on my tongue but held them back. When we had shuffled to and fro to Cody's liking, he gave us a thumbs-up.

I was about to open the door again when Cody added, "Maybe, Deacon, say a couple things before you release the bird. You know, about the charity and what you're doing."

"Good idea," Deacon said with a sage nod.

I wanted so badly to point out how laughable this was but buried it deep. *Just get through the next ten minutes, Dove, and then you can go have the leftover donuts that Frankie baked this morning,* I promised myself. I deserved a treat after all this.

I opened the carrier and grabbed Eddie, holding his wings tucked into his little body.

"Careful," I said as I passed him off to Deacon.

"I got him," Deacon reassured me, and I tried very hard to ignore the way his warm fingers skimmed across the backs of my hands as he took control of the toucan. I tried even harder to not think about how giant his hands were compared to mine.

I swallowed thickly. "Good?"

Deacon nodded and held Eddie a little higher. "I thought toucans had orange beaks."

"You're thinking of a toco toucan. This is a keel-billed."

"Of course, how could I forget?"

I rolled my eyes. There was a time when I would've peppered Deacon with fun facts about keel-billed toucans, but he didn't deserve my fun facts anymore.

"I thought his beak would be heavier. It feels hollow," he said, surprised as Eddie nibbled at Deacon's finger with his serrated beak.

"It is. Their beaks are made of keratin, same as fingernails." *Dammit, Dove! He doesn't deserve your fun facts!* "How would he fly if it were heavier?"

"Good point," Deacon replied. "Huh, look at you teaching me new animal facts. We're practically pals." He smiled at my frown. "Chums? Besties?"

"No."

"We'll get there," he added with a wink that I was sure had dropped a million panties over the years.

"Can you please just focus?"

Deacon looked down at the toucan nibbling his fingers. "At least Eddie here likes me."

"He's trying to attack you," I pointed out. "He's just very weak and unable to peel your skin off the way he wants to. Although, I'm sure if we gave him enough time—"

"Okay, Wednesday Addams," Cody called, making a chopping motion through the air. "Move out of the shot now."

I huffed. "Gladly."

"No." Deacon toed my leg with his shoe. "You should stay.

She should stay," he added to Cody. "We want people to see that the grumpy girl in the viral video and I are friendly now, right?"

"If someone can get that memo to her face, then sure," Cody replied. My frown deepened and he waved me up and down. "My point exactly."

"Dove's actually quite the actress," Deacon countered. "She played one hell of a mischievous tiefling—"

"When we were twelve," I cut in. "But I think I can manage to hide the hatred in my eyes for this one video."

"The role of a lifetime," Deacon said with another panty-dropping wink.

"Alright, let's get this over with," Cody called with a thumbs-up. "Deacon, you ready?"

"Yep." Deacon bobbed his chin in reply to Cody because his hands were filled with a grumpy toucan.

"Eeyore, you ready?"

"I am, dickhead," I sang back with a smile.

Deacon was right. I was an excellent actress.

"Alright . . . and action." Cody pointed at Deacon with a finger gun, as if he were some big shot cinematographer and not a guy filming on his iPhone.

Deacon plastered on that smoldering smile, and I fought every cell in my body not to frown and instead fawn like every girl waiting outside the zoo gates.

"Hi, I'm Deacon Harrow," he started, and I snorted.

Cody grimaced. "Okay, we'll try that one more time."

"Why are you laughing?" Deacon muttered from the corner of his mouth.

"You just sound absurd. 'Hi, I'm Deacon Harrow,'" I mocked in a low voice, laughter rolling out of me. "I'm a grade A asshole who makes animals go extinct, but look at my biceps in this too tight T-shirt and my sexy face."

"You think I have a sexy face?"

I shot him a look. "You ran straight past the point of that statement, didn't you?"

I extracted a grape from my treat pouch and put it on Deacon's hand so that Eddie would double his efforts to attack him. Unfortunately, Eddie managed to grab the treat without doing any major physical harm.

"Kids," Cody snapped. "Go again. Cranky pants, don't laugh this time."

"You got it, jerkface."

Cody pointed at us again, and I thrust my hands into my pockets so I could clench them without the camera seeing.

Deacon started over. "Hi, I'm Deacon Harrow, joined by Lucky Role Conservation Trust's interim director, Dove Lachlan, and this"—he lifted Eddie toward the camera—"is Eddie. Eddie has just come from the vet hospital for his annual checkup and we're releasing him back into his enclosure. Isn't that right, Eddie?" Eddie clicked his beak as if on command. *Traitor*. "If you want even more wildlife news and to make a difference to more critically endangered animals, make sure to subscribe to our socials and join the conservation trust's newsletter."

We had a newsletter? And social media handles already? Wow. The devil worked hard but Cody Novak worked harder.

I had to give it to Deacon too. He nailed that, unscripted, on the first take. Deacon looked back at me in confirmation that he could release Eddie, and I gave him a nod.

"Fly free, Eddie," Deacon said, which I thought might be hamming it up a little *too* much, but I kept my face trained into pleasant neutrality.

Deacon threw Eddie into the air and posed with a smile like the poster boy action hero he was. And Eddie lifted skyward, wings still tucked.

I watched the toucan's wings. Still tucked. Still tucked. Still tucked.

*Any minute now*, I thought as the toucan loaf launched upward. Any minute Eddie would open his wings and majestically fly off . . . except he didn't.

Eddie reached the apex of his toss and, wings still freaking tucked, started to plummet back toward the ground.

"Shit," Deacon said at the same time as I shouted, "Fuck!"

We both scrambled forward, hands out as if we could catch the bird like a football with a giant beak, but we were both too far away. We watched in horror as the stupid bird fell down, down, down to Earth.

*Right* before Eddie collided with the ground, his wings spread and he took flight. The dramatic little piece of shit. Deacon and I both let out exasperated sighs of relief . . . just as Eddie flew smack dab into the chain-link fence and got his beak stuck in a hole.

"Holy crap!" I shouted, running forward and extracting the toucan from the fence. "You are seriously trying to give us all heart attacks today, aren't you?"

Fortunately, the second I retracted Eddie, he ruffled his feathers and flew up to a perch unharmed, searching for more grapes, as if he hadn't just made all of our cortisol levels shoot through the roof.

"I swear to God you are a bad omen," I grumbled at Deacon.

Deacon simply shrugged. "I've been called worse. What now?"

"Now, you go away, please and thank you." I ushered Deacon and Cody to the door.

"Do you need some help?" Deacon offered to my surprise.

"If you're bored, feel free to wander around the zoo, but"—I gave him an incredulous look—"you are the last person I need help from, Deacon."

He gave me another infuriating smile as he wandered to the airlock. "I'm going to change your mind about that, just you wait."

# Chapter Thirteen

Deacon

As I wandered through the zoo, the late afternoon sun dipped below the trees, casting long shadows across the paths. My watch buzzed with a notification, stalling me. It was Luca texting me to tell me that he was waiting in the golf cart to drive me back to the estate. All of the cast and crew had packed up for the day and left, apart from me.

Evelyn had loaned me her office again so I could do remote interviews about the latest season of my Netflix show. The small office was still stuffed with ring lights and a green screen backdrop, ready for even more promo tomorrow morning.

I sighed and stretched my neck side to side, trying to get the blood flowing again after sitting for so long. Four hours of interviews was definitely not my favorite way to end the day after I'd had to be in hair and makeup at 3 am.

But at least the springtime sun was still out as I wandered sleepily down the hill, enjoying the reprieve from constant messages and people swarming me. Here it felt like I was submersed in a jungle—tall trees, twittering birds, the sound of leaves gently blowing on branches. The trees seemed to take a deep breath for me, reminding me to do the same.

Memories danced along with the gently blowing leaves. Summer after summer, I'd always loved wandering the zoo with Dove after all the visitors had left. It had felt like our magical, secret jungle just for us. The adventures we'd had, the reveries we'd dreamed up, the songs we'd sang . . . for it was beneath these same trees that the first song lyrics had come to me along with the very first big dream: I was going to be a songwriter.

Bitterness spoiled that thought. I'd lived that dream once, but not anymore.

I was about to turn toward the café exit when a flash of olive-green khakis to my right caught my eye. Half obscured behind a service area hedge, I wasn't sure which keeper it was until I saw a glimpse of purple hair.

My lips curved, a lightness overtaking me again, and I turned in Dove's direction as she emerged holding a snake around her shoulders.

"Gah!" she exclaimed when she saw me. "Don't scare people holding snakes."

"A good lesson." I tipped an invisible hat at her. "Especially poisonous ones."

"I think you mean venomous." She didn't break stride, walking up the hill as the snake curled around her shoulders.

I followed her a pace behind. "Unless I was talking about the common garter snake, which are, in fact, poisonous."

"How dare you use my own fun facts against me." Her footsteps faltered as she looked at me. "How do you even remember that?" she asked. "I taught you that like centuries ago."

"I remember a lot of things from those summers," I admitted with a shrug.

She clearly didn't know what to do with that admission, so she started walking again and I fell into easy step with her.

"Well then, you know this is a boa constrictor and not a common garter snake," she lectured me. "Deacon, meet Matilda, our four-year-old boa constrictor. Matilda, meet Deacon, certifiable pain in my ass."

She held the snake's head toward me, and I bowed toward it which gained a laugh. "Greetings, Matilda."

We cut through a gate that had been painted to blend in with the surrounding gardens. Dove didn't hold it open for me, but I followed regardless as we moved along the path toward her mother's house.

"Are you still working?" I asked when I realized she had no intention of returning the snake to its enclosure. "Where are you and Matilda going?"

"Movie night at Mom's house," Dove replied as if that were an obvious explanation as to why she was touting a giant snake. When I let out a surprised laugh, she added, "It's been a long day and Matilda is a surprisingly excellent cuddler."

"So no boyfriends to cuddle you then?" *Very subtle, Deacon. Way to play it cool. You could just ask her if she's seeing anyone.*

Dove gave me her patented death stare. "Not currently. I am very content with my boa snuggles at the moment, thanks."

Something twanged in my gut at that. It was the most ridiculous thing in the world—being jealous of a snake for being the one to get to wrap around Dove at the end of a long day.

Clearing my throat, I attempted to push away the thoughts of enveloping her curves with my limbs. *This isn't about Dove, I coached myself. You just really need to get laid. That's all. A few more days of shooting and then you'll be back in New York. Get it together.*

With that wayward bout of lust resolved, I pressed on, trailing after Dove behind the scenes of the zoo. She paused to drop a kiss to Matilda's head and a smile tugged my lips. It was nice seeing this softer side of her again. She'd always loved her animals but let so few people see this gentler person that I knew existed beneath her steely exterior.

"First week as director has been pretty eventful, hm?" I asked, needing to fill the silence between us.

"Mission statements, core values, logo design," she stated, listing things off on her fingers.

"A bungled toucan release," I added with a chuckle.

"That reminds me," she said to herself, deflating a little. "I still need to radio Finch to keep an eye on Eddie after his near-death experience and write up an incident report."

"I can help," I offered. "What other things does the trust need?"

"A permanent director," she lamented, and I wondered again if heaping this massive responsibility on her had been too much. She seemed to love it and loathe it in equal measure. "How long until you find a replacement?"

"We just announced it." I stretched my arms side to side as we walked, wishing I had a snake or something to hold onto. "We will probably need a couple more weeks to line up candidates at least. Maybe after the gala?"

Her forehead creased. "The zoo gala?"

"I forgot about the zoo gala," I replied with a nostalgic laugh. "Those were the best. Remember how we used to sneak into the catering and steal whole platters to eat up by the tiger lookout?"

"We blamed the missing hors d'oeuvres on the twins, but I think Mom knew it was us." Dove smiled at the memory, and it felt like another tiny win for me. "They've become so popular we hold one every season now. The fall one is my favorite; we do a whole spooky pumpkin patch thing. It's great. The springtime one is only in a few weeks. I've ordered an ungodly amount of tulips for it. Pastel everything. A whole host of swanky patrons are coming out for that weekend to party, so hopefully we are able to turn a good profit." She seemed to realize she'd started getting swept away in bragging about her event planning endeavors. I could've listened to her go on, but she refocused. "So if you're not talking about one of the zoo galas, then what?"

"We'll do a big fundraiser party in New York," I explained. "To officially launch Lucky Role Conservation Trust. I have some friends who will be in the city and the guest list will be exclusive, and obviously you will need to be there as director."

She came to a screeching halt again. "What?"

"We're hoping to have big donors in attendance. It's our charity—"

"It's *your* charity!"

"And *you* are my charity's current director, which means you need to be there."

"Oh no, absolutely not."

"Come on," I goaded. "It'll be fun. Walk the red carpet with me." I wasn't going to take this opportunity to tell her that red carpets were a gauntlet of the rudest and most demonic photographers in the world.

"There's going to be a red carpet for a *fundraiser*?" Dove asked.

"There's always a red carpet when celebrities are invited to events."

"There are going to be celebrities?" she balked. "I mean besides you."

I really liked the idea that she'd forgotten I was a celebrity for a moment. I kept wishing Dove would treat me like Deacon, the friend she'd once known, and not Deacon Harrow, the brand.

"You'll be fine," I assured her. "You'll be my date."

"I will *not* be your date," she gritted out, and I swore the blood vessels around her temples might burst along with her protestation. "Attending is one thing. Attending and getting my photo taken is another. And attending as your *date* is entirely out of the question."

"Cody thinks it will look good if we go together," I pleaded. "Show off our alliance."

"No."

I knew it was self-serving. It would make me look good and it wouldn't benefit her in any way. If anything, it would open her up to more public scrutiny. But the idea of her stepping into my world, of her on my arm, of me not having to navigate the shark-infested waters alone was something I couldn't pass up.

"Please?" I begged, clasping my hands together. "What do I have to do to make you say yes?" I reached out toward her but then dropped my hands when Matilda turned her triangular head toward me. "I can't tell if your shoulders are perpetually bunched around your ears or if you just really need a massage."

"Probably both."

"I promise to hook you up with the greatest masseuse in NYC if you come to the fundraiser?"

"No."

Folding my arms, I arched my brow in challenge. "What can I do to convince you?"

She pursed her lips, pondering. "Fine. I'll come." I fist pumped the air. "*If* you let us announce that you're coming to the zoo gala and put your face all over our social media and make a video of you telling everyone to come visit the zoo this summer, *then* I'll be your date. Oh, and you have to pay for an hour-long massage from that fancy masseuse of yours."

I grinned. "Done."

Her mouth fell open, as if she were clearly surprised by my instant agreement. Little did Dove know I had already volunteered to help Evelyn with the zoo gala promotion when I'd first pitched the trust to her. Like mother like daughter, I supposed. But if letting Dove think she was getting the better end of the deal meant she'd come, I wouldn't let on.

"Fine then. I'll be your date." Her brow furrowed. "What?"

"I just never thought I'd have to bargain so hard to get a woman to go on a date with me," I admitted with a chuckle.

"You haven't been hanging around the right women then," Dove quipped.

"Clearly," I replied. "I didn't think we'd ever have a more death-defying quest than raiding that dragon cavern, but this, I think, will be even more of an adventure."

She smiled, and I hoped she was remembering how much fun we'd had that summer that we'd stumbled through my first and only D&D campaign. Did she watch all the *Dimension 20* episodes like I did? Did she think of us when she did? I shook the thought from my head.

"I think this will be one hell of a campaign, Deacon," she said and stuck out her hand. Matilda hung on easily as I shook it. "Just don't die this time," she added with a wink, and she laughed as my expression soured.

I let her walk away with that last little dig. She didn't know that I'd actually cried when I'd asked the Dungeon Master to kill me off our campaign so I could move to New York and start my music career. She didn't know that for three years, I'd missed it every day until life had gotten too busy to think about anything anymore.

I'd relished that exhaustion. I'd tried to reach out to Dove a couple of times, but she'd never replied, and after a while I had just stopped trying. Still, I should've tried harder when her dad died. I should've just gotten on a plane and flown here in the middle of my international tour. No amount of time unspoken between us would ever make it okay that I let her live through those years without knowing I was thinking of her every day.

*Oh well. Just one more thing on my list of never-ending mistakes when it came to Dove Lachlan.*

I stood there backlit by the sunset, watching the space where Dove and Matilda had disappeared for a long time before finally turning around. When I did, I found a very pregnant blonde woman with pink-tipped hair standing directly behind me, looking at me with so much raw excitement in her eyes, I thought she might pass out or start crying . . . or go into labor.

"You must be Hannah," I said, extending my hand.

"Oh my god, Deacon Harrow knows my name!" She shook my hand, her palm exceedingly sweaty. "I'm so, so sorry to bother you. I just have a question for you and I didn't know when would be a good time to ask and it just seemed like now might be that good time and, uh, I ramble a lot, sorry, but I do it with everyone, not just celebrities. I'm kind of a ranter, and, uh . . . what was I saying?"

My smile widened. I could see why she was Dove's best friend. She was like an excited golden retriever to Dove's black cat energy, overly talkative where Dove was monosyllabic, extroverted where Dove was introverted. And I was grateful that Dove had people that clearly loved her and made her life full. The thought caught me off guard.

*I'm just happy for an old friend. Yep, that's all this feeling is.*

With a mounting frustration at my own inner thoughts, I turned back to the bouncing, excited woman in front of me. "What did you want to ask me, Hannah?"

# Chapter Fourteen

Dove

The table was practically full to bursting at **Sunday Funday Fondue** Day, growing year upon year along with **our** family. Lark and Logan sat watching from a laptop at one end of the table, having their morning coffee in New Zealand while we ate our decadently cheesy dinner. Finch and Frankie canoodled beside the laptop while Hawk, Hannah, and I sat on one side of the long rectangular table, Heron, Crane, and Wren across from us.

"It's decided," Mom announced, lifting her glass to **cheers** the air. "I need to buy a bigger dining table."

"We might need to knock down that wall if this gets any bigger," Crane said, sizing up the wall that divided the dining and living rooms in our centuries-old house.

Our family home had been built by my great-grandfather

during the establishment of Prickle Island Zoo. He probably never thought that not only would Prickle Island Zoo still be running a century later, but also that his descendants would be so plentiful that we'd need a bigger house.

"We need space for a highchair," Mom added, nodding to Hannah, who was four days away from her due date and looking like she wanted to murder someone.

Hawk already had their hospital bags packed and hotel room booked, ready for the baby's imminent arrival. This was our last night together. They were officially on baby leave as of tomorrow and would be off island until my nephew's arrival.

Wren scooted her chair over toward Heron and waved at the spot between her and Mom. "We can fit a highchair here."

"But what about all the other future kids and spouses," Mom insisted.

"We can worry about that when the time comes," Finch called from the other end of the table.

"Yeah, Mom," I added. "I don't think we'll need to be setting more spaces at this table for a long time."

Right as I proclaimed that ill-fated statement, I was jinxed by a knock on the door.

Confused, we all looked over as Hannah popped up— which was a feat in her current state—and shouted, "I invited him!" as if she were confessing to a crime.

My stomach plummeted. "Him? Him who?" I had a terrible feeling I already knew.

Hannah slid me an apologetic glance as she moved around the table toward the front door.

"No." I groaned. "Please, dear God, no."

"I'm sorry," she whined. "I'm going to be up to my eyeballs in diapers for the foreseeable future and it was a push present to myself to have dinner with Deacon freaking Harrow, okay?"

"How dare you use my nephew to make me not shout at

you!" I whisper-hissed at her as she pouted and rubbed her belly, knowing full well that it would work.

*Curse my best friend and her adorable, sad, pregnant face!*

Hannah waddled the rest of the way and opened the door. Meanwhile, Mom quickly whisked a chair out from her office and set another place at the table between her and Wren. *Of course he has to sit directly across from me.* By the time Deacon rounded the corner, it appeared a place had been set for him all along.

"Hello, Lachlan clan." Deacon greeted us with a wave. "Thanks for the invite."

He breezed into the room holding a bottle of wine that was probably absurdly expensive and completely wasted on my feral family. He wore a cashmere sweater and gray slacks, looking like he was the face of a Ralph Lauren campaign . . . which he might've been actually. I couldn't remember.

His deep blue eyes landed on me and his stubbled cheeks dimpled. "Good to see you all again," he said to the room but kept staring directly at me.

Hannah erupted into a fit of giggles like he'd just said something hysterical, and Hawk came around to gently steer her back to her seat. "Come on, Hazard," he whispered affectionately.

Deacon took a seat, beaming, like this was his favorite place on Earth. "I missed Sunday Funday Fondue Day. I don't think I've had fondue since."

"You never missed one the entire time you lived here," Mom mused as she gave his muscled arm a playful swat.

"Do you still play 'It's feces but what species?'" he asked, and the table erupted into laughter.

Jeez, none of my family could keep themselves from flirting with him. Crane seemed to forget he was a reptile keeper who was two seats away from a species killer. When had Deacon weaseled his way back into Crane's good graces?

Finch whipped out her phone and showed Deacon a photo of what was clearly kangaroo poo. "Go on, Deacon, it's feces but what species?"

*Even Finch is entertaining him. Finch!* My one hope. But Deacon was like a magical unicorn level of attractive. We were all powerless against it. He totally knew what he was doing too. His eager talk of animal poop was a perfect strategy to con my family into accepting him again. But I spotted his scheming from a mile away.

"Uhhh." Deacon inspected the brown, little circles on Finch's phone.

He shot me a sideways glance and I shook my head. "You *know* I'm not going to help you."

Wren put two fingers on the table and hopped them across her plate in a quick jumping motion.

"Kangaroo!" Deacon proclaimed, and the group cheered as I gave my littlest sister a death stare.

"*Et tu, Brute*?" I mouthed at her.

With an innocent little smile, Wren just shrugged at me.

"So," Deacon said, rubbing his hands together before grabbing a fondue skewer. "What have you all been up to the last fifteen years?"

The whole table laughed again, so easily charmed by him as he swirled a piece of bread in the fondue and ate it, slotting right back in like the little kid who used to constantly be at our house.

Everyone started catching him up on all the latest news. He was ever the politician, even taking time to talk to Lark and Logan on the laptop.

"I'd ask you what you've been up to," Mom said. "But I think we've seen it all splashed around the news."

Deacon chuckled. "Don't believe everything you read."

"I loved you in *Violent Nova*," Mom added. "Dove used to be obsessed with the books and games."

"Oh really?" Deacon turned his smug gaze on me.

I swore to God, if Mom told him I used to have the *Violent Nova* movie poster on my wall, I was moving to the most remote jungles of Brazil and never returning.

"Do you think you'll ever do more Lucky Role songs?" Hannah asked, saving me from my runaway thoughts. "I always loved your music."

Hawk cleared his throat and leaned a little closer to his very pregnant fiancée.

"Never say never," Deacon hedged. "But I don't think my team wants me pursuing new music right now."

I could hear the tinge of disappointment in his voice, as if he didn't get to decide what he did with his career.

Deacon had been "discovered" by a model scout at thirteen, and he and his mom had moved to New York to follow his dreams, splitting the family in two until he was old enough to live there on his own. He'd modeled for a few years before launching a music career under the name Lucky Role. While he'd been doing the whole rock-star thing, he'd started popping up in supporting roles in films, and I'd always figured the acting bug had gotten him.

Now, it was hard to even remember his singing career. He was an action star through and through. His latest role as a monster-killing elf in a Netflix fantasy series was plastered over every billboard. I could begrudgingly admit he was a good actor, but he was an even better singer and I kind of wished he were still making music.

"How's your sister?" I asked. The question came out before I could think better of it.

Deacon looked at me, grateful for the spotlight being shifted off career questions. "Faith's good, still touring with Rusty Sky Reverie," he said with a smile. "Still adamant that we are never mentioned in the same sentence online." He laughed and shook his head. "She always wanted to make her own name for herself and she has."

"I saw they won a Grammy," Mom exclaimed. "Please tell her congratulations from all of us."

"And your brother?"

"Still an electrician," Deacon replied with a grin. "He's not in the least bit drawn in by the flashing lights of Hollywood."

I nodded in approval.

"And Tom and Sheila?" Mom asked. *Of course she remembered the names of one of her kids' best friend's parents from fifteen years ago.*

"Good." Deacon's smile seemed to widen in acknowledgement that Mom had remembered. "They still live in a beat-up little farmhouse in Vermont. I keep offering to pay someone to fix it up for them, but they refuse."

"They're good people," Mom said. "It would be lovely to see them again. If they're ever in the area, you tell them to give me a ring."

"I'm sure they'd love that," Deacon replied.

Hawk rubbed circles down Hannah's back as he said, "Good to have down-to-earth family to keep you grounded."

I snorted. "You think *he's* grounded?"

Mom kicked me under the table, and I plastered on a fake smile to appease her.

"You know." Mom gestured between Deacon and me. "I always thought the two of you would end up together."

My fork clattered onto my plate. "Mom!"

Deacon laughed a little too hard. "Dove and me? Never."

Damn.

That shouldn't have hurt nearly as much as it did. *Never.*

Even if the twenty-seven-year-old Dove agreed with him, the twelve-year-old Dove was devastated. He'd been my first crush, my first kiss. We'd had no idea what we'd been doing and had practically knocked each other's teeth out, but it had been a memory I'd held onto for a long time.

"Never," I echoed, trying to sound indifferent even as a million thoughts whirled in my mind. "Especially not after you cheated on me," I added, and a few of my siblings audibly gasped.

"Whoa!" Deacon leaned into the table. "I did *not* cheat on you."

"You cheated on me in Medovier," I countered.

"That was my rogue assassin character that cheated on you, and that campaign ended fifteen years ago!"

"Still, it started a habit of cheating, didn't it?" I countered.

"Oh my god, you guys are such nerds," Crane said with a laugh.

"It's seriously adorkable," Heron jeered. "You're fighting over a board game."

"It's not a board game!" Deacon and I said at once, which only incensed me further.

The rest of my family clearly didn't understand what a slight it had been. They always acted like I was getting upset over losing Monopoly. But at the time, Deacon and I had told each other *everything,* and even though it was "just a game," it had still hurt. And it had hurt even more when he'd gotten his character killed off to go start a fun new life in New York that I'd known I wouldn't get to be a part of. I'd lost my best friend that day, and he probably hadn't even thought twice about it.

"You know, it's getting late," Deacon said with a sigh, rising from the table.

"Deacon, don't go," Mom pleaded. "Really. Dove's just being, uh . . . Dove."

"Thanks, Mom," I muttered.

Deacon waved to the table. "Thank you for the lovely meal, Mrs. Lachlan."

"I hope you'll come back again," Mom offered.

"Thank you," he replied noncommittally. "It's been a nice walk down memory lane," he added, giving me one last look before he left.

# Chapter Fifteen

Dove

When Deacon shut the front door behind him, the room erupted into a cacophony of everyone shouting over each other.

"You all have completely lost your minds," I screamed to be heard. "You are too charmed by his fame and good looks to remember he is *not* our friend." I turned toward Hannah. "And don't think I won't be bringing this up again in the future!" She cringed and rubbed her belly.

"I mean, you were kind of being extra dickish to him though, Dove," Crane said. "Like, you don't need to go so hard on him for making mistakes at a board game when you were kids."

"It wasn't a board game!" I snapped.

"I mean, he wasn't that bad," Heron echoed. "He was really nice to everyone."

I gaped at the twins.

"We're still on your side," Crane added hastily.

"Well, you're definitely not acting like it!"

"Shit, I'm not on your side anymore," Finch said with a laugh. "Not when you're *clearly* deluding yourself about your feelings for him. I'm with Hannah, Team Deacon all the way . . . . Hannah, you okay?"

Before I could shoot down Finch's suggestion that I had any feelings for Deacon other than hatred, I was halted by her concerned expression. I followed Finch's line of sight and found Hannah zoning out at her plate. "I think . . ." She stood up, revealing wet leggings. "I think my water just broke."

"What?" Hawk shot up. "Okay, okay, uh . . . I guess it's go time."

Everyone leapt up from their chairs as Hawk started barking orders like a military commander. My pulse raced with excitement as we all moved into action.

Hannah groaned, leaning against the table and clenching her stomach. "Holy shit, that was strong." She started panting. "This is nothing like those other ones."

Hawk's eyes flew wide. "What other ones?"

"I mean . . ." She grimaced. "I've been cramping on and off throughout the day, but it hasn't been this intense yet."

"What?!"

Finch's hand landed on Hawk's shoulder. "Bro, chill, you're not helping."

Hannah's face twisted as another contraction came barreling in right after the first. "I wanted to meet Deacon and have a final family dinner together. I figured I'd tell you after we finished eating. They weren't that intense—argh, okay, these ones are though." Her face scrunched up again and then it passed fast as it came. She looked at Hawk. "I figured I'd be in labor for ages. I didn't want to spend the whole time in a hospital bed and miss the chance to meet Deacon Harrow!

Why are you looking at me like that? The book said contractions between three to five minutes apart. It hasn't been that until now. I didn't leave it too late, did I?"

Hawk held Hannah by the cheeks and kissed her to stall her normal spiraling out. "Everything's going to be fine," he assured her, kissing her again and placing his forehead to hers. "Just breathe and think of our little bean."

"Please tell me you didn't name your son little bean," Finch snarked.

Hawk ignored her, rocking with Hannah side to side. "Our son is going to be here soon." His voice got thick as he spoke, overcome with emotion.

"Hopefully not too soon," Heron quipped, and Mom shot them a death stare. *Yeah, I definitely inherited that look from her.*

"Right, okay," Hannah said, taking a deep, calming breath. "Let's go get the hospital ba—" She doubled over with a groan, another contraction coming swiftly after the last.

*That was definitely not three minutes . . . I wasn't an expert on labor—well, not the human kind at least—but these contractions seemed worryingly close together for someone who still had a boat and a car ride to get to the hospital.*

Finch darted a look to Mom. "You know what? Maybe we'll come in the boat with you."

"A nice boat ride," Mom agreed. "Lovely." She sounded way too calm, the kind of calm like when a lion had almost escaped that one time. Fortunately, Hannah hadn't learned that super calm equaled emergency yet, as Mom whispered, "Wren, go grab some towels."

"I'll go get the hospital bag!" Crane volunteered, bolting out the door.

"I'll go get the truck," Heron called as Hannah came crashing into another contraction and my heart leapt into my throat. All of my excitement morphed into sheer panic.

"Petey isn't picking up his phone," Frankie said, hurriedly

texting. "I think his boat is still moored at the west docks just down the hill though."

Hannah's contractions were only a minute apart, coming thick and fast. Hawk held her hand, murmuring calm words in her ear, but when he looked up at me, I could see fear in his eyes.

We could *not* let her have her baby on a rusty boat in the middle of the harbor covered in Petey's snack wrappers.

"Dove, go tell Petey we're taking his boat," Hawk said.

"Oh my god," Hannah whined. "I can't have our baby in Petey's fucking boat."

"Hey, Haze," Hawk calmed her, pulling her into him again as they rocked side to side. "Everything's going to be fine. Finch and Mom are going to come with us just in case you need any support, but we've got plenty of time. We'll get to the hospital, okay?"

"Okay!" she said, a sheen of sweat breaking out on her brow.

I bolted to the door, dashing down the path toward the docks as my eyes pricked with panicked tears. All of my siblings were good in emergencies. It was par for the course when working with wild animals, but while the keeper side of me was calm, the sister, aunt, and best friend in me was completely freaking out.

I ran into the night, using only the light of the moon to navigate as I practically barreled over a broad-shouldered figure ambling away from the zoo.

"Dove?" Deacon called, but I couldn't deal with him or the way he'd said "never" or any of the other feelings exploding out my chest. All I could think about was getting to the boat.

# Chapter Sixteen

Deacon

The stars sparkled brighter in the sky here than anywhere else in the world. I swore the constellations above Prickle Island were my favorite . . . not that I had any intention of ever seeing them again after we finished filming. The family dinner had confirmed it: Dove and I were never going to rekindle our friendship. She was determined to hate me forever, and I probably deserved it.

My watch started vibrating and I looked down to see Zeke was calling me. I fished my phone out of my pocket. Before I could even say hello, Zeke asked, "How quickly can you gain twenty pounds of muscle?"

"What time is it in LA?"

"It's not even midnight, D-man," Zeke said. "And money never sleeps."

"That doesn't make any sense." I pinched the bridge of my nose. "I don't know how quickly I can gain twenty pounds of muscle," I said. "I pay Ricardo to know that stuff."

"He just flew out for a photoshoot with Chris Hemsworth in Australia," Zeke informed me. "He probably won't pick up for another . . . five hours."

"And you need an answer in five hours?"

"I'll just tell them yes."

"Wait—"

"*Hasta luego*, D-money," Zeke sang and hung up before I could reply.

Great. Why did I have a feeling I was about to be relegated to six months of chicken breasts and protein smoothies? God, I wanted to eat some cake and not think about my fucking macros for a few weeks. I hadn't had to think about any of this shit when I'd been a musician. Nowadays, every single role wanted me to be shirtless . . . even one where I was voicing a CGI alien, which they still hadn't quite explained to me.

I was lost in my thoughts of already missing bread and cheese when a figure darted past me through the shadows. Even only in silhouette, I knew it was Dove. Knew it from her height and gait and smell of her lavender shampoo.

"Dove!" I called, darting after her. "What's wrong?" Even being two heads taller than her, I had to jog to keep up. "Dove." Her eyes were wide and frantic as I caught her arm. "What's going on?"

She wrenched her arm free, her eyes scanning back and forth, and I couldn't stop myself. I took her face in both hands and brought her eyes to mine.

"Hey, hey," I hushed, trying to calm her enough to speak to me. "Tell me what's going on." Something about the contact of my hands on her cool cheeks seemed to snap her out of it.

"Hannah's water broke." Her voice thick. "And her contractions are really close together and we're hours from the hospital and oh god, she can't have her baby in that gross ass boat. I haven't cleaned it yet and I—they were supposed to leave the island tomorrow and—"

I released her, already grabbing for my phone. Luca answered on the first ring.

"There's an emergency. Call James and have the chopper ready to lift off immediately," I instructed, trying to remain calm. "Going to . . ." I looked at Dove, whose eyes were still blown wide with panic. "Where?"

"Yale New Haven Hospital."

"Yale New Haven Hospital," I repeated. "When you get off the phone with James, call them so they're ready for her."

"Got it," Luca confirmed and immediately hung up to ring the helicopter pilot.

I thanked every lucky star right then that Cody had insisted we take the chopper to the photoshoot in New York the following morning. I'd wanted to drive, but since we had to be back for shooting the following day, Cody had called the chopper to arrive the night before. Fortunately, the Holloways had a helipad.

Dove was already on her phone, relaying the new information to her family.

"Thank fucking God." I heard Hawk's voice on the other end, the sound of a very much in labor Hannah shouting curses in the background.

That same shout echoed down the hill, and I stared up into the darkness of the nighttime zoo. A truck peeled out and screeched down the back road, speeding toward the Holloway Estate.

"The chopper will be in the air within the next five minutes." My breath curled into the nighttime air. "They'll be at the hospital in no time."

"Can the chopper hold four passengers?" Dove asked, hyperventilating.

"It can."

"Good, uh, Finch is going with them, and Mom." Her voice wobbled. "In case she has the baby in the helicopter." She rubbed her hand over her eyes. "Oh god, she can't have her baby in a helicopter."

"That's a pretty badass story to tell his friends one day," I countered, trying to lighten the mood.

"I guess." Her voice was hoarse, like she was holding back tears.

Dove was a hard one to make panic, at least when it came to herself, but when it came to her family, that was something else entirely.

I took a step forward and rubbed my hands up and down her goose-bump-covered arms. "They're going to be fine. The chopper will be at the hospital before you get back up the hill to your house." Her hands were still shaking as she frantically nodded. "Are you going to be okay?"

"I should go make sure everything is sorted back home," she said but didn't step out of my comforting touch. "They probably left a bunch of doors open in their race to the truck, and, uh, I think I'm going to go crazy if I try to sit still right now."

"When my anxiety gets bad, I can't sit still either," I admitted. "Doing something active sometimes helps. Do you want to go for a walk?"

Her movements were starting to slow, I could see the peak of her panic was slowly ebbing, but I knew her nerves would be boiling over until she heard news of the baby's arrival.

"No, it's fine," she said. "I might just do some diet prep. We'll probably need to all help with some extra keeper work tomorrow, so it would be good to get a head start on the day."

"I like chopping things," I offered. "Put me to work. I won't be able to sleep until I get an update either."

The truth was, I really, really didn't want to leave Dove

alone when she was so clearly in distress. I knew some of her siblings must still be at the zoo, but they might not even know that their sister was freaking out, or maybe they were freaking out just as much and needed a levelheaded person to pull them back into a state of calm.

I also knew Dove was too stubborn to accept my offer if she thought it was out of pity. "Please? I will just be walking around the house in circles and I have no one there to talk to about the latest *Dimension 20* campaign."

Her eyes lit up at that, finally finding mine instead of frantically searching the darkness. I seized that glimmer of recognition, adding, "Did you watch the latest episode? I was literally laughing so hard I thought I was going to pass out."

She cracked a smile, and I felt all of my muscles ease. "It was so good." She grinned, slowly coming back into herself.

I released her arms and took a step toward the zoo, and then we just started walking. Jedi mind-tricking her into talking about our favorite TTRPG show was a surefire way to get her mind off it. There were a lot of things I was proud of, but knowing Dove Lachlan well enough to ease her mind was high on that list.

I pressed my lips together, trying not to smile. I watched more nerves lift off her shoulders with every step as a helicopter took off into the night sky.

# Chapter Seventeen

Dove

Deacon was stacking crates in the room next door when I walked in, phone still in my trembling hands. Pausing at the sound of my approaching footsteps, he turned. His easy smile faded to an expression of concern as he looked from my phone to my face.

"Are you okay? Do you have news?" He asked so quickly it sounded like one word. "Is everyone okay?"

I nodded, so choked up I could barely speak. His shoulders dropped in relief.

"They made it to the hospital in time," I said through thick, bleary eyes. "Hannah and baby are doing great. He was born fifteen minutes after the helicopter landed," I murmured. "If they'd taken the boat . . ."

"They would've had to name him Petey," Deacon teased. "What did they name him?"

I held his gaze as emotions constricted my throat. "They named him Simon."

I began to blubber, and Deacon closed the distance, enveloping me in his arms and pulling me against his warm, broad chest. His chin dropped to the top of my head, and I felt the words vibrating through him as he said, "After your dad."

I nodded, certain I was wiping tears and snot across his T-shirt. The fact he remembered my dad's name made me cry even harder. Deacon had known my dad from when we'd been kids, knew how special he was. I hadn't been expecting Hawk and Hannah to name their son after him. Maybe his middle name, but damn. It hit me in a wave of joy and sorrow. I cried for the new baby and for my dad, light and dark in equal measure. All the while, Deacon held me so tightly that I knew I could easily lift my feet and not drop an inch.

"Shit, Rogue, you're going to make me cry too," Deacon said, dropping a kiss to the top of my head, his voice wobbling. "Well, fuck it." He sniffed and then his chest started shaking too.

It was such a relief, such a comedown from the constant panic and adrenaline. Deacon only shed a few mostly stoic tears while I blubbered into his chest for what felt like hours, but I was grateful he was willing to cry with me.

He held onto me until my arms went numb and still I thought I could've stood there all night long. I didn't want to let go, didn't want to go back to who we were to each other outside of this hug—not the people who would *never* be together, the thought so laughable that it had made Deacon scoff. It felt like that moment at dinner was a lifetime away now. I wished we could stay like this version of ourselves forever, just Dove and Deacon.

"I'm so sorry," Deacon murmured into the quiet.

"For what?" I asked, cheek still pressed against his chest, feeling the outline of some round gemstone or trinket beneath.

"I should've been there for you when he died," Deacon whispered, and my heart twanged anew.

"I was the one who ghosted you, though," I replied. "And you had a big, exciting life by then."

"Doesn't matter," he said, the sounds of his deep words vibrating where our chests pressed together. "I'm sorry, Dove."

I stepped out of his hold, my limbs tingling from being in the same position for so long. Deacon's hands remained poised on my forearms as I looked up at him, and for a second his eyes dipped to my mouth. I wondered what it would be like if I lifted on my toes and kissed him. Twelve-year-old me was begging me to do it, a redo for the teeth-knocking incident the two of us had shared one summer many years ago. But if I kissed him, I wouldn't be able to handle what came next. And the way he'd said "never" at dinner was still ringing in my ears. I was reading into something that just wasn't there.

So, I cleared my throat and took a step back, and Deacon's hands dropped to his sides. I swore I saw the faint look of disappointment in his gaze as I did. Or maybe he was just a really good actor and he was trying to comfort me with his crocodile tears. I never knew with him.

"Thank you," I said softly. "For the helicopter and for . . . everything."

"Anytime you need me," Deacon said, stooping a little to meet my eyeline and emphasize what he was saying. "Anytime you need me, I will be there for you. Even when you hate me and never want to speak to me again, if you need something that I can help with, ask me, got it?"

"Yeah," I said as my throat bobbed again.

He rubbed the back of his neck. "I should head back. I've got to be up at 4 am for a thing in New York," he said, hooking his thumb behind him.

"Okay." I gave him a half wave, unsure of what else to say. Thanks for holding me while I cried? Thanks for knowing I didn't want to be alone but was too stubborn to ask you to stay? Thanks for knowing me better than I know myself even after all this time? As he turned and headed for the door, I called, "Deacon?"

He paused and looked over his shoulder.

"Sometimes I really, really wish I could hate you," I said, and he flashed me a soft smile. "But I don't and I never have. You've always just been *you* to me."

I could see the way that hit him. I was probably one of the few people who knew him like that. Just as he was one of the few people who knew me more intimately than almost anyone. And all of that history couldn't be erased, no matter how many years passed or how much I tried. We'd both made mistakes. We'd both become people we didn't want to become for a while. But I knew who he wanted to be, who he was trying to be in incredible and uncontrollable circumstances. And despite the bravado and many masks he wore, I still saw glimmers of the real him underneath it all.

"You've always been *you* to me too, Dove," he said with a genuine smile, one that was goofy and lopsided and not perfect for camera, just a real smile meant only for me.

And I knew then, as he walked away and my stomach danced with butterflies, that I was in deep, *deep* trouble.

# Chapter Eighteen

Deacon

Our bird release redo was much less eventful than the toucan one, thank God. We even managed to get some nice B-roll footage of Dove and me talking and smiling to each other. After everything that had happened with the helicopter the week before, Dove and I had fallen into friendlier terms. I knew she was still trying to keep me at arm's length, but she couldn't seem to summon quite the same level of vitriol as before, which for me was a huge victory.

After the shorebird release, Dove and I decided to walk back to the zoo since it was only twenty minutes up the beach. Cody disappeared, leaving us in blissful privacy. It was a strange feeling—not having to be on my best behavior, no cameras pointed in my direction.

Apparently, in the off-season, after the last ferry had left for the afternoon, there was barely fifty residents on Prickle Island, which meant no paparazzi or fans or anyone who cared about my IMDB page, just some peace and quiet at the beach.

Dove stretched her arms up to the sun and let out a deep sigh. For once, her shoulders weren't bunched up around her ears.

That night in the prep kitchens replayed in my mind more times than I cared to admit. The way she'd folded into my arms, had cried while I'd held her . . . something had irreversibly shifted in that moment, if not for her then at least for me.

"How's Hannah doing?" I asked as I walked barefoot across the wet sand, the ocean water lapping at my feet.

"Good." Dove let out a sleepy, little hum as if relishing the feeling of the springtime sun on her skin. "Tired, I can imagine, but great. The way they look at Simon . . . I never thought my brother would let anyone in, and now he's got two people who've completely captured his heart." Her smile was infectious as she squinted across the water at the light glinting across the waves. "They're coming home tomorrow. I can't wait to hold him."

"Hawk?"

"No, Simon," she said with a laugh. "But I'll give my brother a hug too."

"It's the best feeling," I said with a grin. "I have three nephews and I cried the first time I held each of them," I admitted. "You know, 'cuz I'm the sensitive, artistic type."

"Uh-huh," she snarked, elbowing me. "Of course you are. Thank you again, by the way." She stole a glance at me and then looked back to the hypnotic horizon. "I don't even want to think about what would've happened if we didn't have your helicopter. I guess you're a hero on and off screen."

"Nothing heroic about it. I'm glad I could help," I replied. "Sometimes it's just fate, I guess. Maybe I was meant to be here."

*With you*, I wanted to add, but I held my tongue. *There I go, being the sensitive, artistic type again.* There were probably song lyrics buried in that sentiment somewhere. Maybe it was time I picked up my songbook and pen again . . .

"It felt pretty lucky that you were about to film a zookeeper movie right when our family needed the money," Dove hedged. "Maybe that was fate too?"

I only hummed in agreement, not wanting to admit that *that* particular situation hadn't been the same kind of serendipity.

"Why did you decide to do a zookeeper rom-com?" she asked skeptically. "Is there even an audience for that kind of sappy stuff? It seems so unlike you."

I laughed and shrugged. "I wanted to show a softer side of myself, I guess," I admitted. "People know me for fight scenes and big stunts. The tone of my last show was so serious. I wanted people to know I could be funny and romantic some-times too."

"If they listened to your music they'd know."

That comment caught me off guard. I wondered how much of my music Dove had listened to. Did she listen to it still? Acting felt a lot less personal than singing. It was easier to fade into someone else's story than share my own, but the music always felt more meaningful to me in that regard too.

"It's true," I mused. "My music was mostly love songs."

"*Lots* of yearning," Dove added, making me laugh.

"I was nineteen," I lamented. "Cut me some slack." I let out a wistful sigh. "Lucky Role feels like a lifetime ago. A lot of people don't even know I'm the same guy. I want them to think Deacon has depth too, you know?"

"I think your hundreds of thousands of die hard Harrow Head fans already know you can be funny and romantic," she said. "You crack one bad joke on a press tour and they think you're the world's greatest comedian. There's like a million fan edits of you on TikTok."

"Oh really?"

"I mean, I just stumbled across them. I wasn't seeking them out," she added defensively.

"Uh-huh," I teased. "Oh well. I guess I just wanted people to know I had more versatility in me."

"You were a model *and* a rock star before you started acting," Dove pointed out. "You've always been a triple threat. You can't suddenly develop comedy chops too or that would just be plain cruel to every other performer out there."

"I suppose so."

"But I know that you're funny," she added.

And I really wanted to reply *that's all that matters* like the sentimental fool I was, but instead, I said, "A comedy fandom of one, excellent."

I'd once been the goofy, funny one, the clown of my family. Many actors started off that way—nerdy theater kids who ended up having the good looks to carry them further than others. It had always been my goal whenever Dove and I had been together to make her laugh because I'd known that if I could make Dove Lachlan laugh, I could make anyone. Her smiles were hard-won and therefore that much sweeter.

Dove stopped, spying a piece of blue sea glass and picking it up. She held it to the sun with a smile before pocketing it.

"Still pilfering treasure from the beach, I see." I tipped my head to a barnacle-covered rock bisecting the beach. "Do you remember that gold coin we found down by the rock pools that one time? You swore it was pirate treasure."

"How could I forget?" She chuckled, lifting her hand to show me her palm.

"I wondered if it would leave a permanent mark." I pressed my lips tightly together after that admission. I was already saying too much.

Taking her hand in mine, I swept my thumb over the scar. She'd cut it open when she'd fallen on the slippery rocks trying to retrieve the coin. She'd been so obstinate that she'd kept going until she'd gotten the coin even while she'd been bleeding onto the sand.

"It's mostly faded," Dove murmured, her voice getting lost on the wind. I realized I was still touching her, but I couldn't seem to let her hand go.

The memory of sitting in the urgent care flashed back to me —the smells of the sterile hospital, the bright fluorescent lights, and the sound of Dove's laughter as her dad had shown us all of his scars and regaled us with stories each more epic and gruesome than the last. Simon Lachlan had been such an incredible storyteller that Dove hadn't even noticed the stitches going in. It should've been a bad day, a bad memory, but I could tell Dove remembered it with the same fondness I did. I hoped the mark never fully disappeared.

Without thinking, I lifted Dove's palm and kissed her scar. I was surprised that she didn't pull away as my lips lingered on her warm skin as if I could feel the memory beneath them. That hug from the previous week echoed in my limbs, the desire to wrap Dove back up in another hug overwhelming now that I knew how good she felt pressed against me, like a piece of a puzzle that I hadn't known was missing.

When I released her, she cleared her throat and kept walking, speeding up a little bit. It had been too much to hope she wouldn't immediately pull away again.

"Seven stitches," Dove said with a stilted laugh.

"Your lucky number."

"You remember that?"

"It was seven because there are seven kids in your family."

"Wow, I'm impressed." She paused to study my face before carrying on down the beach. "Do you still have that coin?"

It took me a second to speak. "Probably somewhere." I

didn't know why I'd lied. But the fact she hadn't run away from me after I'd kissed her palm was a big deal, and I didn't want the truth to scare her away. Everything felt so delicate, teetering on this precipice of something I was too afraid to name . . .

I hadn't realized how much I'd missed having Dove in my life until the last couple of weeks, and I didn't want to do anything to mess it up now. I'd missed her humor and sarcasm and snark and fun. Maybe the conservation trust would give me an excuse to keep this up, keep her in my life somehow.

"I missed this," I finally admitted as we reached the end of the beach and climbed the worn wooden steps onto the road.

"Me too." Her confession made warmth bloom in my chest.

"Why did we lose touch when we were kids?" I asked. "I tried to reach out to you a few times, but you never replied."

"I don't know." Dove sighed. "I guess you were growing into a life that I knew I wouldn't be a part of."

"And you were jealous? I mean, that's understandable—"

"No," she hedged. "I just didn't want the slow distance to pull us apart, fewer messages, fewer hangouts, eventually our friendship just disappearing while your life got too busy for it. I thought I'd just rip the Band-Aid off and give you an out so you didn't have to feel guilty about it."

"What if I didn't want an out?"

"Maybe you didn't," she said. "But eventually you would've left me behind."

I stopped walking for a second, emotions tightening my throat. I wanted to tell her I would've never done that, but the truth was, I probably would have. She knew me better than I knew myself, saw me in ways I didn't want to admit. I'd been a teenager who'd suddenly come into a lot of fame and money, and I'd burned through friendships and relationships and good will with just about everyone I'd known for many years back then. I would've left her behind, even as I carried her memory with me. Maybe she was just stronger than I was for being able to cut it off before the friendship soured.

"It's not a big deal," she added, clearly knowing I hadn't taken it well. "You're not meant to stay in touch with the first girl you kiss."

I laughed. "You know, at the time I thought that was one hell of a kiss," I murmured, and she laughed in agreement. "But now, looking back . . ."

"It was terrible."

"It was terrible," I echoed, and she and I both burst into laughter again. "I wished for a long time that I could travel back and have a redo."

"It was perfectly terrible," she added fondly. "It really set up the next guys after you to seem like great kissers."

"It was a public service," I said, trying to sound carefree even as the thought of the next guys made me twinge with jealousy. I'd bet anything that kissing Dove now would be amazing.

"And I'm sure your first kiss being a gangly, little zookeeper's kid really set up all the supermodels and actresses for you in contrast," she added with a wink.

"Yeah," I said, my voice fading away as I stared back at the ocean. "Well, I'm going this way."

"Cool," she replied, bouncing awkwardly on her toes. "Thanks for the help with the birds."

"You're welcome. Thank you for letting Cody film it."

She shrugged. "It's what interim directors do."

I grinned and gave her a half-wave as I turned down the gravel road to the Holloway Estate. I waited until she'd walked out of view before I fished out my necklace from under my T-shirt and inspected the worn golden coin hanging by a magnet from it—the coin a gangly, little zoo kid had split her hand open trying to retrieve for me.

# Chapter Nineteen

Deacon

"We're losing daylight!" Gavin lamented, practically falling from his director's chair. "Where is she?"

One PA, clearly the sacrificial lamb, finally faced him with a grimace and admitted, "She says she's not coming out of her trailer."

"She what?!"

The PA didn't repeat it, just moved away an inch, half-disappearing into the shrubbery behind her. I rubbed my forehead with a groan, and my makeup artist instantly ran in to touch up the smudged, fake dirt splatters on my face. I had hoped this movie would be a fun, lighthearted break from my more serious projects, but I'd take CGI dragons over Hollywood divas any day.

"Do we even need Ivy for this? It's a simple shot," I called. "There's not even dialogue. We can shoot it with her stand-in."

"Someone call Carol," Gavin shouted.

"She's already left for the day," the PA chimed in, now fully ensconced in the protection of the hedge. By the time she delivered the third piece of bad news, she'd be on the other side of the fence where a bunch of sun lorikeets were currently watching the production.

"We didn't have the budget to keep her until the end of the day? I swear to God, Deacon, I'm never doing you a favor again!" Gavin wrung the script in his hands and looked like he might wallop me with it. "By the time we get her back in hair and makeup, we—"

"Will lose the light," I finished, letting out a long-suffering sigh. I'd been a part of massive studio-sized projects before that were less of a clusterfuck than this one. "What if we—"

I saw Dove trying to dart around the film crew with a bucket full of seeds in one hand and a spray bottle in the other.

"Dove!" I called.

She froze like a deer in headlights before slowly turning to look at me.

Gavin hustled over and looked between us. "Deacon, bud, what are you doing?"

"Finding a solution," I grumbled as Dove wandered over. I slung my arm around her shoulder and held her tightly to my side to keep her from shirking my hold. I looked at Gavin as I waved her up and down. "Solution."

Gavin adjusted his baseball cap and pursed his lips as he considered her.

Dove muttered from the corner of her mouth, "What is going on?"

"I need a favor," I whispered back.

"What kind of favor?"

"I need to borrow your legs."

"My legs?" she snapped, and I finally released her to turn my pleading gaze toward her.

"Ivy won't come out of her trailer and her stand-in has already left for the day. We're losing light, and it's the second to last day of production, and all I'm doing is dipping you and pretending to kiss you." I put a heavy emphasis on the word *pretending*. "My head will be in the way. We don't actually have to kiss. It will only be your cargo shorts and boots and maybe a little hemline of your shirt. It's the climax of the movie. We *have to* get this shot."

Dove seemed entirely unsympathetic to my pleas. "So why not use a blow-up doll or something?"

"You think we just have sex dolls lying around that we can dress up?"

"Hey, you said sex doll, not me," she quipped.

"Please?"

"Don't you puppy eyes me," she snarked. "You already used up all of your 'pleases' to rope me into the conservation trust."

"You owe me for the helicopter," I countered, folding my arms in a mirror position to her.

"Ugh! That is low."

"I'll go low if I have to," I confessed. "You still owe me."

I could see the night of Simon's birth flashing through her mind, see how angry she was that I'd used it as leverage, and I knew I'd won before she even spoke.

"Fine, I'll do it," she groused. "But then we're even. No more calling in favors."

"Deal," I said, giving the director a thumbs-up.

"Yes? Yes!" He fist pumped the air before pointing at a bunch of people to draft up paperwork for our sudden impromptu extra.

"How long is this going to take?" Dove grumbled. "I have a

mountain of work to do now that Hawk and Hannah are both off the roster."

"Ten minutes tops," I promised. "And I'll help you finish your shift."

"Your help is the last thing I need." She pursed her lips at me, taking in my pleading urgency. "Damn, you really do need this shot, huh?"

"Yes."

"What do I do?" Dove eyed the crew as if suddenly realizing they were all there. She held her hands out awkwardly like her sides were made of wet paint.

I chuckled and smoothed my hands down her arms. "Just relax. They won't bite, unlike your co-workers."

"There are like twenty people staring at me," she whispered.

"They're staring at a million other things: the lighting, the juxtaposition of the shot, the costumes," I assured her. "You think they're looking at you, but they're actually just doing their jobs."

"That doesn't comfort me."

"Here." I took her by the shoulders and shuffled her over to her mark so that I was standing in front of her, my back to the camera. My broad shoulders obscured her from view. "Just us now."

She glowered up at me. "For some reason, I don't feel any better."

"Have you ever been dipped before?" I asked.

She screwed up her face. "This might surprise you, but I don't frequent many fairytale balls."

"It's just this." I wrapped one hand around her waist, shifted the other up her back to her neck, and dipped her to the side, taking some of her body weight into my arms as I lunged. "Good?"

We stayed there, her leaning back in my hold to meet my eyes. "Does your face have to be so close to my face?"

"Yeah," I replied with a grin. "We're supposed to be kissing, but we'll film that bit tomorrow when Ivy finally leaves her trailer or her assistant breaks through her barricades."

"She barricaded herself in?"

"She has a flair for the dramatic."

"Actors," Dove muttered as I pivoted us back to a stand.

"Right, when he calls action, I'm going to do that just a little faster, okay?" She nodded and shook her hands out like we were about to start sparring. I winked. "You'll be great."

When Gavin called action, I grabbed her and dipped her . . . apparently with more urgency than she was expecting, and Dove let out a little screech as her arms flew out to catch herself.

"Cut!"

"Okay, that was good," I assured her, trying to drown out the sounds of Gavin bitching behind me. "Just leave your arms at your sides this time, okay?"

"Oh my god, I can't do this," she whined.

"You're doing great."

"Liar."

When Gavin called action again, this time she was prepared. I dipped her without any hand flailing. As we held the position, I tried really, *really* hard not to think about how easy it would be to breach the distance between her mouth and mine.

"Why are we still dipped?" she whispered, her breath hot on my lips.

"Because he hasn't called cut yet," I whispered back. "I think they're slow zooming in."

"I'm sorry my breath smells like Flamin' Hot Cheetos," she replied, and I laughed. "I would've brushed my teeth if I had more warning."

"Cut!" Gavin barked from behind us, and a chorus of whispered groans sprang out across the set. "It's not working. The head is weird, and the angles are wrong. It's just—" The vein in his forehead bulged. "Can you just kiss her? It'll look better from this angle if you just kiss—"

"No. It's unnecessary and I'm not springing that on an actor who hasn't agreed prior." I held up a hand, positioning myself farther between Dove and Gavin. "We can do it as many times as we need to get it right, but I'm not going to—"

"Oh, just kiss me," Dove cut in, making me choke on my words.

I spun toward her. "What?"

"I have *a lot* of work to do today," she said. "And while I appreciate you trying to defend my honor or whatever it is this puffed up gorilla pose is"—she waved at me and I quickly shifted my posture—"I want to spend time with my new nephew. I might implode if we have to do ten more takes, so just kiss me and then it'll be over faster."

"There's my girl," the director cheered as if he knew anything about it. I did *not* like the way he called her "my girl." It made something dark and ugly rise in me as he winked at her and said, "Way to be a team player, Duck."

"Dove," I corrected.

"Whatever," he replied. "Let's reset."

I turned back to my mark and looked down at Dove. "Are you sure about this?"

She looked up at me with those big brown eyes, ones I could easily get lost in. *Pull it together, Deacon.*

"It's just acting, right?" Dove assured me.

Nerves started swirling in my gut. "Right."

"I'll pretend you're Rook Valestrider and you pretend I'm Rogue Hellfire."

"Hellfire for a pyromancer seemed like a very creative name when we were twelve," I joked.

"Hey, you had a sword called Doomfang, so . . ."

"Doomfang is a really cool name—"

"Quiet on the set!" Gavin shouted, and I knew he was pretending to scold some poor crew member when he was in fact yelling at us.

I held my hand lightly on Dove's hip as we waited for him to call action, regretting all of my life choices that had led me up to this point.

I should've just kissed her that night in the prep kitchens. I'd felt something in the air between the two of us and I should've just acted on it. I didn't want our first kiss in fifteen years to happen in front of a bunch of people. I didn't want to pretend she was Rogue Hellfire or Ivy Blanc or anyone else other than Dove Lachlan. And the way she seemed so unbothered by it made it a million times worse. Clearly Dove didn't care about me enough to even mind that I was about to kiss her.

"Nervous?" Dove whispered tauntingly.

I narrowed my eyes, accepting her challenge. "I was going to ask you the same thing."

"So long as you don't knock your teeth into mine this time."

"It was *you* who knocked your teeth into *me*."

"Yeah right, Casanova." She chortled. "You came at me teeth first like you were a horse and I was a carrot."

Before I could protest again, Gavin called, "Action!" and I grabbed Dove with all of that pent-up frustration and even more fervency, determined to prove to her that I'd learned plenty since our first kiss.

I dipped her, my lips crashing into hers with a lust-laced swiftness, but thankfully no teeth. I kissed her deeply, not holding anything back as my hand slid into her hair and held her face to mine. She matched my frenzy with her own as her palms pressed tighter, pulling me closer.

My tongue skimmed the seam of her lips and she opened

for me, our kiss deepening until we were truly devouring each other. A rumble caught in the back of my throat as she clung to me, kissing me like it was her own personal vendetta. A decade and a half of unspoken angst unleashed into that one kiss. She tasted like Flamin' Hot Cheetos and smelled like bird seed and none of that should've been hot, but when she let out a little moan against my lips, I groaned back.

My cock throbbed, a deep, aching lust rising in me and stomping out all other thoughts. *Fuck could she kiss.* Real and raw and passionate and so unlike all of the people I'd been linked up with who kissed as if someone were always watching. Not Dove. She was so attuned to me and I to her that we moved like we'd been doing this for years. Not performing, just melting into each other.

She wasn't the one that got away—she was the one who could've been but never was. With a little more time and age and maturity, what we could've been . . . I let my lips tell her all the things I couldn't say, kissing her like I knew I'd never get another chance. Why couldn't she feel that way about me? Why didn't she also wonder about what could've been?

Gavin called "Cut!" three times before I pulled Dove back to a stand. My head spun as I took in Dove's swollen lips, mussed hair, and glasses askew.

But the spell was quickly broken by Gavin calling, "That's a wrap on Duck."

"Dove," I barked out, my eyes never leaving hers.

"Good job," Dove said, lifting her hand for an awkward high five, and I guffawed as I slapped it.

*A high five?*

"Good job," I echoed, horrified that the all-encompassing kiss that had rocked me to my very core was only casual high-five worthy in her books.

As my libido crashed back down to Earth, Dove hustled to her bucket and spray bottle and darted off without another word. I watched her run away, wishing she felt even half of what I had in that moment, wishing that a million memories and years wasted had flashed through her mind too, wishing she wanted to find another way for my mouth to be on hers as badly as I did. But Dove ran off with quiet determination to finish her shift and didn't glance back once.

# Chapter Twenty

Dove

Deacon did a triple take back and forth between my bucket of raw chicken and the open gate leading to the crocodile moat.

"You can't be serious."

"You said you wanted to help out," I countered.

Deacon had decided to stay on the island for another week after filming had wrapped to prepare for the swanky fundraiser and do more promotional work for Lucky Role Conservation Trust. And every single time I saw him, it took everything in my power not to think about the way he'd kissed me on that film set. I'd known it would be good, but I hadn't expected it to be *that* good. And then I high-fived him . . .

Ugh! That high five would haunt me for the rest of my life!

It would've been far smarter to keep away from him, but no. I kept finding excuses to have him around me. And then whenever he was, I kept him at arm's length. *Curse me to all the hot movie star hells!* At some point, something had to give. I couldn't keep torturing myself with him. Deacon was a drug I craved and a pill I couldn't swallow all at the same time. It made the ebb and flow of tension between us all that much worse.

"I thought *helping* would involve more sweeping and fewer giant, pre-historic water monsters," Deacon argued, keeping his eyes firmly fixed on the murky green water.

I leaned against the open gate smugly. "This from the man who single-handedly battled an entire zombie army."

"Those zombies were computer generated," he replied, never taking his eyes off our old pair of crocodiles, Doris and Clyde. "I was battling a bunch of tennis balls on a green screen sound stage."

"Okay, action hero." I shrugged. "You can stay behind the fence if you'd like. I'm used to doing this shift without help."

"You want to go in by yourself and make me look like a coward?" He puffed up his chest like a grumpy spider monkey. "No. Absolutely not."

I grinned. "There's the superhero of the silver screen I know and barely tolerate."

Deacon ignored that jibe and gestured to the bucket. "You do this every day?"

"Well, usually Crane does it, but all of our routines are kind of messed up right now. We're all pitching in." I latched the lock to the fence and tugged it twice out of habit. "Crane is helping Hawk rebabyproof his house for the hundredth time."

Deacon gave an approving nod. "Well, I'm glad I can pitch in. Just don't tell my agent, or Cody, or Ricardo, or Luca for that matter. I'm pretty sure my next contract with Universal forbids me from risk-taking behaviors, and while feeding crocodiles isn't *explicitly* stated . . ." I chuckled as he weighed his head back and forth. "Better to not tell them."

"Your secret is safe with me," I said, zipping my lips. "Besides, we're perfectly safe."

Deacon snorted. "Yeah right."

I held his gaze for a split second longer than I should. "I wouldn't put you in harm's way."

His smile made my insides melt. He held the gate open for me, and I radioed Heron to let them know that I was entering the croc enclosure. The countdown was officially on, and I had to radio in updates every ten minutes while in close proximity to dangerous animals.

Deacon followed, uncharacteristically quiet as we crept to the edge of the concrete lip that curved down about seven feet before reaching the reed-filled water of the crocodile moat. Beyond the moat was an island holding some of our iguanas and other reptiles, a service bridge already lifted and secured for the night.

I passed Deacon a plastic glove and he put it on. "Having you here is actually kind of nice," I admitted.

Deacon laughed. "Don't sound so surprised."

"I mean, it's hard to feed Doris and Clyde when they're eager and hungry at the same time. Having two people definitely makes it easier."

"Oh, I thought you meant nice as in romantic."

"You think feeding crocodiles raw chicken is romantic?" I asked incredulously.

"Well, it's certainly a unique kind of date," Deacon amended.

"This isn't a date."

He had such a slappably smug look on his face. Oh, how he loved to get a rise out of me.

We picked up our quartered pieces of raw chicken and began lobbing them over the barrier of swamp grasses. I encouraged Doris farther to the left as Deacon threw Clyde's food slightly to the right, keeping the two of them apart long enough that they didn't accidentally snap each other's legs off in their feeding frenzy.

"Wow, they are even more intense than I remembered," Deacon murmured. "And when I was a kid, they seemed like ten times this size to me."

"Doris is particularly moody and ravenous," I said. "So I'm hopeful that we might have a clutch of eggs from her this year. We might need to resegment the moat into multiple enclosures if that's the case," I added. "We have it trisected right now in case we need to separate the two of them for some reason, but they normally have free range of all three."

"This is so cool," Deacon said more to himself than to me. His lips were parted, his eyes wide, his wonder reminding me that it wasn't in fact an everyday occurrence for most people to feed crocodiles.

"Do you remember—"

"Yes," he said, and I laughed.

"You don't even know what I was going to say."

He gave me a sideways glance. "Do I remember the time you snuck us behind the scenes of the cheetah enclosure and I almost had my hand bitten off, but we managed to jump over the fence and get out again without anyone ever noticing?"

I blinked at him. "*How* did you know I was going to say that?"

"Because I know you," he stated with a grin, and my insides turn even mushier.

Damn my hormones. It was entirely unfair when someone as attractive as Deacon said these things. Far stronger women had turned into hot butter at the sight of him.

"To this day, no one knows we did that," I mused. "Nowadays, with the electronic locks and cameras, we would've never gotten away with it."

"Our secret," he whispered conspiratorially, and his eyes roved my face for a split second before looking away.

That kiss flashed through my mind again, and I wondered if he was thinking the same thing. And then I had to go and be so cringey about it. But the way Deacon was looking at my mouth now ...

*Well shit.* That was just plain cruel. Leave it to Deacon Harrow to prove me wrong and make feeding crocodiles sexy. If anyone could do it, it was him.

"Here, wait," he said with a secret smile as he fished his phone out of his pocket. "I need to show you this." He scrolled through his photos and turned the screen to me. "Who does this remind you of?"

It was a selfie of Deacon and a surfer dude with a lazy smile and a mop of blond hair over one eye. I let out a cackle, knowing instantly who this surfer reminded him of. "Our petting zoo llama who spit in your ice cream that one time."

"Yes!"

I doubled over, laughing so hard I had to wipe tears from my eyes. "You found the human version of Garrett? He's still here, you know."

"What? No way."

"Yeah, he's like, what? Eighteen now," I said, looking skyward as I did the math. "An old man and just as grumpy as ever."

"Garrett the llama," Deacon recounted with a belly laugh. "I knew you'd know."

I didn't understand how something could be comforting and unsettling at the same time, but Deacon managed it. After all these years and after such a short time as friends, *how* could he still know me better than almost anyone?

"Ah, good times," he said, going to put his phone away as it slipped from his grip. "Shit!"

He lurched forward, managing to catch it and volley it back into the dirt behind us, but in the process he tumbled forward, down the steep lip, plummeting toward the crocodile moat.

# Chapter Twenty-One

Deacon

As my arms wheeled and I fell like a skater dropping into a half pipe, I saw the front-page headlines flash before my eyes: "Deacon Harrow. Dead at 27. Eaten by Crocodiles."

What a way to go. I saw the in memoriams now. Mostly remembered for roles I didn't really care about and a career I'd just fallen into instead of the music of my soul . . .

That thought swiftly tumbled away as Dove launched forward and caught me by the wrist as my designer loafers scratched down the concrete bowl and splashed into the swampy water below.

She landed roughly on her stomach, eliciting a groan of pain, and I wondered if she might've bruised a rib on the hard lip of the croc moat. But despite the hard fall, she didn't let go of my hand.

"Hang on," she gritted out, face turning bright red as all the blood rushed to her head.

There were many times in my life when being 6'3" had been a curse: flying on airplanes, walking under low ceiling fans, and now, apparently, dangling above crocodile-infested water. I lifted my feet up wildly, scrambling up the slippery side but getting no traction.

"They're going to bite my legs off, aren't they?" I asked, voice frantic and pathetic as I looked up at Dove. *Way to be the suave action hero, Deacon.* "They're going to drown me in this disgusting water. I've seen *Crocodile Hunter*. I know what death rolls are. They're going to death roll me, aren't they—*why* are you laughing at me?"

I looked up to Dove's shoulders bobbing up and down, a wide smile on her pitying face even as she strained to hold me aloft. "There's a fence in the reeds," she explained, biting her lips together to keep from laughing more. "They can't get to you from here."

I twisted my neck around and spied the carefully hidden wrought-iron poles placed at varying heights an inch apart through the swamp grasses.

"Oh, thank all the sweet, sweet crocodilian gods," I said.

"I told you I wouldn't put you in harm's way," Dove chided.

"I thought you meant I was safe *with* you, not *from* the crocodiles," I replied tightly, straining to hang on. I needed to tell Ricardo to add more rock climbing into my workout regimen. My fingers were killing me. "But I appreciate the clarification now that I just squealed at you like a scared little piglet."

"Come on, even piglets aren't that shrill," Dove countered with a laugh. *Oh, she was never going to let me live this down, was she?* Clearly smug with my current predicament, Dove gave my wrist a tug. "I still don't want you getting some crazy bacterial infection from that water, though, so let's get you up, okay?"

"Okay," I said with a deep breath. "Did the fall at least look cool? Like a Legolas slide down the wall and a daring grab for the ledge?"

"You looked nothing like Legolas, unfortunately," she said. Her glasses slid down her nose until she was looking at me over them. "Well . . . maybe Legolas our teenage baboon, but I don't think that's what you were going for."

"Dammit!"

With a laugh, Dove reached down with her other hand and took my free one. I climbed my wobbling loafers up the side and used my leverage to barrel roll over the edge . . . *and* land directly on top of Dove. My body fused with hers, my hips nestled against her, and fuck, I tried really hard not to think about all the places we joined. Crocodiles long forgotten, all I could think about was how electrifying it felt to have her under me, her head bracketed by my arms, her full lips parted in surprise.

I stared down at her mud-speckled face. "Thank you for saving me," I murmured, my chest rising and falling in panting breaths as the adrenaline started to leave my system.

"I told you I'd keep you safe with me," she whispered.

I clenched my jaw with restraint, wanting so badly to kiss her for saying that.

The truth was, Dove Lachlan had *always* made me feel safe, not just from physical harm but safe to let my guard down, to be vulnerable, to be the scariest, most honest version of myself.

"You know," I said with a laugh, my chest rising and falling against hers. "I'm always playing the emotionally distant hero, but in real life, it's you who gets all the great heroic one-liners."

Dove beamed up at me, the warmth in her eyes so beautiful and rare that I wanted to bottle it up and hold onto it forever. For one crazy second, I lowered my head to kiss her, but when Dove winced, I remembered the way she'd come crashing down on the concrete.

"You're hurt."

I scrambled off her and pulled her to a stand. "I'm fine," she said, rubbing her side. "It's just a little bruise. No big deal."

I frantically lifted the hem of her shirt, and she laughed as she shoved it down. "Deacon, really, I'm fine."

"Just let me see." I tugged on her shirt again, and Dove released the hem with a roll of her eyes.

She held her arms out to the sides. "Are you a doctor now?"

"No, but I've played one before," I teased, lifting her shirt another inch and exposing a strip of bare skin. "May I?"

"Be my guest."

Careful so as not to touch her injured side, I revealed the soft curves of her torso and the lower band of her sport bra. A red-and-blue bruise bloomed just above her navel, spreading all the way up to the band on her bra. "Damn."

"It's fine," she assured me. "I'll just go ice it after I close up for the day."

"You should go ice it now," I instructed.

"I don't take advice from TV doctors."

"Touché." I huffed as I studied the purpling wound. "Thank you for heroically saving me from what I thought was near death but was actually just a potential staph infection."

Without thinking, I leaned in and kissed her bruise. *You really need to stop kissing her bare skin!* But I couldn't help myself. Not when it came to Dove. Her skin pebbled with goose bumps in the wake of my lips as I lowered her shirt back down.

"You're, uh, welcome," she said rather breathlessly.

The way she looked up into my eyes, the way she held my gaze, I could've sworn she wanted me to kiss her. But maybe I was projecting. Maybe all of this was in my head. She'd said she loathed me only a few weeks ago after all. I couldn't just kiss her. But she wasn't moving, her gaze oscillating between my eyes and my lips that had just kissed her soft, warm skin . . .

Before I could move, her radio scratched to life.

Heron's voice sounded. "Savannah to birds, I just finished up at the giraffes. Do you need any help down at the crocs?"

Dove picked up her radio. "Nah, we're all good. We're just leaving now."

Both Heron and Mom immediately answered her. "Who's *we*?"

Dove grimaced before replying, "Sorry, just me and my empty buckets. Leaving now."

"Roger," Heron replied in a suspicious voice.

Dove looked at me and pointed uphill. "You're going to have to go that way and cut through the Peckish Peacock so they don't catch us together on the cameras," she ordered.

"Ah yes, I'm well versed in evading cameras." I nodded sagely as Dove laughed.

I was about to step through the gate when she added, "Oh, um, I was going to ask—" and hope bloomed in my chest again.

"Yeah?"

"I was thinking I could get a photo of you with our shingle-back skinks tomorrow." She rubbed the back of her neck. "I could use it for my WAZA proposal for the new Almadran skink breeding program. And you could give it to Cody if he wanted to use it for anything?"

The offer showed how far the two of us had come in only a matter of weeks. I wondered if all of these little tasks and chores she was asking for my help with were because she actually needed my help or because she just wanted an excuse to spend more time together. I hoped the latter. Still, a photoshoot wasn't the offer I'd been hoping for. *What am I hoping for?* I didn't dare say even to myself.

"That's a great idea, director," I said, giving her a salute as I wandered off uphill, avoiding the cameras, before any disappointment showed on my face.

# Chapter Twenty-Two

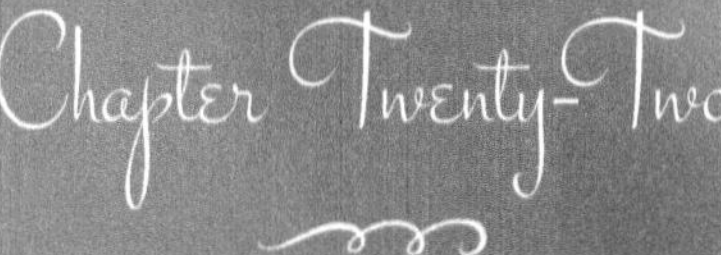

Dove

I discovered a new kind of heaven and hell the night of the springtime zoo gala, when I offered to babysit Simon. I wanted Hannah and Hawk to have a couple hours to walk around, have some fancy canapés, and decompress from newborn life. Hell was the three minutes that Simon woke up and started crying as I tried to quickly change his blowout diaper, only to have him immediately poop again the second I picked him back up.

But what came after was pure heaven. My sweet, pink, little nephew slept on my chest as I rocked back and forth on the deck of Hawk and Hannah's cottage. I patted his little bum in rhythm to the rocking chair, and his chunky, little cheek melted in the warmth of my chest.

As I hummed a little tune to him, I saw the flickers of a

flashlight weaving between the hedges of the path that led to the cottage.

"Did you manage to steal any desserts?" I called out to Heron, who had offered to purloin a tray of catering for me while Frankie wasn't looking.

"I did," the voice replied, but it wasn't my younger sibling.

"Deacon?" I asked to the shadowed figure as it wove the last few steps to the deck and appeared into the light.

*Dear sweet Babybel cheeses.* What I saw made my jaw unhinge like a boa constrictor.

Deacon stood there in a perfectly tailored charcoal-gray suit, fitted satin vest, and purple pocket square that matched the lining of his open jacket. Suddenly, I fully understood all of the "suit porn" Pinterest boards. I'd seen enough photos of Deacon on red carpets and the covers of magazines to know that he looked great in a suit, but seeing it in person was another thing entirely.

"Heron had to give a tour of the hippo enclosure to some big donor so they asked me to bring these to you," he said, coming to sit on the rocking chair beside mine.

"Of course they did," I said, knowing full well that Heron had made up that excuse just to send Deacon over here. But I definitely wasn't about to point out that our zoo did not in fact have hippos. "Did you see Hawk and Hannah?"

"They're having a great time," Deacon answered with a laugh. "Although maybe a little sleep-deprived. They have a bit of a deer in the headlights look about them. It's really cute."

He set the dessert tray down between us, and I eyed all of the little bite-sized treats arranged around the silver base like a confectionary checkerboard. I lifted my bum patting hand to reach for one, and Simon let out a little grunt of protest, and I immediately went back to bum patting, looking forlornly at the tray of food.

Deacon chuckled. "He's already got you wrapped around his finger, doesn't he?"

I twisted a little in the rocking chair to give Deacon a better view of Simon's face. "Could you say no to this face?"

He put a hand to his chest as he took Simon in. "No, you're right. He's already won me over too. And I thought letting my legs go numb when my cat falls asleep on them was bad."

"You have a cat?" I asked.

"Spud."

"Spud is still alive?" I exclaimed, remembering his family's chunky orange tomcat that had traveled to the island with them every summer. "He was old when I knew him."

"Twenty-four," Deacon informed me with a shake of his head. "He has more than nine lives, I think."

"I thought for a second you meant your own cat," I added mildly.

"Nah, maybe one day," he mused, rocking in rhythm to me. "But right now I travel too much to have a pet. It would be someone else looking after them most of the time, and I'd want them to be my pet, not the petsitter's, you know?"

I nodded. "I get it." Deacon lifted a cube of carrot cake and held it out toward me. "What are you doing?"

"Feeding you," he said, as if it were obvious.

"You can't *feed me*. That's too weird."

He laughed louder. "I think you'll get over the weirdness when you taste how good this carrot cake is. Seriously, it's the best I've ever had."

"Curse Frankie and her delicious baking." I'd had her carrot cake before and it was seriously orgasm worthy. "Just lift the platter to my face and I'll eat it off there."

"You are seriously the most stubborn person I've ever met," Deacon admonished with a shake of his head. But at least he obeyed, placing the carrot cake back on the tray and lifting the whole thing toward my face.

I opened my mouth like a ravenous hyena, trying to curl forward over Simon while timing my rocking to swing forward and bite the piece of cake . . . but instead I just got cream cheese frosting on my nose and knocked the three dominos of bite-sized cakes over.

"Aw, man." I groaned as Deacon laughed so hard his whole body shook.

He set the tray back down, swiped the dollop of frosting off my nose, and licked his finger. "Can I *please* just feed it to you now? It won't be weird."

"Go inside and get some chopsticks."

"Dove," he scolded. "My hands are clean and I promise you won't catch my cooties."

"Ugh, fine," I lamented. "I want cake more than I loathe you."

"You don't loathe me," Deacon said softly.

"I know, but it feels good to say," I countered, and he grinned. I couldn't keep on pretending. Too much had transpired between us now. Even as I'd tried to maintain the status quo, Deacon had become my friend again over the past few weeks.

He held the carrot cake up and I opened my mouth for him to feed it to me. My lips closed around his fingers, and for a split second I sucked before realizing what I was doing. I reared my head back, making Simon and I dramatically rock backward.

Deacon let out a soft, husky laugh as he licked the remaining frosting off his fingers—an act that felt incredibly intimate in the quiet night. I had just accidentally sucked Deacon Harrow's fingers. What the hell? And then he'd *licked* said fingers afterwards! The thought made me press my thighs together and shudder.

"Are you cold?" Deacon asked, noticing the action instantly.

"No." I drummed a little faster on Simon's bum. "I've got my little hot water bottle. He seems happiest when we're outside."

Deacon grinned. "Well, he's definitely a Lachlan then."

"Definitely." I smiled back. I took another deep inhale of his sweet baby scent. "God, he smells amazing."

"You look like you're huffing him."

"It's seriously baby crack," I said. "For real. You've got to get in here and smell his head."

Deacon's eyes crinkled as he stood and leaned over to sniff Simon's head, his cheek grazing across my own as he did. He let out a satisfied hum as he returned to his chair. "Oh boy. I shouldn't have done that."

"Why not?"

"Because he smells too good and now I'm going to want to have one of my own."

I guffawed. "I think that is biology working its magic on you. You're no match for baby pheromones." I shook my head as he held my gaze. "I could see it though, for you, one day, being a dad. I think you'd be good at it."

"Yeah." He rubbed the back of his neck. "Maybe one day when life calms down, if I ever find the right person."

"I'm sure there's a bevy of supermodels who would line up to have your babies. You'd have to come up with some ridiculous celebrity baby name, though," I joked. "Suitcase Harrow? Apostrophe Harrow?"

"You know, Apostrophe has a nice ring to it," he teased. "No, I don't think that's for me. If I can't have a cat with my lifestyle now, I definitely can't have a baby. And just because there might be a few volunteers," he added with a chuckle. "I guess I'm a traditional sap. I'd want to fall in love, get married, have a life together just the two of us first. It would be nice to put down roots somewhere—somewhere far from cities and paparazzi— and *then* maybe have a family." He cleared his throat, leaning his elbows on his knees and looking out into the shadowed garden. "Is that . . . something you'd ever want? A family, I mean."

My stomach flipped at the way he so delicately asked that question. "I think the bigger question is could I ever find someone who'd want to settle down with someone like me."

"I can't imagine that would be hard," he mused, and I rolled my eyes. "I'm serious! You're a catch. You're funny and smart and beautiful—and terrifying," he added, and we both laughed. "Although the dating pool must be awfully small on an island."

I shrugged, trying not to think too hard about the way he'd called me funny, smart, *and* beautiful. *Ever the charmer.*

"Prickle Island just might be the world's smallest dating pool," I said with a huff. "But I don't think I'm going to live here forever."

Deacon stilled. "You're not?"

"I mean, maybe I'd keep Prickle Island Zoo as a home base, but I want to travel and see the world and have jobs that take me to new places and do large scale conservation work, more than I can achieve here," I said. "I don't know. What I want my life to be and what I think it's actually going to be are two very different things."

Deacon nodded. "Now *that* I understand."

I shot him a look. "How?"

"It's the world's tiniest violin, I know." He let out a long sigh. "But sometimes I feel like I'm the ambassador for someone else's dream." I could feel the weariness in his words as he spoke. "I mean, I don't want to complain. I have so much and—"

"You're allowed to complain with me," I cut in. "I know I'm hard on you but—"

"That's putting it lightly."

"*But* it's just because I know who you really are. I guess I want to hold you to that standard," I admitted. "But that doesn't mean you can't have bad days. You can be real with me. *Especially* me."

He looked at me, grateful. "I just feel like I'm being given all these opportunities and I have no choice but to take them because so many people work so hard their whole lives and never get this lucky." He stared up at the starry night sky. "But I keep wondering, what now? I've achieved all of my career goals in the first quarter of my life. Like, am I meant to just keep grinding because I should always want more? Is there a bottomless pit I'm meant to be filling for the rest of my life? When do I get to step off this treadmill? When do I get to eat cake?"

"Whoa." I blinked at him. "I didn't realize you were feeling that way."

"I sound like such a douchebag, I know." He scrubbed a hand down his face. "I don't want to seem ungrateful."

"You don't seem that way to me."

"You thought I was a worthless waste of space a few weeks ago."

My gut clenched. "Yeah, I should've never said that. I was just angry."

"You were right," he said with a shrug. "I have teams of people who are always trying to shift the blame off of me, who've taught me to never admit my faults. And sometimes I don't think I like who I've become very much," he admitted. "I don't actually know if I really want things anymore or if I've just been told I should want them enough times that I've started believing it."

"You can't live your whole life based on other people's expectations of you. There is no winning that game. They will move the goal posts every time you reach them." He hummed in agreement. "Maybe it's time to figure out what you'd want if no one was telling you what you should want," I said, and his eyes hooked with mine. "Maybe it's time to figure out who you want to be."

Our gazes held, and I felt myself tumbling into his stare and knew in the pit of my stomach he was about to say something that would shift what existed between us forever. So like a coward, I quickly cut him off and said, "Now feed me another piece of cake."

Spell snapped, Deacon laughed and grabbed another dessert from the tray.

# Chapter Twenty-Three

Deacon

I slept in a strange, slanted concrete room with a drain in the center of it—one that I remembered once housing capuchin monkeys. One wall was entirely chain-link fence with a curtain rod affixed to it for a modicum of privacy. No wonder Dove had gotten out of here when the twins had moved in. Still, I was grateful that they'd given me a place to stay, and the bed was surprisingly comfortable.

A whoop of laughter filtered up from the kitchen and I let out a grumble at the loud echo that carried through the house.

How I longed for my room at the Holloway Estate. I missed all the soft furnishings that ate up the sound. I'd take the creepy cherubs over chain-link any day. Unfortunately, the place was no longer available for rent, and since I'd sent the team back to New York, I would've been completely spooked to have that entire cavernous place to myself. Not that this place didn't freak me out. I'd traded *The Shining* for *Saw*. The whole night I'd kept dreaming that chainsaw-wielding monkeys were strangling me with their prehensile tails.

Note to self: next time I visit Prickle Island, don't take Evelyn Lachlan up on her offer of staying in their "spare room."

I stumbled, tired, down to the makeshift kitchen and found that a good portion of the Lachlan clan had crammed themselves into the place—Crane, Heron, Finch, and Frankie all stood in a circle around the countertop, eating egg and cheese sandwiches that smelled amazing. Meanwhile, Wren sat perched in an old recliner in the corner, crocheting what appeared to be a Christmas stocking.

"Coffee?" Crane offered, sliding a mug across the stainless-steel countertop.

"Yeah, thanks," I said groggily. "You're all up early."

The four of them laughed.

"We've been up for hours," Finch said with a chuckle. "We usually do the rounds before breakfast. Frankie was making egg sandwiches for us, and we thought we'd bring the kiddos some."

"We're twenty-two," Heron said flatly.

"I said what I said. You'll still be kiddos when I'm fifty-one and you're forty-two," she added with a wink.

I wandered over and perched on a barstool as Frankie dished me up a plate of sandwiches and fresh fruit.

"This is wonderful, thank you," I murmured groggily.

Crane gave Frankie a half hug as he kept eating. "We used to eat dry ramen bricks for breakfast before Frankie took pity on us."

"Honestly, the spider monkeys have a more refined palette than these two." Frankie pointed between the twins.

"Is Dove up?" I asked, looking out the window that faced their family home on the top of the hill.

Crane let out a low whistle. "Can't have her out of his sights for even a day. Yep, he's got it bad."

"*He* is sitting directly in front of you," Heron pointed out as Finch smacked her little brother over the head with a tea towel.

"So, you and Dove, huh?" Crane asked.

"I know what's happening," I muttered, wiping crumbs from my lips. "You all came back from your shifts this morning to interrogate me."

"See, I told you he gets us," Crane quipped.

"That's because I've known you all for a very long time," I explained.

Frankie leaned in. "What was Finch like as a kid?"

"I'll pay you fifty bucks not to answer that," Finch cut in.

I grinned. "She was a hellion just as she is now. Sarcastic. Funny. Didn't give a crap what other people thought but cared a whole hell of a lot about her animals."

Frankie leaned into Finch and kissed her shoulder. "Yep, that sounds about right."

"And these two." I pointed my fork between the twins before spearing a cube of cantaloupe. "Were only seven years old the last time I saw them, but they were already absolutely feral."

Frankie's smile stretched as Finch wrapped an arm around her. "So nothing's changed there either."

"Nothing except their facial hair," I joked.

I pointed to Wren in the corner. "And she had just learned how to make daisy chains and spent her days carrying around a crayon box like a briefcase."

"I forgot about your crayon box thing!" Finch crooned. She wandered over to the recliner to ruffle Wren's hair. With a practiced swat, Wren smacked her sister's hand away and kept her eyes focused on her project.

"I remember little flashes of you," Heron said, considering me. "You and Dove making up secret code words at dinner. You and Dove running around the café, reading books about drag-ons. You and Dove rock-pooling at the beach. The two of you were always trying to ditch us."

"That's because you were insufferable," I retorted with a sweet, mocking smile.

"Fair."

"But just because you were a family friend when we were kids, doesn't mean we will go any less hard on you than Logan or Hannah or Frankie, got it?"

I blinked at them, wondering why they would put me in the same category as their siblings' partners. There was definitely some magic energy between Dove and me—well, at least, *I* felt there was—but I didn't know if I'd ever have the guts to confess my feelings outright to her, let alone whether she would ever reciprocate them. But her siblings saw it too, saw that there was a spark between us, and even if Dove and I never acknowledged it, I was grateful to know I wasn't the only one who thought it was there.

This was a lot more than my tired morning brain could convey, though, so instead I asked, "You're going to be hard on me?"

Heron pointed a spatula at me, making a serious face despite their chosen implement. "Don't break our sister's heart," they said. "Or we will feed you to the crocodiles."

"I thought the crocodiles get better quality meat than me?"

Finch snorted. "I see Dove has already told you that family joke," she said. "Well, gang, we're going to have to finally come up with some new ones."

"Finally." Frankie let out a mocking laugh.

"And don't think about trying to sneak off to bang in the zoo, okay?" Crane said, and Finch smacked him again. "We know all the places. The restaurant, the lookouts, the back alley, the Jeep."

"The Jeep?" I scoffed. "The others make sense, but the Jeep is right out in the open between the lion and tiger enclosures."

"Yeah, Hawk and Hannah have *definitely* banged in that Jeep," Crane continued.

Finch weighed her head side to side as if debating the truth in that statement. "I'd put money on it."

"How much?" Heron asked, intrigued.

"You all need to stop betting on your siblings' relationships," Frankie scolded them.

"We live on a tiny island," Crane offered. "There is very little entertainment here in the off-season. Hence the intimidating of the movie star."

"When does the intimidating part begin?" I joked as I took another long sip of coffee.

"Listen, pretty boy," Crane said, and the rest of us laughed. "If you hurt Dove, we will—"

"What?" I cut in. "Put a tarantula in my bed? Put meal worms in my pockets? Hide crickets in my food? You've done all of those things to me before."

"Okay, no more childhood friends are allowed into the family," Heron decreed, waving their arms into an X.

"And to further add to your point," I said to the four of them. "Dove is a grown woman who makes her own decisions, and she has made it very clear that she wants nothing to do with me anymore."

That—*apparently*—was the funniest thing I'd ever said. All five of them laughed uproariously for several minutes before I could even get a response to the question, "What's so funny?"

"Uh, besides the fact that the two of you have been in love with each other since you were kids?" Finch asked.

"What?" I exclaimed.

"Look at you! Can you even see yourself?" Finch huffed as she waved me up and down. "You are still *clearly* in love with her. Normal people don't sleep in old monkey enclosures for their *friends*."

"And she is definitely still in love with him too," Frankie murmured as she spooned more fruit salad onto my plate.

"You really think she is?" I asked, trying to sound more curious than hopeful.

"Um, hello? Obviously," Finch said. "Everyone knows except the two of you. You were always like two little aliens from the same planet. I've never seen two people more suited to each other." Frankie pretended to pout, and Finch slung an arm around her. "Except for us, of course, Goldilocks."

"Of course," Frankie said, kissing her.

"Maybe we once were close," I hedged. "But not anymore. Stop laughing!" I shouted, exasperated, but was drowned out by a chorus of more laughter. Even Wren had decided to join in.

I grabbed my coffee and headed out with a shake of my head. But when I opened the door to the monkey enclosure, Evelyn was already standing there.

"Evie, hi," I greeted, raising my mug to her in toast.

"Hey." With the sharpness of a bomb sniffer dog, she narrowed her eyes and peered around me into the house, spying the others. "Aren't you all meant to be getting Daisy ready for that endoscopy?" she asked knowingly.

"Gotta go!" Finch called, and they all scattered like their speakeasy was being raided. "Nice seeing you, Deeks."

Evelyn shook her head, smiling albeit exasperated. "Dove's going to get the truck," she said. "I'll drive you two down to your private yacht. So fancy," she added with a laugh. "I know she's really excited about the fundraiser."

"Thank you for letting me borrow her for the night, Evie," I said. "I promise to have her back tomorrow night."

With a gentle smile, Evelyn reached out and hugged me. It was the perfect kind of mom hug, warm and comforting, and it made me make a mental note to call my mom. I'd been slack with checking in lately. I'd bet Evie and my mom would pick up as if fifteen years hadn't passed just like Dove and I had.

"I know you're used to all this flashy stuff," Evelyn continued in her breezy way. "But look out for Dove, will you? These sorts of big events really freak her out, and I know she really wants to do a good job and impress you."

"I'll take care of her," I vowed.

Evelyn beamed up at me. "You're a good guy, Deacon," she said. "More than you give yourself credit for, I think."

I didn't know what to do with that statement. It was as if she'd both complimented me and issued me a challenge. These Lachlans really knew how to play mind games. I wandered heedlessly back inside to get my bag, still reeling from what Finch had said. Despite the kiss Dove and I had shared, and the inside jokes, and knowing looks, and the friendship we'd eventually fallen back into, I still hadn't dared to dream that she still carried a flame for me.

Nerves filled me anew. A dangerous sort of hope grew in my chest. *Maybe.* Maybe I'd have the courage to ask her if she felt about me the way I'd always felt about her, *still felt*, even after all this time.

I held a hand to my chest, feeling the outline of the coin beneath my palm—two aliens from the same planet, as Finch had put it. The other side to my coin.

# Chapter Twenty-Four

Dove

As the black SUV navigated the gridlocked streets of New York, my nerves increased with each creeping turn. I stared out the tinted windows as the puzzlework of glass-plated skyscrapers and flickering billboards whizzed past. Rambling, I wondered if Deacon knew I was anxious or if he'd suddenly just developed an overwhelming interest in the mating habits of frigate birds. He'd peppered me with ornithological questions for most of the ride and kept asking me follow-up questions that I was happy to blather on about to keep my anxiety in check.

In a momentary lull in my lecture about plumage, Deacon checked his phone and leaned forward to speak to his driver. "Change of plans. We're going straight to the venue."

I looked down at my zoo-branded hoodie and sweatpants. I only owned two types of bottoms: khaki cargo shorts and pilling old sweatpants, and right then I wished I'd selected the shorts this morning. "But . . . I need to change and check into the hotel—"

Deacon's brows furrowed. "What hotel?"

"The hotel I'm staying in tonight?" I asked. "Luca said he organized my accommodations for me?"

"You're staying with me," Deacon balked as if it would be offensive to stay anywhere else.

My stomach curdled at the thought of being *alone* in an apartment with Deacon, especially with all of the dangerously alluring thoughts I'd been having about him recently. I really shouldn't have been so flippant about kissing him. There was no way my traitorous lips could be trusted around him now.

"I'm not staying with you," I said flatly.

"My apartment is right around the corner from the venue," he countered. "And I have a feeling it will be quite late by the time we leave—especially for an early bird like you. Do you want another half-hour car ride through Saturday night traffic to get to a decent hotel?"

"I don't mind taking the subway—"

"You are *not* taking the subway."

I scoffed. "Afraid I can't handle myself?"

"Afraid I'll have to bail you out of jail at 2 am because you went full rabid raccoon on someone who catcalled you," he replied with a begrudging smile.

"Damn straight."

"It's a three bedroom," Deacon added. "You can have your own room and en suite just like a hotel, and the kitchen's fully stocked, and the water pressure is amazing."

"It will be weird."

He arched a brow. "I promise it won't be any weirder than sleeping in an old monkey enclosure."

I gave him an incredulous look, hating that he already knew what I was thinking. But the idea of Deacon and me being alone in an apartment together made my heart skip a beat. I got nervous and jittery whenever he and I were alone together, but at least then we always had the constant interruption of siblings and publicists to buffer any awkwardness.

But to be truly alone with him . . . It felt like standing on a cliffside and thinking my body might involuntarily fling itself off the edge, but instead I feared involuntarily launching forward and kissing him. Especially after on set the other day . . . Now that I knew how good of a kisser he was, I was bound to trip and fall directly into his mouth, *especially* if we were alone.

But my protestations were getting less and less robust when it came to Deacon. After the conservation trust fundraiser tonight, he'd stay in New York and I'd take the train home and that would be it. We probably wouldn't see or speak to each other again except for the occasional board meetings he deigned to attend, if ever. And once I passed the torch on to the permanent director, he and I might never cross paths again. So maybe it wouldn't matter how weird tonight was anyway.

. . . and I had to admit I was very curious to see what his apartment looked like.

"Luca's already arranged for your outfit to be delivered to the venue, and the hair and makeup teams will meet us there."

"Teams? As in plural?" I asked, feeling like a complete fish out of water. What was this life? Did I need whole *teams* of people to make me look red carpet worthy?

"Your dress has already arrived. I'm doing an Armani campaign right now, so I hope that's okay?" I just stared at him like he was slowly morphing into a fluorescent green alien. "Dove?"

"Did you just ask me if an Armani gown was *okay*?"

He laughed, looking me up and down. "I did. I'm sorry we couldn't get it fitted, but they have your measurements so it should be fine."

"*How* did they get my measurements?"

Deacon's smile widened. "I have my ways."

My mind started wheeling through the memories of the past few weeks, when it snagged on one. "Wren!" I exclaimed. "She said she needed to measure me for a sewing project. That little traitor. Why didn't she just tell me?"

"I think she liked being an accomplice to Luca's shenanigans," Deacon said with a wink. "And if she told you what it was really for, you would've freaked out."

I folded my arms tightly across my chest. "I don't know how I feel about you being in cahoots with my siblings," I muttered. "But like, is a dress even necessary?"

"And this right here is exactly why Wren lied," Deacon jeered.

I let out a little groan. "I kind of thought maybe as director, I should just go in my zoo uniform and a blazer or something," I said. "It's more official that way. That's what Baz Madigan does with his charities."

"It's not what his wife and kids do," Deacon countered. "They are designer brand people all the way."

I shot him a look. "Keeping up with the Madigans, are we?"

"Stop evading the point I'm trying to make," Deacon taunted. "If a dress really makes you that uncomfortable, I can make a call and we can pull some other options."

"A dress is fine," I conceded. "I suppose I can rally for one night."

He smiled at me ruefully. "Being my date is a great hardship, I know. I appreciate your sacrifice."

"I just want this night to be perfect and for the trust to raise a bunch of money and for us to save a ton of wildlife and for me to not embarrass myself or you or my family or the Prickle Island Zoo legacy or—"

"Whoa." Deacon took my hand in his, threading his fingers through my own. "I know you're not a big fan of the spotlight, but it's going to be great," he assured me, squeezing my hand. "More importantly, it's going to be fun, okay?"

"Okay," I gave in, letting out a nervous breath as the car pulled into an underground parking garage flanked by security guards.

"Just pretend it's only you and me."

I offered Deacon a weak smile, not telling him that imagining that would only make my nerves a million times worse.

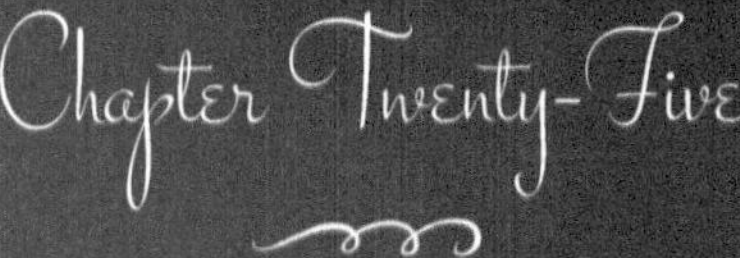

# Chapter Twenty-Five

Deacon

I waited for Dove in the foyer of the cordoned off suites. The bustle of photographers and event staff echoed up the stairs from the venue below. I unbuttoned and re-buttoned my jacket three times, a surprising bout of nerves tying my stomach in knots as Zeke talked a mile a minute in my ear. He had managed to "find time in his schedule" to fly out for the fundraiser, and I was sure it had nothing to do with the bevy of actors, artists, and models who were in attendance—some of whom were looking for new representation.

"So that script should be coming in the next week," he drawled, and I had no idea what he was talking about because I was so focused on the closed door that I knew Dove was behind.

I hoped she was okay. I knew this whole thing was really

intense for her, but I wasn't sure if demanding to stand next to her while she got her hair and makeup done would seem like I was being the overprotective boyfriend.

*As if she would ever allow that.*

Maybe I shouldn't have made her come to this event. Maybe I was pushing too hard. I'd gotten so hung up on the idea of her on my arm, showing her my world, having her fall in love with all of it and see me, maybe, in a new light. But I should've known better than to think Dove could be wooed by all the glitz and glamor.

I was an expert at delusional fantasies, but this one was going to only hurt me in the end. Even after what Dove's siblings had said, I really needed to lower my expectations. Dove was headstrong, confident, and she knew what she wanted out of life, and it had nothing to do with glitz and glamor . . . and I highly doubted that it had anything to do with me either.

"Earth to Deacon." Zeke waved in front of my face, and I finally broke my staring contest with the closed door.

"I think I might want to take a little time off after the next project," I admitted with a sigh, crossing my legs at the ankles and leaning against the wall.

Zeke looked at me like I'd just told him I wanted to move to Mars. "Time off?"

"Yeah, or maybe focus on some projects for my—"

"Please don't say art. You're not going down the tortured indie artist path on me, are you?" Zeke ran an anxious hand through his hair. "I swear to God, if you start going method and wearing turtlenecks and talking about your fucking *craft*."

"I'm not. I just want—"

"If you say an Oscar, I'm going to lose my mind." Zeke groaned. "You know how political that shit is? I'd have better luck making you the King of England. Let's just keep our heads down and focus on Batman right now. Stick to the plan, right?"

"Right," I muttered, knowing it wasn't worth the battle. The path had been laid out for me. All I had to do was walk it. It shouldn't be that hard.

The door opened and I stood straight, waiting with bated breath as Dove walked out. Even as I braced with anticipation, I wasn't ready for what I saw. The sight of her hit me like a freight train.

Dove strode out wearing an emerald-green corset gown, a slit running up the side all the way to the top of her thigh. All the air stole from my lungs as I trailed my eyes up her satin-clad body to her face. Her hair was pulled back, teardrop crystals hanging from her ears and a matching necklace glittering across her chest. Her lips were a deep red, and her eyes ended in dramatic wings. At first glance, she looked like the epitome of Hollywood vixen, but there was so much more depth to her beauty because it wasn't just a façade layered upon her. It radiated out of her. The lighthouse in my storm.

"Damn," Zeke said, adjusting his collar as his eyes scanned Dove up and down.

For a split second, I questioned whether it was an overreaction to punch him just for appreciating how beautiful Dove looked. "Damn indeed."

Dove searched the corridor until her gaze hooked with my own and a soft, little smile curved her lips. To be the guy she smiled at felt like more of a victory than every award on my shelf. I pushed off the wall and straightened my suit as she sized me up with similar appreciation. Whatever she was feeling in that moment, I hoped it was even half of what I was feeling toward her.

She was absolutely stunning. Always. Unequivocally. Irrevocably. Stunning. In khakis or sweatpants or designer gowns. And I knew then for certain the thing that I'd been terrified of happening when I returned to Prickle Island after fifteen years had come true: I was in love with her. I'd never *stopped* being in love with her; the feeling had just grown and matured right along with me. But I'd known from the moment she'd stormed into her mother's office, she had my whole heart whether she wanted it or not.

It took me several seconds of gaping at her before I realized someone was speaking to me.

"What?" I turned and found Ivy Blanc standing there, her hand on her hip, looking annoyed.

"I said, are you ready for the carpet?" she grumbled, wringing her rhinestone-studded clutch in her hands.

"Ivy, I . . . didn't know you were going to be here? I'm walking the carpet with Dove," I said, confused.

Zeke jumped in and clapped me on the shoulder. "We want you and Ivy to be the canoodling costars for your new movie," he announced. "The trailer is about to drop. Stick to the plan, remember?"

I glared at Zeke before I looked back at Dove's too-wide eyes. She stepped back an inch, as if she didn't want to interrupt the conversation, a mixture of fear and disappointment on her face.

*No, nope, absolutely not. I'm not going to throw her to the wolves and make her handle this treacherous obstacle course solo. And there's no way I'm letting her hang on the arm of any other guy tonight besides me, because she's mine.*

*She's always been mine.*

"Ivy," I said cooly, holding my anger in check. "I am so glad you were able to attend this fundraiser."

"Like I had a choice," she muttered.

"But the focus of this event is on the charity." I gave Zeke a look that told him if he meddled a second longer, I'd fire him. "So I will be walking the carpet with the charity director as intended."

I stretched out a hand to Dove and she gratefully took it. I wrapped her hand over my forearm, escorting her through the room as she wobbled on her high heels. She smelled amazing, like she'd been spritzed with a rich French perfume. Everything in me eased when she was finally by my side again.

"I look better on my own anyway," Ivy huffed, bristling as Dove and I walked past her. "It'll look cute in the press, you with her," she added, looking Dove over with disdain. "Deacon Harrow, two-time Sexiest Man Alive, with the doe-eyed charity case."

I could see Dove shrink an inch at that statement and it incensed me. Normally, Dove would've had something sharp-tongued and pointed to spit back, but this snake pit was one she didn't know how to navigate . . . unlike an actual snake pit which she'd probably love. But if she could save me from literal crocodiles, I could save her from Ivy Blanc.

I debated all kinds of retaliation, but instead, I just simply guffawed. "You really are a spiteful bitch, aren't you, Ivy?" I asked in a mocking tone. "I know your breakup stung, but maybe consider your target a little more carefully next time. You just called the most beautiful woman in the room a charity case."

I walked Dove down the hallway and out into the open foyer, leaving Zeke to rush in and apologize to Ivy on my behalf. I really didn't care. Too many people in my life now thought that they could talk down to everyone and anyone and I couldn't stand it.

"Thank you for that," Dove murmured.

"Ivy is just miserable and wants to make everyone around her miserable too," I gritted out.

"But you don't need to lie for me," Dove added. "She's a freaking supermodel." I raised my eyebrows, halting us, and Dove teetered on her high heels at the abrupt stop. "What?"

I pointed to the giant gilt mirror hanging in the entryway. "Look." She glanced at our reflections before quickly looking away. "I wasn't lying."

"That is very sweet," she murmured, eyes darting everywhere but the mirror. "But there are like ten of the most beautiful women in Hollywood going up and down that hallway right now. And I really don't care. I have no desire to be the most beautiful woman in the room. That sounds daunting and awful."

"I know you don't, but that doesn't change the fact that it's true."

She shot me a look. "How many drinks have you had?"

I held my hand to my chest in mock offense. "One glass of whisky."

I turned her fully, standing behind her so that she had no choice but to stare at our reflections. One hand snaked around her waist to her lower abdomen, and I thought about how dangerously close my fingers were to that slit in her dress, how easy it would be for me to dip them underneath the fabric and touch her. I swallowed thickly as she and I stared at our reflections.

"Deacon," she whispered, and the sound of my name on her lips made me ache. "You don't need to prove anything to me."

"Tell me you don't look beautiful," I insisted. "Tell me you aren't the right person to have on my arm tonight. Ivy and I don't make sense even in works of fiction. Tell me you and I don't look perfect together." I leaned down, my lips caressing the lobe of her ear as I whispered, "But you won't because you know it's true."

She shuddered at the rush of my breath against her ear, turning her head ever so slowly toward me, her full red lips only a hair's breadth from my own. And I wanted to tell her then, tell her all of the secrets of my heart—

But then Zeke came barreling around the corner, clapping his hands like a football coach. "Right, D-money, your audience awaits." He paused, rubbing his hands together. "Deacon and Dove." He chuckled to himself. "Double D-money tonight."

"Thank you for ruining a perfectly nice moment, Zeke," I murmured only loud enough for Dove to hear. I straightened and extended my arm out to her again. "Ready?"

"Nope," she said with a tight smile.

"Great, let's go."

# Chapter Twenty-Six

Deacon

I knew Dove Lachlan could handle snakes and lions and crocodiles, but now I knew she could handle the most dangerous animals of all: paparazzi. She was a natural. Now I was convinced there was no situation in the world that she couldn't deal with—the same of which couldn't be said for me. And damn if it didn't make my chest ache watching her easily wade through the treacherous waters, unintimidated, beautiful, confident, *everything I always wanted and never thought I would have.*

Only the slightest pinch in Dove's eyes let me know that she didn't realize she was doing as good of a job navigating the red carpet and mingling through the fundraiser as she was. But truly, she was perfect. I should've known she would be. Despite never having any official media training, she'd been born into a family that was running a popular customer-facing business. She'd been handling thousands of people per day from all over the world since she'd been old enough to give a bird talk. Now, she had a million diplomatic retorts and animal fun facts in her back pocket, skilled at bringing the conversation back to the charity at hand and away from reporters drudging up her viral video or questions about my dating life.

I could tell Cody, who stood a few paces behind us, was impressed too. Not once did he have to dive in and rescue her from a rogue question. He even gave me a thumbs-up when Dove managed to turn a question about what diet she was on into a heartfelt discussion about the importance of food abundance for critically endangered wildlife. It was truly masterful.

At the start of the night, I thought I would have to take the lead, but after a few hours, Dove was flying solo, navigating through the crowded ballroom all on her own. Meanwhile, I was downing more and more glasses of liquid courage, wondering if I'd ever have enough to cross the room and ask her to dance with me.

The emerald green complimented the purple in her hair perfectly, her figure on full display, the milky skin of her thigh peeking out of the slit in her dress. *That fucking dress.* I held my hand to my chest, feeling the familiar shape of the coin against my heart through my heavily starched shirt.

"Well, look what the cat dragged in," a soft female voice said, sidling over to me. "You clean up nice, big brother."

I turned, brows lifting in surprise as I took in my sister, Faith. "Wh-what are you doing here?" I asked, my smile stretching wider as I pulled her into a tight hug.

"Dove invited me," she informed me, sweeping her long, wavy blonde hair over her shoulder. She wore a long-sleeve, floral-print dress, modern but with nods to her folk music roots.

"She did, did she?"

Faith eyed me. "I thought you knew."

"You usually say no to these sorts of things," I replied.

Faith pursed her lips, considering. "You know, I think Rusty Sky has enough of a name for itself now," she said with a grin. "I'm sorry I had to go it on my own for a while there. I just didn't want to be known as Lucky Role's little sister. Sorry."

"Don't be," I said with a shake of my head. "You've been incredible. You're a Grammy award winning band. Lucky Role could never," I added with a chuckle. "Your music is amazing. You know how proud I am of you, right?"

"Thank you." Her nose wrinkled as if she couldn't quite take the compliment. "Does it make you want to pick up the guitar again?"

"Yeah," I hedged. "Maybe one day."

Faith cocked her head at me. "Maybe one day should be sooner rather than later."

I hummed. "That would make a great song lyric."

"Maybe we should cowrite it," she offered. "An indie pop, folk crossover. People would love it."

I smiled down at my little sister. She was the first person to give me hell for doing something stupid, but she was also the first one to pick me back up when I fell. Our relationship reminded me a lot of the Lachlan siblings. It didn't surprise me that Dove had thought to invite her.

"Batman doesn't write love songs," I grumbled. "That's what Cody tells me at least."

"Cody is a narcissistic psychopath," Faith replied with a sweet smile.

I guffawed. "Tell me how you really feel."

She shook her head, taking in the room. "This is really nice, Deacon," she said. "This charity was a great idea. I think it'll be good for you. I'm proud of you too, bro."

That meant a lot to me, especially coming from Faith, who never pulled her punches. My little sister's gaze fell across the room, and she let out a low whistle. "Wow, she is freaking stunning," she said as her eyes landed on Dove.

"Easy," I warned.

"Why? Is she taken?" Faith gave me a smug knowing look.

"Don't look at me like that."

"Don't look at you like I've known you my entire life and can read you like an open book, hm?" She nudged me with her elbow. "All I'm saying is if you don't go ask her to dance, that horde of hungry looking men will. I'd throw my hat in the ring too, but I'm taking off now, got an early flight back to LA. Plus, Dove is a sweetheart and I like 'em meaner."

I chuckled. "Fine, I'll go ask her." I turned and hugged my sister. "I'll see you at Mom and Dad's for his birthday weekend?"

"See you then," she replied with a nod. "And congratulations again, Deacon." I thought she was going to say on the charity, but she added, "Dove is a good one and she's *way* out of your league."

With that, I watched my sister wander off through the crowd. I turned to see the pack of leering men prowling closer around Dove and I rushed across the room to cut in.

"Gentlemen," I said, and Dove looked up at me with grateful eyes as I extended a hand. "I believe this woman owes me a dance."

The crowd parted, and I swept Dove out onto the dance floor. "I *owe* you a dance?"

"It's romantic, just go with it," I whispered back, and she laughed. "I was trying to rescue you."

"I appreciate it," she replied. "I was about to punch that dude in the nose for staring at my tits during our entire conversation, but that wouldn't have been very director-ly of me."

I turned swiftly. "Which one?"

Dove barked out a laugh, practically dragging me back

toward the dance floor. "Save the testosterone for someone who needs it," she said. "I can handle a few creepy men."

"I've seen you stare down a pack of literal hyenas," I joked. "I know you can handle it, but I still like defending you because —" *You're my person*, I thought, but said aloud, "—because you're my friend."

"Fine, I'll let you puff up and drum on your chest to defend my honor next time, okay?" she said lightly, not knowing all of the emotions swirling inside of me.

"Fine," I relented as I pulled her against me, taking one hand in mine and placing the other on the small of her back. "You know who I just bumped into?"

"Who?" she asked a little more breathlessly as we swayed side to side.

"My sister."

She couldn't quite contain her smile. "Oh."

"Oh?" I asked. "That's all you've got for me? *Oh?* What were you just saying about me being in cahoots with Wren, hypocrite?"

"Guilty."

"How did you even have her number?"

Dove's smile widened. "She and I text every so often. We kept in touch."

"You kept in touch with my sister but not me? I'm wounded."

"If you call a couple messages a year *in touch*," she replied. "Your older brother and Hawk still comment on each other's Instagrams. Apparently, our moms still send each other Christmas cards too."

"So all the Harrows and Lachlans have been keeping in touch this whole time apart from you and me?" I asked with a shake of my head. "I don't know who to be more angry at, you, my mother, or my sister. Meddlesome trio you are." She laughed lightly. "I think Faith only said yes to this because you invited her by the way. She's never said yes to any of my invites."

"I'm very convincing," Dove flaunted as we circled the room. We moved in an easy rhythm, her body feeling so good pressed against mine, her skin so soft. "You're a good dancer."

"Only after many drinks," I admitted.

"You do look a bit glassy-eyed." She chuckled as she looked between my eyes. "We should grab some painkillers and Gatorade before we go home."

*Before we go home.* She didn't know what that statement did to me. For a moment, I pretended she said that to me all the time, like we always went home together at the end of a big night out, like my home was always hers.

"Don't worry, I can hold my liquor." At that inopportune moment, I stood on her foot. "Sorry."

She laughed. "Forgiven. Honestly, it's nice when you're clumsy. It's a relief to know you're not perfect."

"I'm so far from perfect."

She let out a yawn and leaned her cheek against my lapel. "Not to me."

I had the terrible urge to lean down and kiss the top of her head. But a million eyes were on the two of us and already the way we held each other was close enough to arch some eyebrows.

"Sleepy?" I asked, and Dove let out a hum, her eyelids drooping to half-mast.

"I'm normally asleep by eight and it's almost midnight." She yawned again.

Sleep tugged on me, pulled under by the warmth of the crowded room and the way Dove and I lazily rocked side to side. Luca caught my eye and I nodded, letting him know to ring my driver. Boneless, Dove leaned further into me.

"Tonight has been amazing," she complimented. "I can't think of anything that would've made it better."

"I can think of one thing."

She perked up a little. "What's that?"

"How does popcorn, TV, and sweatpants sound?"

"Heaven," she replied with a satisfying groan. "Even though I'm exhausted, I need to decompress a little before I go to bed."

"I always need to do the same." As my eyes searched her face, I hoped I wasn't gazing down at her like a lovesick fool, but when it came to Dove, I couldn't quite contain it. All of my acting flew straight out the window. She cracked me right open and made everything more real.

"I have the perfect show in mind," she said, stepping out of my hold.

I couldn't bear not touching her. Without thinking, I took her hand and threaded it with my own. "Then let's get out of here."

She shook her head at me. "What a line."

# Chapter Twenty-Seven

Dove

When we arrived at the apartment, Deacon busied himself with calling the concierge—something I thought only hotels had—while I wandered off in the direction he pointed. I found my suitcase neatly placed on a luggage rack beside a queen-sized bed. His guest room was austere but expensive-looking, designed in shades of sage green and cobalt gray.

The city lights twinkled in the gaps of the thick curtains, the world beyond this luxurious apartment feeling so far away as I unzipped my tight dress. I let out a moan of relief as I rolled down my shapewear, wadded it up, and threw it across the room onto my suitcase.

Deacon's apartment seemed more like a hybrid between a hotel and an art museum than an actual home. Apart from the catalogue racks of comic books and a framed map of Middle-earth on the far wall, nothing about the place seemed like Deacon. I wondered how many days of the year he even got to spend here. The three bed, two and a half bath property had probably cost him millions and he didn't even get to enjoy it.

I slipped into my trusty sweatpants and hoodie, grateful to take off all the elaborate and suffocating clothes and the layers of caked on makeup that made me feel like I was drowning in my own skin. The fact I managed to find a cozy blanket stashed in the bottom of the linen cupboard was a miracle. I wondered if Deacon even knew it was there or if whoever had designed and furnished the apartment had done it for him.

When I came out, I found that Deacon had on old episodes of *Game Changer* on the TV. I flopped onto the couch, pulled the soft blanket over my lap, and surveyed the spread of food across the coffee table.

Deacon had called up for snacks and, to my surprise, the concierge had brought up two buckets of movie theater popcorn, candy, and fountain sodas. I wondered if some poor staff member had had to run to the nearest movie theater at midnight to obtain them. Somewhere even being *open* at midnight felt unfathomable to me on my little island. If I suddenly had a craving on Prickle Island for something that Lighthouse Lane General Store didn't stock, I'd have to take a ferry into town to acquire it.

I laughed and shook my head as I opened a box of Butterfinger bites. "Designer clothes and luxury cars are fine," I said, "but this is the coolest perk of being rich and famous I've seen so far."

Deacon grinned at me, sweeping his hair off his face. "I've been wanting to do this with you for a long time."

My stomach flipped. It should be illegal for such husky words to come out of the mouth of someone as attractive as he was. I was certain the many glasses of Champagne, whisky, and complimentary cocktails had loosened his tongue. He'd shucked off his jacket, his bowtie and belt abandoned and his collar unbuttoned to mid-chest, making him look like a sexy, disheveled assassin.

*Move over James Bond, Deacon Harrow has entered the building.*

Deacon stood in stark juxtaposition to me in every way, but especially now while I wore a faded hoodie and he looked like he'd just foiled the world-ending plot of an evil supervillain.

Deacon fell onto the couch beside me, and I collapsed into his side. We ate popcorn and watched our favorite shows until midnight became 2 am. And despite my exhaustion, I didn't want to sleep. I wanted to keep laughing and swapping inside jokes and sharing fun facts and just simply letting the conversation flow on forever. I didn't want this magical moment between us to end and my carriage to turn back into a pumpkin just yet.

When the food had been devoured, Deacon pulled the leather cord of his necklace out from the neckline of his undershirt, pulling a coin off a magnetic clasp. I scrutinized it as he toyed with it in his fingers for a second before I finally caught a clear enough glance and gasped.

"You *do* still have that!" I exclaimed, looking down at the golden coin in his grip. My mind spun. "You've been wearing it this whole time?"

I'd hoped he'd kept it. I'd hoped the memory had been as special to him as it had to me. Suddenly, all of the times Deacon had rubbed his hand to his chest took on a whole new meaning. I'd thought it had been some sort of meditation tool, some yogi-appointed gemstone or something, but no, it was the coin—*our coin*—that he'd been touching this whole time. My heart thumped faster at the thought.

Deacon grinned. "I've almost lost this thing more times than I can count," he said with a chuckle as he flicked it up with his thumb and caught it again. "I finally had a jeweler make a magnetized clasp for me so I didn't keep losing it in my pockets."

"Why didn't you tell me?"

"I don't know." He tossed the coin up again and when he caught it, his eyes landed on mine and snagged. "Maybe I was afraid."

"Afraid of what?" I asked as he passed it between his knuckles with practiced ease. "Oh, come on, you have to tell me."

He weighed his head back and forth. "Maybe I should let the coin decide," he said. "Heads or tails?"

"Uh . . . tails."

He flicked it up in the air, caught it, and slapped it onto the back of his hand. He peeked at it before showing me. "Tails."

I cheered, bouncing on the couch in a goofy victory dance. When I looked back at him, he was just staring at me. My brow furrowed. "So what it is you were so afraid—"

Before I could get the whole question out, he grabbed me by the back of the neck and kissed me.

My insides exploded, fireworks filling my body as his lips slid over mine. He let out a satisfied sound at the back of his throat that had my hands delving into his hair, pulling him closer. He tasted like popcorn and whisky—because he was drunk and not thinking straight.

*He's drunk and not thinking straight!*

The reality of the moment crashed into me and I pulled my mouth from his.

Deacon dropped his forehead to mine. "I've been wanting to do that for a really, *really* long time," he murmured, moving in to kiss me again.

I lurched backward, warring with myself to make the sensible choice.

"Wait." I put a hand on his chest . . . and then slid it down to his cut abs because I wasn't a fucking saint and when else was I going to have a chance? Still, I said, "You're drunk right now and you will regret this in the morning."

He shook his head, his thumb sweeping across my cheek as he held onto me. I couldn't help but lean into his touch.

"I'm not that drunk," he refuted, trying to close the distance between us again. He managed one more amazing, world-shattering kiss before I rose to my feet, putting the couch between us so I didn't climb him like a freaking mountain goat.

"Deacon, this is the alcohol talking. You probably won't even remember this in the morning."

He leaned back, tousled hair falling into his eyes and a smile on his swollen lips as he slung an arm over the back of the couch. "You don't know how wrong you are, love."

"How dare you say such a hot thing right now!" I let out a frustrated groan, balling my hands to keep from touching him. "You probably won't even remember that you called me love."

I started anxiously bouncing on the balls of my feet. Was this really happening? This couldn't be really happening. There was no circle of hell where I would say no to Deacon trying to kiss me, was there?

"I will remember." Deacon cocked his head at me. "*Why* are you freaking out right now?"

I shook my hands out. "Because you're *you*! Look at you!" I screeched, gaping at him like he'd seriously lost his mind. "You don't date girls like me."

"No," he said. "I fall in love with girls like you."

"Oh my god," I whined. "Screw you for being so damn romantic! You are a hopeless flirt when you're drunk."

"I'm not doing this because I'm drunk," he argued with an exasperated laugh. At least he was able to make light of the situation, even if I was utterly panicking.

"Then why did you say 'never'?" I paced back and forth across his perfectly shined wooden floorboards.

"What?"

"At family dinner," I clarified. "Why did you say 'Dove and I? Never.'" I mocked his voice, unsure why I delivered the line with robot arms, but right now that was the least of my concerns.

"Because you are incredibly stubborn." He drunkenly waved me up and down. "Case and point." He shook his head. "And I thought you'd never forgive me for the skink thing. So I said never because I knew you'd never let me in, never give us a chance, well, at least I thought that until you kissed me, and then I thought maybe there was still hope."

I crossed my arms. "Well, you should've been more explicit with that sentiment then. It was very confusing."

"Dove."

"Deacon, we can't do this!" I exclaimed. "I don't think you understand. You do not go for people like me. There's a reason why celebrities date celebrities. I mean, come on, you date women who need fake IDs to get into bars!"

He winced. "Those were all fake relationships," he said, holding up a defensive hand. "Not that I'm saying I've been a monk or haven't been playing the field, but yeah, none of the relationships that have been public have been real."

"Still," I said, pacing faster, searching for ways to make him understand that he and I were not the same. "I'm older than you!"

He rolled his eyes. "By five months."

"You date supermodels. With zero cellulite and blindingly white teeth. *And* millions of Instagram followers," I countered. "I'm not in the same universe as you, let alone league."

His head reared back. "You think *I'm* too good for *you*?" he asked in disbelief. "Dove, you have absolutely no idea how incredible you are. Ivy picked on you because she's horribly jealous of the fact that you don't even care that you're ridiculously gorgeous. You are smart and funny and nerdy and hardworking, and you have an amazing family and job and wit, and you care so much about making a difference in the world." He held a hand to his chest like it made his heart hurt. "If anything, I am unworthy of you."

"You don't really want this, Deacon." I retreated another step. "You don't want me."

"Could you please stop telling me what I want? I know what I want," he demanded, his face growing more serious as he held my gaze. "I've known since I was twelve years old." I felt tears pricking my eyes, my heart constricting as I tried not to believe him. "Are you saying you don't have feelings for me?"

"Of course I have feelings for you!" I erupted, unable to deny it any longer. "You were my best friend—funny and smart and creative and daring—and how could kid version of me not develop feelings for kid version of you?" He laughed. "What?"

He shrugged. "I think you're the only person in the world who wouldn't have led with rich, famous, and handsome, and that is one of the many, many reasons why I really want to kiss you right now." He stood, ambling over to me.

"Don't you come over here with that sexy smolder face and your perfectly kissable lips," I scolded him. "Your looks might be lower down on my priority list of things I like about you, but come on! You *know* you're the most gorgeous man in the world, so *please* don't test me."

"What if I want to test you?" He flashed that mischievous smile and my pussy fluttered.

*Fuck, fuck, fuck.*

This was the worst kind of torture. Was he this devilishly charming with every model and actress he'd brought back to this apartment after a few too many drinks? I bet I was the only woman ever who didn't immediately get naked for him even though I *desperately* wanted to.

Why—*why!*—did I have to be the bigger person right now?

"You are drunk," I repeated slowly, holding Deacon by the shoulders so he didn't come any closer.

"I really wish I didn't have any celebratory drinks tonight." He sighed, scrubbing a hand down his face, and I suddenly felt the pull of sleep surrounding us and the fact it was 2 am, which was insanely late for someone who routinely woke up at 5. "What can I do to make you believe that I'm not just saying this 'cuz I'm drunk?"

"Okay, how about this?" I proposed, knowing I needed to get both of us to bed and reset whatever sloppy, drunken, melodrama was playing out between us. "If you still want to kiss me in the morning, then you go right ahead, okay?" I offered. "But chances are you won't even remember this conversation."

"I will remember," he slurred, suddenly more obviously intoxicated now that he was on his feet. I was pretty sure he was seeing two of me, which only reconfirmed my decision not to take things further.

"Sure you will, big guy." I patted him on the shoulder. "Let's get you to bed before you crash into something, okay?"

"You could sleep in my bed tonight?" He held up his hands. "Nothing would happen. It would just be nice to have you there."

Yeah, and have him wake up thinking we'd slept together when he couldn't remember any of this and have to come up with some awkward excuse as to why it was all a big mistake.

"Another night."

"Okay." He gently rubbed his knuckles across my cheeks. "I'll hold you to that."

I smiled. "Tonight was perfect. Really. Thank you."

"You might be the only person in the world who has the same definition of perfect as me," he said. Which almost made sense and made my chest constrict with its sweetness.

With that, he wandered off, leaving me reeling. All the things he'd said to me, I knew, would be erased with the daylight, but God did it feel good to hear them. I probably should've just let him kiss me, but knowing he was spurred on by alcohol hurt too much. It would just be a crazy memory I could tuck away when I headed back to Prickle Island tomorrow. Deacon would go on being one of the most famous men in the world, but for a little while in the wee hours of the night, it had been fun to pretend that he was mine.

# Chapter Twenty-Eight

Dove

I sat on the countertop next to the coffee maker, swinging my legs as my third cup of espresso was churning out of the machine beside me. In a baggy old zoo shirt and checker-print sleep shorts, I was too tired to navigate to the dining table until at least my third cup. I'd managed to sleep in until 8 am which, for me, was massive. I wondered if Deacon would even wake up before I had to leave to catch my train in a couple hours. Maybe it would be better if I just skirted out the door before he woke . . .

*One more coffee. Then I'll leave.*

My mind was sleep-addled, still hazy from the whir of events that had taken place the day before. What a night. The fundraiser had been nerve-wracking and glitzy and over-whelmingly successful, but the part I would treasure the most was the simple act of sitting on a couch with my old best friend, watching our favorite shows together, and eating popcorn. That would be the part I'd miss most when I got on the train, more than the glamor, more than even that scorching drunken kiss we'd shared. I'd miss the way he felt so right sitting beside me, being my person, easy as that. In another universe, maybe he would've been.

I pulled my mug out from under the machine and started pouring milk into it, when Deacon's bedroom door opened.

He emerged rubbing a hand down his face, lines still streaking his cheek from his pillow. His expression looked somewhat hungover, but not nearly as bad as some of my siblings after a night out at the Salty Dog. Lark would forever win for world's worst hangover, but the memory of that day tumbled from my mind as Deacon stepped into the room. He wore low slung gray sweatpants and a tight black T-shirt. My stomach flipped at the sight of him all sleepy and disheveled.

"Morning," I said cheerily, determined not to bring up last night or ruin our reigniting friendship by telling him all the things he'd said. "I'll let you have this cup of coffee. There's also some painkillers and a giant water on the island, which you should definitely drink, and before you ask, no, I am not taking my own advice."

Deacon seemed to ignore that statement as he sleepily wandered over toward the coffee maker. But instead of going for the coffee, his eyes hooked with mine and he started walking faster.

"I remember," he said and grabbed me and kissed me.

It took a second for me to catch up to his words, frozen and reeling as his lips slid across mine. He remembered what he'd said to me last night.

*He remembered.*

He remembered all of those sweet, heartbreaking words, all the things he thought about me, all the things he felt for me and me for him in return. He remembered . . . and he *meant it?*

My body finally caught up and my hands snaked up his back as my mouth fused to his. The kiss was a frenzy fifteen years in the making. We unleashed ourselves on each other, and all the while my brain kept singing: *this is real, this is real, this is real!*

Deacon Harrow, the first boy I'd ever kissed. Deacon Harrow, my best friend. Deacon Harrow, the movie star and rock star and nerd who my twelve-year-old heart never truly recovered from, was *kissing me.*

Deacon groaned into my mouth as his hands roved down my curves and kneaded into my ass, pulling my hips flush with his. I let out a surprised gasp at his possessive grip as he rocked me against his growing erection.

"Tell me you want me." He groaned, his mouth drifting from mine to kiss down my neck.

"I want you," I urged as I frantically grabbed the hem of his shirt and tugged. "I've always wanted you."

He let me yank his T-shirt off and throw it across the room, a hungry smile on his lips. My eyes dropped to the coin hanging around his neck, rising and falling with each heaving breath. I leaned in and planted a kiss directly above it.

"Dove," Deacon panted. "I—"

"Take me to your bedroom," I cut in, terrified that I knew exactly what he was about to say and not knowing if I'd be able to survive hearing it.

Deacon didn't need to be asked twice. My wicked smile stretched as he scooped me up by the ass. I wrapped my legs around his hips, needing us to be so much closer, trying to fuse us together. Our mouths collided again as Deacon blindly stumbled across his apartment and we collapsed onto his bed. His warm chest pinned me into the mattress as his hips nestled between mine, and he kissed me so deeply it felt like my world titled on its axis. Everything was suddenly upside down . . . or maybe, for the first time in my life, it was right side up.

Deacon started pulling my shirt up and I instinctively pushed it back down. Suddenly, I remembered that this guy was used to getting into bed with Victoria's Secret models and a flash of nerves shot through me. What if hot celebrity sex was different? What if I wasn't good enough? What if he expected me to rival them? What if one failed fuck ruined all of the building tension between us?

Even as my emotions roiled up within me, I realized I was still rocking against him, unable to stay still with him on top of me.

Deacon tried to lift my shirt again. "Don't you dare pull away from me," he rumbled as he nibbled on my earlobe. "Never with me, Dove. I want all of you."

My heart ached with that pleading, how badly he wanted me to bare myself to him—not just my body but my heart. I saw it in his eyes more than the lust or hunger, more than everything else. He was begging me to trust him, to *love* him.

And despite all my nerves and reservations, I wanted him to know that I did trust him, knew that he would never fumble my heart. I yanked my shirt up as he grabbed the waistband of my shorts, and I lifted my hips so he could pull them off. Pajamas discarded, I lay there bare before him.

"You are so beautiful," he whispered, eyes devouring me. "God, I imagined this moment so many times," he confessed with a disbelieving shake of his head. "But even my fantasies never did you justice."

"I've thought about this so many times too," I confessed.

My eyes fell to Deacon's sizable erection as he slid off his sweatpants, a little sound lodging at the back of my throat. He was more beautiful than a Grecian statue, so perfectly sculpted he might as well have been made of marble. My throat went dry at the sight of him, my pussy throbbing in anticipation.

*I need to send Ricardo the biggest fucking gift basket.*

Deacon's eyes trailed up my body to meet mine and held as he prowled over me. The feeling of his warm skin on my own was ecstasy. He kissed me, his tongue dipping into my mouth before he trailed kisses back down my body. His head dipped to my breast, and he pulled one peaked nipple into his mouth. I moaned as he sucked, rolling his tongue over the sensitive bud. His hand lifted to my sex, cupping it as I tilted my hips into his touch. He trailed one finger down me, spreading me further and finding my pussy flooded.

"You're so wet for me," he whispered against my skin.

I was practically vibrating with need now. "Please tell me you have condoms here."

Deacon let out a dark laugh and released me to prowl across the bed and reach into his bedside drawer. He pulled out a condom, ripping the foil with his teeth and rolling it on while he watched me.

His lips were swollen and parted, his face filled with lust, but they quirked, too, as if he couldn't contain the joy of it. I let out a breathless laugh. Him and me. After all this time.

He crawled back toward me, hovering over me as he guided the tip of his cock to my entrance. I hitched my knee on his hip, and his hand kneaded the flesh of my thigh as he pushed in.

I let out a cry of pleasure as he pushed in deeper and deeper, filling me until my vision began to spot, so overcome with roiling sensation that I could barely think.

"You feel so good." He groaned against my neck. "You okay, baby?"

"Yes," I panted. "Please."

I felt his smile against my ear. "Please what?"

"Please fuck me," I begged. "Now."

His throaty, little laugh made my skin tingle as he pulled out of me and thrust back in. Another moan pulled from my lips as he began to move, picking up the pace with each roll of his hips. I'd had good sex before, but *never* had it been like this. The way he moved inside of me had my eyes rolling back. My fingernails clawed into him, holding on in eager desperation as he pushed me higher and higher into euphoria.

I'd spent so many nights touching myself and imagining my hand was his, imagining the way Deacon would fuck me as I came alone in the dark, but this was more than even my fantasies could conjure. Each low groan he made, each reverent whisper of my name, I knew, as unbelievable as it was, Deacon needed this just as badly as I did. I hadn't believed in fate before, but now I knew this moment between us had been inevitable. There was no universe, no timeline where he and I didn't end up joined like this.

If ever there was such a thing as soulmates, he was mine.

I angled my hips to take him deeper, rocking myself with each thrust. This feeling was so amazing and addictive and all-consuming, I hoped it would never end. But the need in me kept building higher and higher, until I couldn't deny it any longer. With one final thrust, I shattered, crying out Deacon's name as my pussy clenched around him. He barked out a final groan as he came, the two of us tumbling into ecstasy together. On and on, pleasure shot through me like bolts of lightning, a feverish high that left me panting and sated and sweaty.

Deacon collapsed to my side and pulled me in close, folding me into his arms as I pressed another kiss to his chest. And I'd never felt more right in the world than right now, wrapped up in my best friend's arms.

# Chapter Twenty-Nine

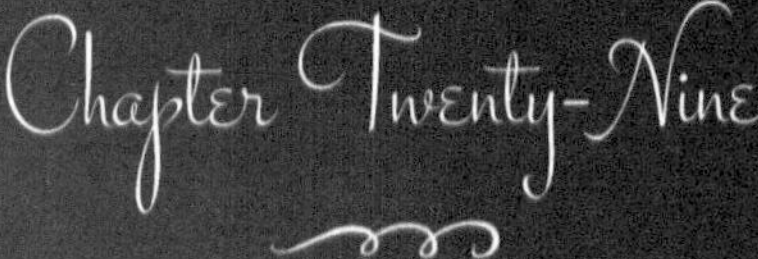

Deacon

Dove's cheek rose and fell against my chest, her body curved against mine. She toyed with the coin hanging from my neck, pulling apart and reattaching the magnetic clasp again and again. Every so often, she'd let out a satisfied, little hum. She probably didn't even realize she was making it.

I'd never known such perfect bliss as this moment. Dove Lachlan's naked body against mine, the smell of her lavender shampoo, the feel of her fingers tracing lines across my skin, and knowing that everything in the world suddenly felt right.

Dove started to roll away and my arm wrapped tighter around her waist.

She laughed. "As much as I'd love to stay, I need to go or I'll miss my train."

"Don't take the train," I grumbled, circling my fingers down her bare back.

"I need to get home. It's all hands on deck at the zoo right now." She let out a frustrated grumble. "Even as much as I wished I could freeze time and stay."

That made me smile. She wanted to stay. She wanted this— *us*. A few weeks ago, I hadn't dared to hope, and now it felt foolish I hadn't seen it before. There had always been this buzzing energy between us. Whether we called it love or even sometimes hate, it had always been there. Inevitable. I should've known the second I'd taken her frantic phone call that this was where we'd end up.

"I'll have my driver take us back," I insisted.

Dove propped her head up in her hand to get a better look at me. I loved the way her eyes roved my face, her swollen lips and sated expression. "Us?"

My hand roamed lower to her hip and squeezed. "I'm not letting you ghost me this time," I informed her, lifting my head to kiss her. "No running away. No slowly fizzling out. I don't want to lose you again."

"Deacon," she admonished with a little grumble. "This was incredible, but we need to be realistic."

"I am being realistic."

"But—"

"No buts." I kissed her pouting lips until she was smiling again.

"I'm not trying to run away, but I have to go home and you have a life that needs to keep rolling on without me."

There were no two words I hated more than the way she said "without me." I knew it was a lot to ask of her. I knew my life was a lot to take on. But if anyone could handle it, it was Dove Lachlan. I held her tighter, as if my arms were trying to prove to her that I wasn't going to let her go.

"My life can wait right now," I pushed. "Let's focus on the

zoo first. I'm coming with you." Dove opened her mouth to protest, and I sat up fully. "Dove, I meant what I said last night. You and me. I'm all in."

"But you have work," she protested.

"I'll cancel it."

"Deacon!"

"Dove!" I mocked. "Let me take you home. I have nothing big going on this week. I'll have Luca shift things around, and next Sunday we'll make a game plan, okay?"

Finally, she relented, collapsing back down against me. "And you call me stubborn." I grinned victoriously as her eyes drifted to the guitar in the corner of the room. "Do you ever still write?"

"Sometimes," I hedged. "Not that I'll do anything with the songs. It's just a hobby now."

Her bedroom eyes lifted to me. "Do you want it just to be a hobby now?"

"When it comes to my career, it doesn't matter what I want."

"Of course it does! It should matter more than anything," she argued. "What do you want?"

I sighed. "I want to make movies that mean something to me, I guess," I confessed. "And I want to start making music again. I want to spend less time working and more time on the things I love."

"And what things do you love?"

"Searching for treasure on the beach, binge-watching episodes of *Dimension 20*, texting my best friend that I saw someone that looked exactly like the grumpy petting zoo llama . . ."

"Garrett."

"That's the one." I chuckled. "I want to do all the things I love with the person I love."

Her lips curved. "And who is that person?"

"She's a Russian supermodel," I teased wistfully.

Dove's wandering fingertips stalled. "Oh."

"*That* was a joke," I said, recapturing her hand. "I realize now that was terrible timing. I was talking about you, if that wasn't clear. I've been madly in love with you since I first saw you at ten years old. I've been in love with you longer than I'd known what love is, and I never stopped."

"Well, I wish I could say the same," she lamented, and my heart sunk for a second. "And I can because I've been madly in love with you since I was ten years old too."

She let out a squeak as I rolled over until I was pinning her into the mattress, kissing her deeply. "We are just as bad as each other," I said with a laugh. I lifted up to search her eyes, wanting to tumble into her gaze as I said, "I love you."

"I love you," she echoed, reaching up to pull me back into another kiss.

She loved me. And with that thought, everything in the world felt complete.

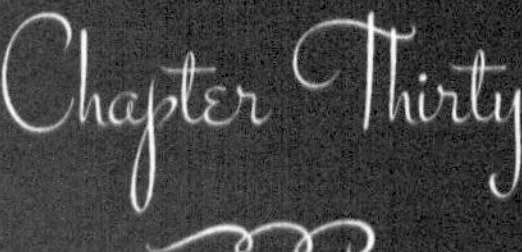

# Chapter Thirty

Deacon

The rain lashed against the car windows as the driver pulled up to Petey's boat shed.

"Are you sure you want me to leave you here, sir?" the driver asked, looking at me skeptically through the rearview mirror. "I can take you to a hotel or something for the night if—"

"We can stay in the boathouse. It's fine," Dove assured. I gaped from the rusted tin shed back to her confused expression. "What? He has a cot and some sleeping bags. The twins and I used to sleep over here all the time as teens. And then we'll be ready to catch the boat in the morning."

And here I was thinking the monkey house was bad . . .

I shook my head. A sudden springtime thunderstorm had blown in on the drive up from New York. Dove and I hadn't managed to get out of my bed for another eight blissful hours, and so by the time we'd made it to the shoreline, it had already been nightfall, and with the storm, there would be no passage across to Prickle Island until the morning.

Still, Dove had insisted that we get there at first light to help out at the zoo. There was that dogged loyalty to her family again. It was one of the many, *many* things I loved about her. She and I both knew the importance of family, and for a brief second I wondered what kind of one the two of us could make together. My squeeze of her hand was my only acknowledgment.

When Dove went to open the door, I tugged her back into the car. "Are you sure about this?" I shouted to be heard over the galing winds. "You want to stay in a *boathouse* during a *hurricane*?"

"It's a mild thunderstorm," she countered as a loud roll of thunder made the whole SUV tremble. "If you want to go stay in a fancy hotel, you can, but I'm going to stay here so I can get back to the island at dawn."

Defeated, I scrubbed a hand down my face, knowing every second with her was going to be an adventure.

"Alright," I relented. "I guess we're staying here tonight."

She smiled at me as lightning flashed overhead. The driver went to get out, and Dove called, "We've got it, Mike. You don't want to drive back all wet." She gave him a pat on the shoulder before opening her door again to the torrent of rain. "Have a safe drive home."

"Thank you, Ms. Lachlan," Mike replied.

When had Dove learned his name? The car service switched drivers all the time, and at some point I'd just stopped asking. It was one of those jarring moments for me, as if I suddenly realized what my life had become. So many people wanted a piece of me that I'd started treating everyone like they did. I didn't want to be that way anymore. Like a sharp jolt of awareness, it took Dove being in my life to finally wake me up.

"Thanks, Mike," I said as I raced to the trunk of the car to grab our bags.

Dove was already attempting to carry both, and I swiftly scooped them out of her grip as we dashed to the front door, huddled together under the tiny overhang to avoid the rain.

"Please tell me you have a key," I pleaded as Mike pulled away, leaving us plunged into darkness. I pulled out my phone and used the flashlight to illuminate the door.

Dove lifted on her toes, fingers feeling across the lip of the door. She adorably stuck her tongue out in concentration as she felt her way along the ledge. "Got it," she declared, holding out the key in victory.

"Very safe."

"Who's going to break into a dilapidated old boathouse?" she asked incredulously. "What are they going to steal, Petey's rusty tools and expired tins of food?"

"You're really not selling me on this place."

"Apologies, it's not the Ritz," she jeered, opening the door.

We stumbled inside, and she found a few candles in a drawer, lighting them until the shadows disappeared, revealing the boat shed. It was something straight out of *Hoarders*. There were boxes of tools and knickknacks stacked to one side, a cot, a balled-up inflatable mattress, and some blankets to the other. Old built-in cabinets were pulling on rusty nails, hanging from the wall. And a beat-up armchair sat in the corner next to the smallest TV I'd ever seen.

As I surveyed the space, I murmured, "You know, this reminds me a lot of my first apartment in New York. Except cleaner and probably with fewer pests."

Dove chuckled. "See? Just like home." She wrung out her dripping wet hair. "We should probably get changed into some warmer clothes."

I bridged the distance, pulling her into a slow, lingering kiss. "I have a better way to heat each other up."

She laughed. "First we need to eat," she rebuffed, holding aloft the plastic bag of Chinese food that we'd made Mike pull over to acquire. Steam swirled from the containers in the chilly room. "No one wants to eat cold fried rice."

"Agreed. And I doubt there's a microwave in here."

"Nope," she replied as I rubbed my hands together. "There are a couple fleece jackets hanging on the hook over there." She pointed to the coatrack in the corner stuffed with all sorts of rain jackets and winter coats.

We sat in Petey's giant fleece jackets and ate takeout on the creaking floor, surrounded by the light of a dozen candle nubs. The sound of waves lashing against the shore roared outside, the occasional sea spray misting the fogged windows. It was like Dove and I were in another world.

After a satisfying meal, we blew up the air mattress and sat watching the storm through the windows. Peeks of moonlight were starting to appear as the rain died down.

"Sunrise will be beautiful," Dove mused. "Nothing like a sunrise after a storm."

I hummed, leaning my shoulder into her as I put my hands in my fleece pockets. There was something crinkly in there, like an old receipt. I ignored it as we kept watching the last flashes of lighting in the sky, but then suddenly, a horrifying realization dawned on me: it wasn't crinkling under my fingers . . . it was *moving*.

"Gah!" I exclaimed as I pulled my hand out of my pocket to reveal a wolf spider clinging to my palm.

"What?" Dove screamed as I flung the spider across the room, and we both leapt up onto the cot.

"Ughhhh, it was hairy! Why was it so hairy?!" I shouted as Dove doubled over laughing and clutching her stomach.

"Oh my god, don't do that," she managed through fits of laughter. "I thought there was an axe murderer outside or something. It was just a spider."

"I'd rather an axe murderer. That spider and I were holding hands for like ten minutes before I realized," I whined, wiping my hands down my shirt, my skin crawling. I unzipped the fleece and flung it across the room as the giant spider disappeared in the cracks in the floorboard.

"It wasn't trying to hurt you," she soothed. "It was hiding from the storm."

I glared at her. "You are entirely too calm about this."

"We're in a boat shed," she said with a jovial shrug. "Of course there's spiders. Why do you think Crane always wanted to come out here?" She bit her lips together, her shoulders still shaking with restrained laughter. "What would all your adoring fans think about zombie hunter and sword-wielding superhero Deacon Harrow squealing at the sight of a spider?"

"If you told them, I'd deny it," I warned as I shook my hands out. "I feel like they're crawling all over me."

"They're not."

My hand shot to the back of my neck as something touched it, and I barked out a cry as I grabbed a fistful of shirt and whipped it off, making Dove laugh even harder.

"There's nothing on you," she said, smoothing a warm hand down my bare back. "It was probably just the tag."

"We're not all spider people, okay?" I finally laughed along with her as she soothed her arms across my skin.

"I know," she comforted, kissing my shoulder.

"I should be the one heroically rescuing you from spiders." I dropped a kiss to her hair.

"You can rescue me from all the other things," she suggested. "You rescued me from Ivy Blanc. I'd take a spider over her any day." She kissed across my skin as I laughed. "We'll take turns on who has to be the brave one. Right now, it's mine."

I smiled, turning and pulling her flush against me as her

hands continued to rove up and down my sides. "You make me want to be all the best parts of myself," I murmured.

Her gaze softened, deeper emotions blooming to replace the lighthearted ones. "You make me want to be all the best parts of myself too," she whispered, dropping her cheek to my chest.

We stood there slowly rocking, the storm our only soundtrack. And I knew this was one of those moments that anyone else would think of as small and inconsequential, but for me, it would forever be on loop in the highlight reel of my life. In that second, I knew for certain the thing I'd wondered when I'd first knocked teeth with her—maybe I'd just found the love of my life. Maybe soulmates were the ones who made us want to be the very best version of ourselves. Even twelve-year-old me had known—this was what love felt like.

When Dove finally released me with a yawn, I slid my hands down her sides. "You should sleep," I offered. "I will hold vigil against the army of hairy spiders."

She laughed. "Why don't you just come to bed too?"

"There's no way I'm going to be able to sleep tonight knowing those things are creeping around the place," I admitted.

"Hmm. Maybe I have better ways we can pass the time," Dove suggested, and suddenly I forgot all about the spiders as she lifted on her tiptoes and kissed me. Any place where Dove Lachlan's lips were on mine was paradise.

# Chapter Thirty-One

Dove

Instead of heading straight to the zoo the following morning, Deacon led us down the road that curled around the parking lot and down a private beachside drive. To one side were rolling hills of pebbled shoreline scattered with patches of seaweed and driftwood. A boardwalk cut across the dunes, leading all the way to the northern point of the island. In the summer months, it would be filled with joggers and cyclists getting their morning workouts in, but in the off-season it was a picturesque, private landscape. We followed the gravel to the very end before turning down a narrow lane to a white picket fence.

I paused, looking at the periwinkle shutters, window boxes overgrown with wildflowers, and pearlescent abalone shells tinkling from the garden gate. The first peeks of sunrise kissed the wind-worn shingles of the beach house, adorning it in a golden glow.

I took it all in with a sigh, admiring the beauty for a split second before turning to Deacon curiously. "Why are we at the Sea Pearl?"

"You know this place?" Deacon asked, and I shot him a look. "Right. Small island. Of course you know this place." He set the bags down and opened the front gate to the stone-lined path that led to the front door. Drifts of orange wildflowers danced in clumps throughout the rock garden. "I've rented it for the week."

"You rented a house? When?" I answered my own question before Deacon replied, "Luca."

*That explains why he was hastily texting him in the car yesterday.*

"Nothing as palatial as the Holloway Estate," Deacon replied as he carried our bags toward the front door. "Thank God, that place was creepy. I swear it was haunted by a bunch of posh ghosts."

"I believe it."

"This seemed just as beautiful but far more cozy." He gave me a sideways look. "I thought I'd get ahead of it before your mom offered for me to sleep in the monkey house again."

I let out a sharp laugh. "I don't blame you."

Deacon fished his phone out of his pocket. "Luca sent me through the code for the lock box—"

"It's 3441," I chimed in. Deacon's head whipped up, brow arched in question. "We come run the water in winter, make sure the pipes haven't frozen and stuff. I think the twins were once in charge of weeding but . . ." I waved a hand over the yard. "Seems like they have forgotten."

Deacon huffed. "I think I like it like this, wild and a little chaotic." He slung his arm around my shoulders. "Just like you."

"What a ringing endorsement," I teased, leaning into his hold. "The owners haven't been on the island in years. They mostly just use it for weekend vacation rentals now. A shame, it's such a beautiful house." I admired the little driftwood and abalone sign beside the door proclaiming it the Sea Pearl.

"Well, it's ours for the next week." Deacon brushed a kiss to the side of my head.

"Ours?"

"You're staying with me." He hesitated. "Unless . . . that's too much? Too fast? If you want to stay at the zoo, I understand. I just thought that—"

I lifted onto my tiptoes and kissed him, pausing his frantic words. "Oh, I'm staying here with you," I murmured against his mouth.

"Good." He smiled against my lips, cradling the back of my neck. I could see it in his eyes: the last two days together, all of the feelings bubbling up to the surface. "And this way I can have you all to myself." With a mischievous grin, he dropped his mouth to the shell of my ear. "I'm going to have you on every surface of this house." I bit my lip, my cheeks flushing with heat. "You'll be grateful for the roar of the waves when I make you come so hard you scream my name."

My hands twisted in the fabric of Deacon's shirt as I swallowed thickly. "Maybe I can start my shift late today . . ."

Deacon let out a husky laugh, placing a slow, lavish kiss to my lips. "You'll be very glad to not have your siblings' constant interruption when I—"

"Well, if it isn't Freaky Deaky!" Finch called, her faint voice cutting over the roll of waves crashing onto the stony shore.

"You've *got* to be kidding me," I gritted out. "She's like freaking Beetlejuice."

Deacon and I turned to find Finch and Frankie on the boardwalk a few yards beyond the house's gate. Simon was in a baby carrier strapped to Frankie's chest while Finch pushed an empty stroller filled with what appeared to be an entire toy shop full of baby toys.

"What are you two doing here?" I shouted as they abandoned the stroller and wandered over the rocks toward the house.

Finch took out her phone as if texting someone. "Heron owes me twenty bucks."

Frankie swatted the phone down. "I thought you were going to stop betting about your siblings' love lives?"

"I made no such promises," Finch said with a wink.

I crossed my arms. "You just *had* to be walking past this house at . . ." I checked my watch. "5:30 in the morning?"

Frankie swayed side to side as she spoke. "Simon is only sleeping while he's moving at the moment," she announced, doing a half-rock, half-squat movement like some kind of crazed, interpretive Oompa-Loompa dance. "My internal clock is set to 4 am anyway—baker's curse—and since there's no more café work until summertime, I offered to take him so Hawk and Hannah could get some sleep."

"But enough about us," Finch cut in with a shit-eating grin. "What are *you two* up to?"

I rolled my eyes. "I think you already know."

"Oh, we *all* already knew," Finch replied with a laugh. "We were just waiting for you two to catch up."

"Wonderful," I bit out, my frustration only making Finch smile wider. "Well, I'll be up for my shift in half an hour, so see you then." I wheeled my hands, not-so-subtly trying to shoo her away.

Finch chuckled. "Alright, alright, we're going. You two have fun." She turned and added over her shoulder, "And make sure to draw the curtains before jumping each other, there are families around here."

"Finch!"

"Toodles." She waggled her fingers and she and Frankie

started walking back to the boardwalk, whispering and laughing between themselves.

"What was that about us not getting interrupted here?" I asked quizzically as Deacon unlocked the front door. "You have clearly underestimated the Lachlans' penchant for annoyance."

"What was that about you having half an hour before your shift?" he countered, hooking his finger in my belt loop and tugging me across the threshold.

"Make it an hour." I wrapped my arms around his neck and kissed him as he kicked the door closed behind us. "I can be a little late just this once."

# Chapter Thirty-Two

Deacon

I stood at the top of the hill with my phone to my ear, trying to understand Cody's string of unintelligible curses.

"I'm just taking a couple weeks off, Cody," I assured him. "You need to chill."

"Just a couple weeks with *no notice*, Deacon," Cody argued. "I have no idea how I'm going to spin this. Rehab? Mental health, something about mental health."

"I'm sorry I had to cancel a couple obligations, but the schedule was light," I justified. "And I just finished filming. I should be able to get a couple weeks off."

"Yeah, on a *planned* vacation to Monaco or something where we get photos of you and Ivy sunbathing on a mega yacht. The team is completely freaking out over here," Cody complained.

"They think you're completely in love with this bird girl and she's going to Yoko your career."

"I am in love with her." Warmth bloomed in my chest at the proclamation, even as Cody muttered another string of curses under his breath. "And people really need to give Yoko a break already."

"Oh god." Cody groaned. "I really wish you hadn't just said that to me. I've *just* finalized the plan for next quarter. We can't get this time back after this all ends terribly. Think with your head and not your dick, Deacon."

"I am," I replied tightly. "I've been in love with her forever and finally the stars aligned and she wants to be with me too. She's the one, Cody."

"*The one?*" Cody made a gagging sound. "But you're still going to act like Ivy is *the one* for the promotion of this movie, right? I've worked to the point of exhaustion on this plan. You signed off on it just a few weeks ago!"

My gut clenched. Acting was one thing, but I didn't want to leverage my personal life into letting people think I was in love with anyone other than Dove anymore. That was a step too far. I didn't want to pretend. Not when everything finally made sense.

"Your silence is deafening," Cody snapped. "Please, Deacon. I'm sorry I'm being harsh right now, but I *need* you on board with this Ivy thing. Six years we've been working together. And now you're one of the highest paid actors in Hollywood, and I know I'm not your agent, but I'd like to think I played a small part in that."

"You did," I admitted.

"So . . . we already have a whole promo tour planned based on you and Ivy being loved up. It's what we agreed upon when you decided to produce a *romantic comedy* of all things. This was our compromise, remember?"

I pinched the bridge of my nose. "I remember."

"So we stick to the plan."

"We can find a new plan," I pleaded.

"Get serious, Deac—"

"No," I growled, finally having enough.

He always did this. He always lured me in with guilt to keep me in line. And in the end, I always conceded. But nothing was more important to me than protecting what I'd just found with Dove. If she wanted me, I was hers. Simple as that.

"I don't work for you, Cody. You work for me," I gritted out. "I'm in love with Dove and I'm not going to ruin the rest of my future in order to sell some B-grade movie we're only making because I promised Dove I'd use this place as a filming location, understand?"

The line was dead for a long time before Cody finally said coldly, "Understood. I'll find a way to fix it."

"Thank you." I hung up and turned to find Dove frozen halfway down the path. A bucket of green waste was in her hand, her eyes filled with cautionary concern.

"You what?"

My mind reeled as I realized what I'd just said.

"I . . ."

Dove dropped the bucket and folded her arms. "This movie." She searched the air as if looking for answers. "Deacon, please tell me that this whole movie wasn't just so you had an *excuse* to give me money."

I blew out a long breath. No point lying now. It was clear from her expression that she already knew the truth.

"You wouldn't have taken it if I just gave it to you." Her mouth fell open, and I scrambled to explain myself. "The fact you even called me told me how dire the situation was," I pushed. "They were going to sell the zoo. You were going to lose your *home*, your family's legacy." I took a step forward, hands clasped and pleading. "And I was afraid you still wouldn't take the money from pride alone, so when you called and asked if I could use the zoo for a filming location, I panicked and said yes." I panted, barely able to get the words out fast enough. "And then I went to work green-lighting this thing because I wanted to make this happen for you. *Please*." I took her hands in mine. "Don't hate me for this. I'm sorry I didn't tell you."

To my relief, she didn't pull away. "You know, I always thought the amount you were paying to use the zoo was insane." Brows pinched, she shook her head. "I had a feeling you were padding the numbers to give us more, but . . . making a whole movie just for the zoo?"

"For you," I clarified. "I'd do anything for you, Dove. Always. That's how much you mean to me."

Her eyes welled, and I was so relieved for a split second before she said, "I don't want to Yoko your career."

"You heard that too, huh?"

"I don't want to kill your dream."

"Baby," I murmured, wiping a tear as it slipped down her cheek. "You could never do that."

"Listen, Deacon, these last two days have been incredible," she started. "But we need to talk about the elephant in the room."

"I didn't think you had elephants."

"Not right now."

"Okay." I chuckled, making a mocking serious face.

"You know we can't be a couple."

My muscles constricted, fear spiking in me. "Of course we can."

"You have an image to keep up."

"First of all, fuck my image," I asserted. "Secondly, the only image I want people to have of me is a man madly in love with his childhood sweetheart, of an actor who is hopelessly devoted to the love of his life. *That* is the image I want."

"I like that image," she said with a sniff. I hated that she was crying but loved that she was willing to show all of her emotions to me. I knew how rare that was. "But you and I have very different lives. I want—"

"You want to make a big impact in the world of wildlife conservation," I supplied.

"Yes."

"You want to travel the world and see new places and discover new things."

"Yes."

I held her cheeks and kissed her, murmuring across her lips. "And I'm the perfect person to do all those things with." I rested my forehead to hers. "You can be the permanent director of the trust—you're the best person for the job," I continued before she could protest. "And you could travel with me on promo tours and to film festivals and shooting on location all over the world while doing your conservation work."

"You've thought about this."

"Every day since you walked back into my life," I confessed. "Every day, I started thinking of all the ways I could make you happy, of all the ways we could be together."

Her tears fell heavier and I kissed them away. "Be mine, Dove Lachlan," I pleaded.

"I already am," she said and kissed me.

# Chapter Thirty-Three

Dove

I danced into the backyard, holding a bottle of sparkling wine and two plastic cups. "Guess what?"

Deacon looked up from where he sat frowning at a thick script, looking perplexed as if translating a foreign language. I could see the relief lifting off him as his eyes landed on me. It made my stomach flip every time. There was nothing like the way he looked at me. Even his best acting paled in comparison. It felt like Cupid's arrow to the heart every time.

"Are we celebrating?" he asked, tossing the script on the worn outdoor table and leaning back in his chair.

The evening breeze twirled through the private back garden —mostly a continuation of beach rocks along with a few strate- gically placed garden beds and a driftwood walkway that bisected the yard, leading out to a large table under a honeysuckle pergola. It was the most perfect seaside secret garden, the smell heavenly.

I closed the distance to Deacon, leaning against his chair. "I just got a call from the species coordinator."

Deacon's eyebrows shot up, his excitement uncontainable. "And?"

"And Prickle Island Zoo in conjunction with the Lucky Role Conservation Trust has officially been green-lit for the Almadran skink breeding program!"

"Yes!" he cheered, grabbing me around the waist and pulling me into his lap. "You did it!"

"We did it," I corrected with a laugh. "And this is just the beginning."

Deacon plucked the cups and wine from my hands and set them on the table behind him.

"What are you—"

He silenced my question with a kiss, taking my face in his hands and pulling me tighter into him. "I'm so proud of you," he said between kisses. He pulled back to look at me, beaming. "You are spectacular in every way, you know that?"

"I don't think—"

"You are," he pushed, twisting me around in his lap until I was straddling him. "You are the most amazing thing. I can't believe that I get to be yours."

My smile doubled in size as I wrapped my hand around his neck and pulled him back into another kiss. My other hand roved up his chest, neck, and delved into his hair.

He let out a throaty groan as my tongue dipped into his mouth. His hands wrapped around my ass and he stood, easily carrying me back toward the house, bottle of sparkling wine forgotten.

I was already unbuttoning his shirt before we even made it through the back door. We stumbled into the living room and tumbled backward onto the couch. Deacon made quick work of my T-shirt and shorts, shucking my clothes off with haste as I laughed.

His responding smile turned wicked as he hooked his hands behind my knees and tugged me to the end of the sofa. My eyelids drooped, lips parted as he dropped his mouth to my pussy. I moaned with the first lick of his tongue. He swirled it over my clit, making my head fall back as I titled my hips against him.

*God, that mouth.* I was already barely hanging on as he expertly worked me into a dizzying state of pleasure. He hummed against my sensitive bud as if I were the tastiest meal he'd ever eaten. I shuddered against him.

Moaning, I reached for him. "Deacon . . . I . . ."

He released me, looking up at me through my legs. "I want you to come on my tongue."

His rasping words made my pussy flutter. As he lowered his mouth again, his fingers circled my entrance, taunting me once, twice before pushing into my flooded core. Deacon pumped his fingers in and out of me as he moved his tongue faster. I cried out, the sensation so overwhelming, I was seeing stars. I shattered, voice going hoarse as I cried out Deacon's name. My inner walls clenched around his fingers again and again as the waves of my orgasm roared through me.

When I came down long enough to catch my breath, Deacon released me, licking his lips with a lust-filled grin. He rose from his knees and prowled on top of me.

"That was one hell of a way to celebrate." I panted as he kissed up my neck.

His hot breath in my ear made me shudder again. "Oh, that was just the beginning of our celebrations."

# Chapter Thirty-Four

Dove

It took a great force of will to unfold myself from Deacon's arms in the morning. Waking up next to him was a new kind of bliss. I awoke to a beautiful sunrise as I hastily donned my work boots and grabbed an iced coffee from the fridge, leaving Deacon to sleep in as I dashed off to start work for the day. I skipped up the hill toward Mom's house to grab my radio, humming an old Lucky Role tune as I went.

But when I wandered up the front porch into the kitchen and saw my family anxiously gathered, whispering frantically to each other, I knew ready or not, the blissful bubble had burst.

"What's going on?" I asked.

"Whoa!" Finch exclaimed, holding her arms out wide and preventing me from seeing the newspaper behind her.

I tried to peer around her to the kitchen island, and she lifted on her toes, raising her arms like a basketball player guarding me. "What are you doing?"

"Softening the blow," she replied with a grimace.

"Oh god, what happened?" I skirted around her and shot forward to see a cluster of newspapers and laptops and phones all strewn across the marble . . . all of them with photos of me.

Photos of *us*—Deacon and me.

On the beach, the red carpet, the zoo, stolen looks and glances between us that were meant to be used to promote the conservation trust but instead were twisted and morphed to make it look like dates. And the way I looked at him . . . it was so obvious I was completely in love with him, meanwhile every single photo, he was looking away, split-second moments that made it look like a completely different situation than it actually was—as if I were a deranged fangirl and Deacon a cold, detached heartthrob.

The first headline read, "Deacon Harrow Caught Cheating on Girlfriend Ivy Blanc with Zookeeper."

"What the hell is this?" I screeched, grabbing Mom's phone and flicking through more images. "Did you Google alert my name? Oh my god, there are hundreds of articles! Why would they print this?"

Horrified, I scrolled through more headlines:

"Bad Boy Deacon Harrow Caught in Another Cheating Scandal."

"Deacon Says He was Manipulated into an Affair. Is He Being Blackmailed?"

"Hope for the Normal Girls, Even Zookeepers Can Snag Movie Stars. Take this Test to see if your Star Sign is Ready for True Love."

"Meet the Other Woman: Everything You Need to Know About the Zookeeper Deacon is Keeping on the Down-low from Ivy."

"Deacon's Secret Baby with Zookeeper. Ten Baby Names for Deacon and Dove's Future Brood."

"It's not true," I spluttered, looking between my siblings and Mom. "He and Ivy were never even a thing. Oh my god." I kept scrolling, seeing all these op-eds about me.

"Who is Deacon Harrow's New Mistress?"

"Mistress?" I balked. "They didn't even get my name right! Who the fuck is Duck Loblin?"

"This one says you're thirty-seven." Wren showed me her phone. "They're calling you a cougar."

"Not helping, Wren," Finch said, pulling Wren back behind her.

"It's all lies," I insisted, searching through the article. "People can't seriously believe this. It will go away, won't it?"

"Dove." Hawk scrubbed a weary hand down his face. "We've decided we need to hire a security team for everyone's safety."

"What?" I glared at them. "On the island? On the off-season? That's ridiculous. This is just—"

"These are only the headlines," Hawk started. "You've been getting a lot of hate from these articles, too, and you've seen what fans of Deacon are like. They hired a private yacht to camp out at the zoo in hopes of seeing him for crying out loud!"

"They were only there for a couple days and then they gave up," I pushed, folding my arms tightly to keep my limbs from shaking. I tried to put on a brave face, but I could feel the entire world crumbling around me.

"It's not just jealous teens, hon," Mom added gently, her whole face creased in pity. "It's—"

"Death threats," Wren finished.

"What?!" I yelped, feeling like my soul left my body. This was my fault. I'd brought this upon my family. A terrible question echoed in my mind: *what have I done?*

"Not helping, Wren," Finch gritted out, tucking Wren

behind her again. "We're supposed to be breaking this to her gently, guys."

"Death threats?" I asked, horrified. "But those are just keyboard warriors online. That's not . . . not a real concern. Is it?"

"We've had a couple calls from the shoreline police station." Hawk sighed. "They know where you live because you live where you work and where you work is in every headline in every major news site today."

"Not the kind of publicity the zoo was hoping for," Mom said, trying to make it sound like a joke, but it was more like a groan.

"It makes you a target," Hawk continued. "Some of these things sound credible, and I'm not taking a risk with my family."

"This is crazy." I shook my head. "We have electric fences and cameras at every entrance and . . . What is even happening right now?"

"This is what happens when you date one of the most famous men in Hollywood," Finch said with a shrug. "But we'll figure it out, Dovey. It will be okay."

"This is too much," I whispered, eyes pricking with tears. "I can't. I can't do this. I can't do this to all of you."

Wren gasped at her phone. "Oh my god."

"Whatever you've just seen, Wren, we don't need to know about it," Finch grumbled. Wren showed her phone to Finch. "You've got to be fucking kidding me!" she exclaimed.

"What?" My heart thundered in my chest as Wren showed her phone to Hawk.

"He fucked a Madigan?" Hawk shouted.

"What?!" I screamed, lurching forward and grabbing the phone from Wren's grip.

On it was grainy footage of a couple on the beach, the title reading: "Does Deacon Harrow Have a Type? Old Footage of

Deacon Harrow Kissing Lynx Madigan Surfaces Amid Latest Cheating Drama."

I watched the clip all the way through twice, tears welling in my eyes before my mother gently extracted the phone from my grip.

"Honey, I—"

"Don't," I said, voice wobbling.

Mom's phone buzzed and she picked up. "Kirby? You okay? I thought you were still in Greece." Mom looked at me. "Yeah, she's seen it." Her eyes flared. "They've been trying to reach you at the Salty Dog? Why? There's no story there."

"Oh my god." I dropped my elbows onto the countertop, head in my hands as Finch circled her palm down my back in calming strokes.

"Kirby," Mom continued. "Petey's calling me. I've got to go. Okay. Bye." She switched lines. "Petey, hi. Yes. She's seen it. How did they get your number? What?" Mom exclaimed, covering the speaker and looking at Hawk. "Someone is trying to hire Petey to drive them around the island and take photos of us."

"What did he say?"

"I normally wouldn't repeat what he said," Mom hedged. "But since this is kind of an emergency, he said, 'Get fucked.'"

"Well done," Finch said with a huff.

"They are offering him a lot of money for any stories he might have on Dove, too."

"They're probably calling every person I've ever known in my entire life right now." I groaned. "I don't understand why this happened all at once. I thought he had a team that dealt with this stuff. Why now?"

"I have no idea," Finch said. "But it's going to be okay, Dove. We've been through worse."

"Worse than this?" I shouted, unable to contain my panic.

"We can't—we can't—I won't put you all through this. I won't put you in danger. This is insane. I . . ."

"Maybe you should sit down," Hawk suggested, taking me by the elbow. "You look like you're going to pass out."

"I can't do this," I said again, voice breaking as I burst into panicked tears.

"Somebody needs to call Deacon," Mom urged.

"This is all that bastard's fault," Hawk growled. "He pulled Dove into this and threw her to the fucking wolves. He—"

The door opened before Hawk could finish that thought and Deacon rushed in. "I'm here."

# Chapter Thirty-Five

Deacon

My heartbeat drummed in my ears. My whole body shook in silent rage as the phone rang and rang and rang and Cody never answered.

Finally, I got one text message: I quit.

Reading that message was like being smacked with a wall of ice.

*No, no, no. This couldn't be happening. How could he do this to me? After all these years?*

I gripped my phone so tightly I thought I might break it as I left the house still yanking my T-shirt on. I stormed across the gravel road and up the hill toward the zoo, finding a suspicious number of boats in the harbor as I went.

*Shit.* I'd been afraid this would happen. I had wanted a slow, controlled announcement of our relationship. Instead, Cody had mutinied me. Luca was already on the phone with my lawyer. I was going to sue the shit out of that son of a bitch.

But lawsuits could wait. My first concern was warning Dove before she saw any of the vitriol being printed about her. Running barefoot up the cold pavement, I braced against the morning chill as steam curled from my lips. I ran up the front steps of the old house—the one filled with thousands of memories—as Evelyn's old dog, Phoebe, announced my arrival with a chorus of barks.

"I'm here." I threw open the door, not bothering to knock, and tumbled into the kitchen to find five members of the Lachlan clan staring daggers at me and, behind them, Dove with red-rimmed eyes. My heart shattered at the sight of her.

A white-hot knot lodged in my throat. "Can I talk to you?" My chest rose and fell in heaves. "Cody just rage quit and released a bunch of nonsense to the media, and we're hiring a crisis PR team and going to sue his ass and we're going to deal with it—"

Hawk took a step forward, crossing his arms tightly across his chest, his eyes filled with the kind of rage that made me take a step back. He was definitely about to punch me. "Did you sleep with Lynx Madigan?"

All the blood drained from my face at that question. "What? I . . . How did you . . ."

Finch tossed her phone to me and on the screen was a grainy video of twenty-three-year-old me kissing Lynx Madigan on a not-so-private Queensland beach.

"That son of a bitch," I growled. "How could he do this to me? I thought he'd killed that story years ago. But of course, he kept it just in case he ever needed it."

I hadn't realized I'd said all of that out loud until the group around me collectively grumbled, inching closer, as if they might mob me like a troop of baboons. I looked at Dove pleadingly. "It was a long time ago. We—"

"I think you should leave, Deacon," Finch snarled, rising an inch, and I wondered if she was thinking about all the ways she could kill me and make it look like an accident.

"No," I choked out. "Dove, please, talk to me."

Hawk took another step, and I was certain then that I was about to get my ass kicked, when Dove barked, "Stop." She moved around her brother, eyes downcast, not meeting mine. "It's fine, guys. Let's just talk outside."

I thanked every spirit in existence for that as I followed her quietly out the door and down the main path, away from view of her inevitably prying family.

"I am so sorry about these stories," I said. "I promise they'll all die down in a week or two. Luca is already on top of it. We'll have a new team hired in the next hour and—" I reached for her, and when she stepped away, it felt like someone cleaved my chest in half.

She wiped angry tears from her eyes. "Explain the Madigan thing to me," she demanded. "You *knew* my family hated them. How did your paths ever even cross? Unless it's true you have a weird fetish thing for zookeepers."

"Dove," I begged. "It's not like that. We met on a photoshoot when I was touring Australia as Lucky Role," I explained, scrubbing a hand down my face. "It was an Australian tourism campaign. I was still making a name for myself and it was good money and—"

"Did you sleep with her?"

"I . . ."

"That's not a no," she said tightly. "So that's how it is."

"It was five years ago." I reached out and again she stepped away. "Just a one-night thing. It meant nothing. I was a rock star, for fuck's sake. I mean, we've both had other people."

"Oh, spare me," she gritted out. "I don't care if you were elbows deep in pussy for the last decade, you don't just accidentally fuck your best friends' archenemy. You did it for a reason, why?"

"Because I missed you!" I erupted. "And I thought I could feel something about her as a substitute since you never answered my messages and cut me out of your life. I wanted to feel something like what I felt for you, and it was immediately clear to me how stupid that was, and that was it. I never talked to her again. I—"

"You fucked her because *you missed me*?" Dove seethed. "You've got to be kidding me. And the photos?"

"Lynx called the paps."

"Of course she did," Dove said with a bitter laugh. "I could've told you that she'd do that. She's been chasing fame her entire life. You should've known better."

"I got Cody to pay them off to kill the story," I offered. "I didn't think it would pop up again. I'm sorry."

"I forgive you," she muttered.

I reared my head back. "What? Really?" I was prepared for a long punishment and many acts of penance, not her instant forgiveness.

"Yeah," she murmured, wiping under her eyes. "I mean, I'm still pissed about it, but we all did some really dumb shit when we were younger. And the Madigans are total manipulative snakes."

"Then why are you crying?" I reached for her, and she took another step away. "Dove, please. Why are you pulling away from me?"

"Because all of those articles are true." A sob wracked through her. "In some small ways, they're right. Him with *her*? All those comments."

"You know better than to read the comments—"

"I can't live with the entire world hating me forever," she cried. "Even if I don't have social media or never go online, I can't deal with having every girl who's ever fantasized about you wishing I were *dead,* threatening to hurt my family. I can't travel the world with you always worrying that I've put them in danger just because I was too selfish to give you up."

"I will keep them safe," I pleaded. "I'll hire a full-time security team. This place will be Fort Knox for as long as it needs to be. But this will all die down soon, you'll see. The internet has a shorter memory than a goldfish."

"Goldfishes' memories aren't actually that short," she retorted, so stubborn she had to correct my animal facts even as she was crying.

I gave her a soft smile. "It will quiet down. I promise you."

"But it will always be there," she said. "And I can't be that person for you. You know I don't want to live in a spotlight. I don't know if I can survive all that comes with it."

"I'll quit acting," I announced, carrying on even as Dove shook her head. "I just got everything I ever wanted and I'm not giving it up. I'll quit today. Consider me retired."

"No. You can't—"

"Dove, please," I begged. "I don't care about anything as much as I care about being with you."

"I'm not going to ruin your career." Her voice cracked. "You've got songs to write. The world deserves your music, Deacon. It's your calling, your passion. I know you want that, and I won't be the one to take it from you. You are made for this life."

"I'm made for you." The words caught in my throat as my eyes began to well. "I love you more than any of it, Dove. I want this more. Please, I love you."

"You can't love me anymore," she replied definitively, her words a knife to my heart. *As if it were a switch I could just flip.* "It will only hurt us both in the end, more than it already has. I'm taking myself out of this equation."

"You're pulling away from me before I can let you down

again. But I promise I won't," I vowed. "I won't move on from this, from us, please. Don't do this."

I grabbed her, and for one split second I thought she'd change her mind as she lifted on her toes and kissed me. Salty tears coated our lips, and I tried to silently tell her all the things I felt, all the memories only she and I shared, all the dreams I knew we still shared together too.

But when she lowered back down, she choked out, "Please don't follow me." She took another step. "Goodbye, Deacon."

I saw my heart rip in two as she walked away, half of my soul going after her, half staying put. I watched as the ghost of me followed her and took her hand and we wandered off into a life of love, marriage, a family one day, a quieter life. I'd write the music that spoke to the deepest parts of me, and she'd save the world one endangered species at a time. I felt in my bones what it would be like to live that life more viscerally than I felt my feet on the ground now, and I watched as that future flickered away, out of sight.

# Chapter Thirty-Six

Deacon

I holed up in my apartment, not answering calls or responding to messages for a week . . . not that that meant I was entirely unreachable. Luca had his own key, and I'd suspiciously find the liquor cabinet restocked and that my piles of laundry had disappeared when I woke up each morning. I didn't like it. I would've preferred the squalor around me to reflect the dimness in my heart.

"What's the point?" I asked the ceiling aloud, rubbing a hand over my aching forehead.

I clutched the neck of a half-drunk bottle of whiskey in my hand as I paced across the shined floors of my apartment.

"What's the point of anything if I can't be with her?"

Fame was a cruel beast. It had given me access to the things

I loved most and taken them away from me in one fell swoop. Now I had everything I could ever want apart from one thing— the only thing that mattered.

I had money, fame, adoring fans, a career with enough open field ahead of me that I could make the projects I wanted to and pivot in any direction I saw fit. But the mountain of benefits of this life were so easily dwarfed by one simple truth: Dove Lachlan wasn't in it.

My phone started ringing, and I stared across the apartment in the direction of the Rusty Sky Reverie song emanating from the speakers—their first number one single. I could've sworn I'd put my phone on silent, but Luca must've turned the notifications back on again.

Great. The media was still in a frenzy over the Dove news, paparazzi camping at every entrance in and out of my apartment building, hoping to catch a glimpse. I'd hired a private team to patrol the waters around Prickle Island. Evelyn was the only one who knew, and I made her promise not to tell Dove. Even if Dove wanted to be out of the equation, I was still always going to protect her.

I stumbled through the apartment and fished my still-ringing phone out of my sweatpants pocket. "What?" I barked.

"D-money!" Zeke greeted. "You've had a week to be in your feels, my brother, but now we need to talk."

"No."

"Wait! Don't hang up," Zeke said, his tone changing from the normally smarmy, bro-y one to something more like what I imagined his real voice to be. "Listen, the new PR firm has been all over the zookeeper stuff. Very respectfully and without dragging her name, they've been putting out new stories of some of their other clients who are very excited to be splashed across the front pages. The story is going to be dead before you know it, m'kay? The news is a fickle mistress," he added with a chuckle. "They've scrubbed the worst of it and redirected attention from the rest. All that stuff is going to be long forgotten by next month, so hang tight, bud."

The tension in my shoulders eased a little. "Good. I'm glad."

"Good. So . . . Ivy's in New York," Zeke hedged. "And they think it would be good if the two of you went to dinner or something. The best way to get over a breakup is to distract yourself, my man. Get back to the plan, you know."

"Zeke," I groaned.

"Deacon, brother, you've got to let her go," he urged. "Either you need to be with this girl, and we can figure out how to make that work for you and your career, or you need to move on and get back to the original plan."

I rubbed my fingers in my swollen, red eyes. How could I ever let her go? I needed to but couldn't. Never would. My tight grip on what the future could hold for Dove and me had calcified that way. I didn't want anything else. Even if she'd never take me back, I couldn't go on the way that I had been. My life had changed forever when she'd walked back into it.

"New plan," I said to Zeke. "This film with Ivy is going to be my last for a long time, Zeke, maybe forever. I want to go back to making music."

"Okay."

I practically dropped the bottle from my grip. "Okay?"

"Yeah," Zeke replied. "I was wondering when this news was coming. Cody was the one who was hell-bent on getting you Batman, not me," he said. "Even though it's literally *my* job. I'll be honest with you, Deacon. You have made me a shit ton of money and I know you will continue to do so whether you're movie star Deacon Harrow or musician Lucky Role, okay?"

"Okay," I agreed, still disbelieving that I had his support. "I guess, yeah. That's the new plan then. I'm taking a step back from acting, working on new music again."

"Great," he said. "Have Luca organize a call for us with the new team later next week. Time for a new game plan, bud."

"Time for a new game plan," I echoed, and Zeke hung up.

The phone buzzed only a split second later and I picked it up, assuming it was Zeke again. "Forgot something?"

"Is this how you answer your phone now? 'Cuz it's weird," Faith answered flatly.

"Faith, hey," I choked out, emotions suddenly constricting my throat. Everything that had happened between Dove and me came flooding back.

"You sound like shit."

"Yeah, well, I feel like it too," I replied. "What's up?"

"Mom called me," she started, and I groaned. "Not that she needed to. I've seen all the news and already knew something was up. I'm sorry about D—"

"Don't, please." My voice got thicker. "I can't handle your kindness right now."

She snorted. "Well, that's too fucking bad because I've got something I need to ask you."

"There she is," I said. "What's up?"

"Open your door," she told me.

"What?"

"Open your door," she repeated like I was a disobedient dog.

I rolled my eyes as I unlocked my front door. "I swear to God, if you sent me a fruit basket—"

But when I opened it, I found my little sister standing there, looking up at me. "Who sends a fruit basket? That's so lame." She lifted a plastic bag of snacks, and I spied a packet of Skittles and Flamin' Hot Cheetos amongst it. "I brought you something that isn't boiled chicken and broccoli." My eyes welled, emotions I'd been battling to keep at bay brimming over, and then she landed the killing blow when she said, "I thought you might need a hug."

I let out a half laugh, half sob, and she dropped the bag of snacks to hug me so tightly she might've cracked a rib. And I cried my heart out into my sister's shoulder in the threshold of my apartment.

273

# Chapter Thirty-Seven

Dove

Working all day until my fingers bled and sobbing all night into my pillow seemed to be part of a long-standing Lachlan family tradition—work until we were too tired to feel all the pain.

After two weeks apart, I wanted to wish I'd never known Deacon. I wanted to erase every single memory that we'd shared. But he was so intertwined with all of my formative years that erasing him meant erasing *me*. Deacon Harrow, that stupid, handsome, insufferable dork, was inextricably linked to my soul.

I hated him for making me be the one to call it for what it was. I hated that I'd had to be the voice of reason. But there was just no way we could be together. Especially not now at the height of his fame. Even if I could bear the scrutiny of living in such a bright spotlight, despised by every fangirl and media outlet in existence, I didn't want to put my family through the ringer for it too.

I thought of little Simon, fear coursing through me that something could happen to my perfect little nephew because some psycho had broken into the zoo. All my worst fears swirled through me. I couldn't drag my family into this maelstrom.

Maybe one day if I quit my job and moved far from Prickle Island. Maybe one day if Deacon became a relic of a different era and—*no.* I couldn't go down this path of what-ifs and maybes. This reality was the only one that I had.

And I wouldn't let Deacon grow to slowly resent me, wouldn't let him see the way I couldn't keep up with his life— red carpets and parties and events and paparazzi—until he wished he'd never shared his heart with me. And I definitely wouldn't watch him throw away the things he loved most, his incredible art and talent and voice, just because he thought he loved me more. He'd come to resent that one day too.

No, the only way forward was apart. I'd known it that night in his apartment, in every time my stomach had fluttered with butterflies but I'd pulled away. I'd had good reasons for keeping him at arm's length after all.

Maybe one day when we were old and gray, we could have a chance at a life together . . . but by then he'd probably be married to some beautiful celebrity who could handle his fame, and I'd have to watch from the shadows as he loved her, married her, had children with her, all splashed across every front page to torture me for the rest of my life. The thought brought more tears to my eyes.

Everything hurt. Everything reminded me of him. I couldn't watch my favorite shows because they were his too. I couldn't focus on my new interim director role because it was *his* charity. I couldn't look at Eddie the toucan because Deacon had once held him. I couldn't even *wash my hands* without seeing the scar on my palm and starting to blubber again at the way he'd kept that coin all these years . . . and that he hadn't been wearing the necklace in his latest paparazzi photos.

I shouldn't have looked. I should've buried my head in the sand. Maybe I was a sadist or just trapped in the horror of watching this train crash, but I kept checking my news feed with rapt terror, and what I saw made my heart shatter all over again.

The news about Deacon and I had swiftly shifted after two weeks—the headlines now saying how gracious Ivy was for taking a cheater like him back after his "one-night stand" with me. I didn't know how he'd done it. He was a better actor than I ever knew—smiling in paparazzi photos, holding Ivy's hand as they left posh restaurants together, taking off a necklace he'd worn for fifteen years as if sending a personal message directly to me: *I'm really letting you go.*

It shouldn't have hurt how quickly he'd moved on, even if it was all pretend, especially since I was the one who'd ended things between us. The narrative had swiftly been turned back into one that favored Deacon again. His new PR team was apparently worth their weight in gold. My name dropped out of the headlines as quickly as it had arrived there. Some tech wizard had worked some serious SEO magic. Now, the top search when I typed in my name and Deacon Harrow were articles about the Lucky Role Conservation Trust and their hunt for a permanent director. It was as if the past few weeks had never happened. The only tangible aftermath was my broken heart.

Hannah and I sat on rocking chairs while Finch and Frankie

gently swung back and forth on the porch swing, holding Simon and sniffing his glorious head.

"I think we might need to have one of these ourselves one day," Finch murmured.

"I think so too," Frankie agreed, leaning farther into her.

"After I make you my wife," Finch added, kissing Frankie's hair.

"Hey! No love talk," Hannah piped up, snapping a finger at the two of them. "Don't make me get the spray bottle."

I let out a half-hearted laugh. "I appreciate the loyalty, but you *are* still allowed to be in love in front of me. I'm doing just fine."

Finch guffawed. "Yeah, I know that kind of just fine. I wouldn't wish that kind of just fine on my worst enemy."

"There's nothing that can be done." I gritted my teeth, shoulders bunching around my ears. "I'll get over it eventually."

"He won't always be that famous, you know," Hannah said tentatively. "Remember when we were all obsessed with Oliver James?"

"Who?" Finch asked.

"Exactly," Hannah replied smugly. "Maybe one day, you—"

"No. No maybe one days," I refuted. "I don't want to think about that. It hurts too much to hang onto something I need to let go."

"You're right, screw him," Hannah said definitively, and I loved how she immediately switched tact to support me. "We should print out a bunch of photos of him and burn them."

"I can Google hexes?" Frankie offered.

"We are not going to *hex* him." I slapped a hand to my forehead and rubbed the headache building behind my eyes. "That's what makes this all so hard," I lamented. It would've been so much easier if Deacon had done something unforgivable. I wish I could blame him for everything falling apart, but there were forces beyond his control at work. It just made everything all the harder to accept. "He didn't do anything wrong. I ended things. He's faultless."

"Apart from sleeping with a Madigan," Finch cut in. "That is completely unforgivable."

"Oh, come on," Frankie bemoaned. "Lynx may be crazy, but she's also crazy hot. And he was a rock star *and* single *and* he and Dove hadn't talked in over a decade at that point. I think you need to cut the guy some slack."

"Never," Finch vowed.

"Rehashing all of this really isn't helping," I grumbled.

"You know, normally my comforting would involve something a lot stronger than tea," Finch added, nodding to the mug in my hand. "Why don't we go to the Salty Dog for drinks tonight? I have the key to go water the plants, and there's some wonderful vintages just sitting lonely on the shelves."

I gave my older sister a weak smile. "That's okay. I just need some space, I think."

The three of them all tsked and clicked their tongues as if they'd heard the lie before it had even come out of my mouth.

Hannah stood up out of the rocking chair and turned toward me. She grabbed me by the hand and pulled me to a stand, wrapping me up in the warmest, fiercest hug. "You've taken care of me so much the last few months," she murmured as tears pricked my eyes. "Let us take care of you now, okay?"

With that, I dropped my head into her shoulder and cried. Frankie and Finch scrambled out of the porch swing, carrying Simon over and wrapping us up in a group hug.

"We've got you, Dovey," Finch soothed, rubbing a hand down my back.

And I knew in that moment that no matter how badly my heart shattered, no matter how many scars this left me with, it wouldn't break me. I'd always have my family to help put me back together. I took a shaking breath and squeezed them back.

"Okay, I think I need to hold Simon again," I said, and they all laughed.

I took my sweet nephew from Frankie and felt all of the tension in my muscles ease. Even in the depths of heartbreak, I was surrounded by so much love.

I sniffed as I looked down at him. "I'm going to be okay." And I wished more than anything that I believed it.

# Chapter Thirty-Eight

Deacon

Ivy Blanc and I sat across from each other in the latest swanky New York hot spot, smiling at each other like we both had sexy secrets.

"I swear to God, if I go to one more restaurant that serves foam as food, I'm going to have a complete breakdown," I muttered, staring down at a bubbling froth on my plate.

"My cheeks hurt," Ivy murmured through her smile. "Men have it so lucky. You can just smirk."

"My cheeks hurt too if it's any consolation," I added.

"Someone's always watching," Ivy complained in a tight singsong. "At least we're not alone under this microscope."

A woman wandered over, and Ivy's bodyguard, Sergei, was about to intervene when I gave him a mild head shake and he allowed her to pass.

"Hi," the middle-aged woman said, giving us a half-wave. "So sorry to interrupt, but . . ."

"It's absolutely fine," Ivy said. "Did you want us to sign that?" She nodded to the woman's hands tightly clutching a pen and a napkin.

"Uh, just Deacon, please." The woman rushed forward and placed the napkin and pen in front of me. "I loved you in *One Man's Call*," she gushed, and Ivy smiled, ignoring the slight.

"Thank you," I replied with a broad, fake—but believable— smile. "What's your name? I'll sign it to you."

"Oh, it's not for me," she said, and I wondered if she was going to try to sell this napkin. "It's for my daughter," she added. "She's had your posters up in her bedroom since she was ten." I wanted to say that none of my movies were appropriate for a ten-year-old but refrained. "You can make it out to Sophie. S-O-P-H-I-E."

The woman leaned over my shoulder, casually putting a hand on me and running it down my back as if I were an object just for her to touch. I was starting to feel like one of those statues where my biceps had been rubbed and fondled so many times they'd turned to shiny gold. I let out a little laugh as I twisted, moving out of her touch and passing the napkin back to her.

"There you go.".

"Thank you," she hedged, and I could tell she was waiting to say more. "Could I have a hug?"

My smile tightened as I said, "Of course."

I'd learned the hard way, celebrities weren't allowed to say no to hugs without being labelled as arrogant or rude. Apparently, my body no longer belonged to me, and I knew that Ivy had it a million times worse. Men were allowed to be "dark and brooding," whereas women were just called divas. Ivy and I were made for public consumption now. It felt like I was taking more and more pieces of myself to give to everyone else until I had nothing left—a stump like the Giving Tree. In a world where everyone wanted to take, Dove had filled me up. She'd been the one that had made me bloom instead of hacking away at me. I was more acutely aware of it now in her absence.

I ached thinking about her again as I leaned over to hug the woman. She lingered, and Sergei took a step in, placing a hand on the woman's back to gently extract her. "Thank you," the woman said, voice shaking with nerves. "You are just so handsome and firm."

I laughed lightly. "You have a good night."

Sergei started ushering the woman away and pulled the curtain between us and the rest of the guests, keeping us still visible to the bay window and the row of flashing camera lights.

"Remember when this used to be fun?" Ivy asked, swirling her straw around her drink, still keeping a mildly amused look on her face.

"It still is sometimes, isn't it?"

"The fact you have to ask says plenty."

"I mean, I'm grateful—"

"Yes, yes," Ivy said, wheeling her hands. "We're all grateful." She picked up her cutlery again and began cutting her steak before neatly setting the utensils down.

"You're not going to eat?" I asked.

"I'm a vegetarian."

"Then why are we at a steakhouse?"

"We're here to be photographed," she explained. "They can just throw this out when we leave."

My mind immediately flashed to Dove and her hatred of food waste. She would've demanded a to-go box at least. The thought of food waste shouldn't choke me up, yet here I was, wanting to cry over the smallest thing. I wished I could go back to a time when I'd thought Dove and I could never be together, when I'd thought she'd never want me. Longing was far better than heartbreak.

"I'm sorry I'm being terrible company," Ivy finally said, looking delicately down at her plate. "I should be over Eliza already. It's been over a month. It's your turn to be the grumpy, sad one."

"At least we can be messes together." I huffed out a laugh. "So, dating life is not going better for you, I take it?"

"Nope," she said, popping her P. "The number of lesbians in the industry is already slim, and the ones who are out even slimmer." She moved her mashed potatoes around with her fork, raking the tines across it like a mediation garden. "Sometimes it feels impossible to find someone who can keep up with this lifestyle."

"Now *that* I understand," I said wistfully.

"Oh please." Ivy rolled her eyes. "This isn't the same. You had a good thing and you let it get away."

I lifted my head, uncaring about my facial expressions. "What?"

"You and Dove were great together. Obviously." She waved me up and down. "Not many people could handle being in this fishbowl," she added. "But I think someone who wrangles snakes for a living just might be one of them. I saw her on the red carpet. She was in full control. You should've hung on to her. She was cool."

"She was *cool*?" I echoed incredulously.

"I mean, yeah. Like, the first media storm is scary, but she would've gotten through it."

"You don't know what you're talking about," I grumbled. "This is too much to ask someone to take on."

"I don't know about that. With a little time and coaching . . ." Ivy shrugged. "She handled me and I'm awful."

"You *really* are," I said, and she grinned. "But Dove told me she doesn't want to be in the spotlight. She said it's all too much for her and her family."

"So she freaked out for a second," Ivy countered. "Who

hasn't? If anything, her family business will thrive with you attached to it. Look at those Australian people, the Mulligans—"

"Madigans," I said tightly. "And I would caution you that making that comparison could lead to being public enemy number one with the Lachlan family."

"Whatever," Ivy continued, unbothered. "What I'm saying is, don't take no for an answer. Go after her."

"I can't," I said. "Not if she asked me not to. Not if this isn't what she really wants."

"What do any of us know about what we really want," she groused, taking another sip of her martini.

"I'm doing what's best for her."

"Ugh. How chivalrous of you to leave her alone to navigate all of this notoriety without the teams or protection that you have," she snarked, and that hit me like a sucker punch. "If you actually wanted to respect her wishes, you would've helped her disentangle her life from yours."

"I have."

"Oh really?" Ivy asked, cocking her head. "Then who is the current director of your new charity, hm?" I glared at her. "That's what I thought. You're too chicken to win her back and too chicken to let her go."

I wanted to drop my face in my hands and rub my eyes in frustration, but I knew that someone would grab a photo and it would all be twisted in some unfavorable way. "You're right. Maybe I should dissolve the trust. Make it so Dove isn't tied to me in any way anymore."

Ivy frowned. "That's not what I was—"

"I need to give her the choice," I carried on. "A real choice, not one sprung on her by the tabloids."

Ivy's eyes narrowed. "Yeah, I don't understand what you're saying now."

"Does it matter?"

"No, I suppose it doesn't," she said, eating the olive from the dregs of her glass. "I'm just miserable and wish at least one of us had a chance at a happily ever after."

"I think both of us do."

"Don't hold your breath. Where am I going to find a hot gay girl who has her own busy work life so she can understand mine, who is okay with being in the limelight, *and* has a job that would let her jet around the world with me when I'm working?"

I grinned, leaning back in my chair. "You know, Ivy, I think I should introduce you to my sister."

# Chapter Thirty-Nine

Dove

"Thank you for all your help with this paperwork," Mom said, tapping the manila folder on the kitchen table once before putting it back in her bag. "It's been a lot lately. I feel bad making you work through lunch though."

"I volunteered, Mom. It's fine."

"I don't think the zoo has ever been so up-to-date on its admin," Mom replied with a chuckle.

I was determined to keep myself busy but was running out of tasks. I'd helped Crane construct a new gibbon viewing platform and now he had locked the tool shed because I kept stealing his construction tasks. Aya had practically banned me from the prep kitchens upon her return from Greece because she'd discovered I'd kept rearranging the stock at night. Wren had even attempted to teach me how to knit but had given up on me after I'd used three skeins of yarn to make a lumpy, unwearable sweater. I tried to support Hannah—folding laundry, washing dishes, changing diapers—but now even she was starting to tell me to go home and that she didn't need more help.

In a job and family where there was *always* more to do, I was beginning to think the tasks of running the place weren't infinite after all. And soon Lark and Logan would be arriving for the summer, and Lark would inevitably be just as anal and hardworking as I was, which meant even less for me to keep busy with.

Mom's hand covered mine, and I knew before she even spoke that she was going to say something that I didn't want to hear. "Honey—"

"I don't want to talk about him, Mom. It just makes everything hurt," I admitted.

"But—"

"Letting him go was the right decision." The saying had become my own personal mantra. I wondered if I said it enough times, if maybe I'd start to believe it. "I couldn't endanger our family."

"The zoo is a very safe place, honey. We'd be okay," Mom said. "Besides, the twins would've loved to patrol with tranquilizer darts at night."

"That's not the only reason." I dropped my chin into my hands. "I couldn't let him sacrifice everything to be with me either."

Mom let out a long-suffering sigh. "You know, I was in law school when I met your father."

"Yeah?" I asked, wondering what that had to do with anything.

"He told me we couldn't be together." Her eyes crinkled as she looked through the window as if looking back to her fondest memories of him. "He knew his life's mission was here

—taking care of our animals, using whatever money we could earn to protect animals in the wild and conserve natural habitats."

"I know?"

"And he said being with him was too big of a sacrifice for me to make. To leave my career. To move to an island no less," Mom said with a chuckle. "But what he called *sacrifices*, I called *choices*. I chose the future I wanted. I wanted the one with him in it and I never regretted it, not even for a second."

"Mom, Deacon abandoning his career is not the same as you leaving law school."

"Maybe not." Mom let out a contemplative hum. "Who knows what my life would've been if I turned a different direction at every fork in the road. I've made a lot of wrong choices in my life, but choosing love wasn't one of them," she said. "Just don't be afraid to choose the future that you want for yourself, okay?"

"Yeah." My shoulders drooped as I let her words sink in. "Thanks, Mom."

"You're welcome." Her eyes softened. "And since you want to work through lunch, I will gift you with the task of completing some more of my paperwork." She squeezed my shoulder. "I've got a new induction form I need to write up."

"A new induction form this time of year? Why?"

The lines around her eyes deepened as she smiled. "Because I've hired a new keeper."

"A new keeper?"

"Yeah," Mom said, as if that weren't massive news that we all should've been talking about for months and months before making any such decision. "I figured now that Hawk and Hannah have their hands full with Simon, we could use an extra staff member. She's a country girl from Wyoming. She'll be perfect to take over hoof stock."

"Hoof stock? Where's Heron going?"

"To birds," Mom informed me.

"And *where* am I going?" I asked, perplexed.

"On to other things," Mom said with a shrug. "I've known since you were a kid. I thought you'd be out the door long before Lark to be honest. And don't get me wrong, I've loved all this extra time I've had with you, but I think it's time for some new adventures in your life. Being here right now doesn't seem to be healing you. If anything, I think it's making it worse." That hurt to hear, hurt because she was right. "I think a fresh start would be good for you, hon."

"Probably," I murmured. "Not that there's any town in the world where I could completely run away from someone as famous as Deacon Harrow."

"Do you want me to call my friends in Borneo?" she asked, taking out her phone. "You could go do some field research for a while? Can't be haunted by Deacon Harrow where there's no electricity."

"Tempting," I admitted with a huff. "But I think I'll manage to survive." Mom's eyes widened for a second as she stared at her phone. "What's up?"

"Uh, nothing," she said cooly, and I narrowed my eyes at her. She was a good liar, but not that good. "Seriously," she added as if sensing my wariness. "Just an invoice that was higher than expected. I'll need to call the fruit supplier again."

"Do you want me to do it?" I offered, hopeful to be put to work again.

"That's alright, sweetie." Mom smiled. "Oh, and I've sorted the last of the LRCT paperwork," she said, clearly not wanting to mention Lucky Role Conservation Trust but needing to.

Two weeks after he'd left, Deacon had closed down the trust. Mom had helped with the documentation for it in my stead because even looking at the charity right now hurt too much. I should've known Deacon would abandon the charity without a new director at the helm. It was too complicated now having my name attached to his. It shouldn't have surprised me but was still disappointing. For a brief flicker of a moment there, I'd thought he'd returned to the guy I'd once known. But maybe his good-heartedness had just been another performance.

"I just need to sign some things and then it's official," she said, sweeping her stray gray hairs off her face. "I have them printed out in my office, if you could just swing by on your way down to return the buckets."

"Yeah, no problem," I agreed, grateful she was giving me something to do other than sit and stew.

She gave me one last hug. "I'm proud of you, honey. You were an amazing director, and I know that you will be just as amazing at whatever you do next."

"Thanks, Mom." I leaned into her hug.

I wandered down the hill, wondering what I would do next. Maybe I'd move to a city for a while. Maybe I'd try to get a job at a big NGO. We had family connections at a few different places. Maybe I could reach out to a few of Mom's old contacts at Singapore Zoo. The thought gave me a little flicker of excitement, a feeling that had been muted in me for weeks but now was revived at the thought of a new challenge.

Mom knew me too well. It was time for something else.

I wandered through the prep kitchens toward Mom's office, and fortunately Aya wasn't there to ward me away from her inventory systems. But the radio was still on, playing an old Lucky Role song, and my heart twinged at the sound of Deacon's voice. I'd never told him how many times I'd listened and relistened to the entirety of his music catalogue. I'd fallen in love with the man behind every song and had wished like a heartsick teenager that one day he'd fall in love with me. But every girl in the entire world daydreamed about the angsty rock star falling for her. I'd gotten to have it for a split second, and it had all fallen apart. If only they knew what loving someone like him came with, maybe they wouldn't want it so much.

"An oldie but a goodie," the radio announcer said. "This comes after Deacon Harrow's shock announcement that he is taking a step back from acting." I froze, turning to the radio. "What do you think he'll get up to next, Paula?"

"Hopefully more music," a feminine voice replied. "Or maybe he wants to get behind the camera and do some directing. Who knows?"

I stared at the radio as the next song played, wishing it would suddenly give me more answers. He had officially announced he was taking a step back from acting? *I can't believe he really did it.* I hoped that meant he'd make more music. He was probably off in a studio somewhere right now recording new songs.

I sighed, the tension in my chest easing a little. I was glad he'd taken that step for himself. Just because he had great success at something that wasn't his passion, didn't mean he had to keep pursuing it. I hoped he was proud of himself, too, for moving back to the music. That had been his first love.

I jogged up the steps to Mom's office, feeling the bittersweetness of it all lingering in the air. I mindlessly opened the door and practically fell forward at what I saw. There, sat in Mom's desk chair, was Deacon motherfucking Harrow.

He leaned back in the chair and smirked at me, smug at my surprise. "Hello, Rogue."

# Chapter Forty

Deacon

I kept my hands tightly clasped beneath the desk to stop them from shaking. It took everything within me not to get up and go to her.

"Deacon," she said breathlessly. "Wh-what are you doing here?"

*Winning you back*, I wanted desperately to say, but I knew she would just launch into all the reasons she couldn't be with me again. It was time I gave her a choice. A real one.

"I had some paperwork for you to sign." I pushed a stack of papers across the table.

"And you came all the way out here to have me sign it?"

I shrugged. "I was flying up to Boston." It *technically* wasn't a lie. "Figured I'd make a detour."

"Oh." Her shoulders slumped in clear disappointment.

"Right," she said, wandering over and sitting across from me. "You're dissolving the trust."

"I am." I balled my fists tighter. "I'm transferring the funds to other organizations. More established ones and a new one."

Her brows furrowed. "A new one?"

"That is the other reason I came in person," I said, nodding to the sheets of paper in front of her. The moment she read it, Dove let out a half gasp, half sob. I watched as her eyes scanned over and over the title of the document: The Simon Lachlan Conservation Fund.

"What is this?" she asked, eyes welling with tears.

"What it always should have been. Your dad worked so hard to protect wildlife. It should be in his name. The fund will be operated in conjunction with Prickle Island Zoo." Dove wiped tears from her eyes. "It means you can still start that breeding program. It means you can fund a bunch of other breeding programs at other organizations too. It means the zoo will be protected for years to come."

*It means you can do your dream job without it being attached to me.*

She wiped her sleeve under her eyes. "Thank you."

"It's what I should've done from the beginning," I admitted. "I should've never made it about me. I surrounded myself with people who only wanted me to cover my own ass, who didn't care if I was ever a good person, not like the way you made me a good person. And your father was a good person too," I said, voice growing thick. "I wanted your family to have this."

"It means a lot." Her bottom lip trembled as she nodded.

"And there's another thing I wanted to tell you."

"Yeah?"

"All the proceeds from the film we shot here will be donated to the Simon Lachlan Conservation Fund."

"I . . . Wow." She could barely get the words out as her eyes welled more. "You have no idea how much this means to us."

"I was thinking, maybe . . . ," I hedged. "Maybe you'd want to be my date to the premiere?"

"Deacon," she said quickly, shaking her head. "I—we—"

"It's the last film premiere for a long time, I think," I continued. "I got a call from Faith. I'll be working on a new album with her. We're going on tour next year. It's already planned. Her band and Lucky Role doing all our old hits, and we'll perform the new album together too."

"You're really doing it," she praised, smiling. Smiling for me, happy for me, even through tears, and it made my heart hurt.

"Thanks to you," I said.

She waved that away. "I just made a call."

"Well, now you are the head of a new conservation fund. Congratulations, director." I rose to a stand. "It's not attached to me in any way, and you can run it without being reminded of me if that's what you want."

"Everything reminds me of you," she confessed, and I felt it like a sucker punch. "The ocean, the animals, Eddie the toucan and Garret the llama. My music, my shows, my hand."

She cried harder, and I couldn't contain myself. I moved around to her chair and lifted her hand and kissed her scar, just like I had that day on the beach. I dropped to my knees in front of her, holding her hand to my lips, frozen in this moment where I wasn't sure I could bear to ever let her go again.

"I came here to say goodbye," I said, choking on my words. "I came here to give you a clean break from me." My pleading eyes met hers. "But I can't just let you go. There's just no world where you and I weren't meant to be together." Dove opened her mouth to speak, but I pushed on. "I can protect your family. I can protect you. I *want* to disappear into my music and get out of the headlines and I want you to come with me."

"Deacon . . ." She shook her head as I pulled my necklace out from under the neckline of my shirt and pulled the coin from the magnetic clasp. Dove looked at me through bleary eyes. "What are you doing?"

"Heads, you come with me," I offered, brandishing the coin.

"What?"

"If it lands on heads, you come on tour with me," I clarified. "You can work on the road. We can travel the world. You can be mine. Agreed?"

"You want to let a coin flip decide if we end up together?" she asked with a watery laugh.

I wiped her tear with my knuckle. "Agreed?"

She considered me for a long time before she finally said, "Fuck it. Heads and I come with you."

I grinned and tossed the coin up with my thumb. Dove caught it in midair before it could even reach the apex of its flight. She held it tight in her palm as she met my gaze.

"It was heads," she said, grabbing me by the back of the neck and pulling me into a burning kiss.

# Chapter Forty-One

A few years later . . .

Dove

Deacon's hand gently guided me down the red carpet as the lights of a million flashbulbs strobed in my eyes. It didn't feel as jarring anymore. Being on tour with him had prepared me for this gauntlet—the last one for a long time. As much fun as the last few years had been, I was ready to stay in one location for more than a day, and Deacon was too. One last hurrah and then we'd get a much-needed rest before the next adventure. Wanderlust sated for the time being, Deacon had rented out the Sea Pearl on Prickle Island for the next six months, and I couldn't wait to have a quiet Christmas at home with him.

"Deacon! Deacon!" a journalist shouted, and Deacon and me split in two, him going to answer one reporter while I replied to another.

"Dove, how does it feel to be walking the red carpet on the arm of Deacon Harrow?" the young reporter asked me.

"Wonderful, as always," I answered honestly.

I was used to being treated like being Deacon's girlfriend was an honor I didn't deserve, like I'd somehow struck gold and that meant every "average" girl now had a chance with him. It was a narrative they liked to spin, but exposure to it over time had desensitized me to it. I leveraged it into attention for our charity and more visitors to the zoo with practiced ease. As Deacon shifted back to music and as our relationship continued to thrive, people seemed to get over the shock of heartthrob Deacon Harrow being a happily taken man.

"Now, this is reported to be Deacon's last film project for some time," the tight-smiled journalist said. "What does this movie mean to you?"

"Well, as you know, all the proceeds for the film are going to the Simon Lachlan Conservation Fund," I replied, bringing the conversation back to my message at hand. "And as the charity director, I know that it will mean a lot to all of the future animals we'll be able to help. We've just started a very successful reintroduction program for the Almadran skinks, and this money will go a long way to helping them." I leaned into the microphone and added, "And Deacon isn't disappearing from the limelight, just shifting his focus back onto his music."

"Did you know the soundtrack for this film is trending on Spotify?"

"It's a collaboration between Rusty Sky Reverie and Lucky Role," I explained, beaming and winking into the camera lens behind her. "You'll love it. Go listen."

"You and Deacon have been together for a while now," the

journalist prodded, and I already knew exactly what she was going to ask. "When are we going to hear those wedding bells?"

I let out a laugh as Deacon came and took my arm, rescuing me from the awkward question.

The reporter seized her opportunity. "Deacon, why no ring? Getting cold feet?"

It was an incredibly rude thing to ask, and I could tell by the pinch in his face that he wanted to give an honest reply, but instead he just smiled. "Oh, believe me, I have plans, and I absolutely won't be sharing them." My stomach fluttered as he slid his gaze to me. "I've been in love with the same girl since I was ten years old, and I want to spend the rest of my life with her."

The journalist swooned, and my smile widened as he guided me down the red carpet and into the theater.

Deacon leaned down and pressed his lips to my ear, whispering, "I can't wait to peel this dress off when we get home."

"So that you can help me into my sweatpants and rub my feet while we watch Dropout?" I asked with a grin.

He winked at me. "I've already requested the popcorn."

"You're not coming to the party at Teak?" Faith pouted as she escorted Ivy across the carpet to us. "The after-party is going to be wild."

"I've had enough wild to last a lifetime," I quipped.

"Why would I want to go to an after-party when I could be on the couch with this gorgeous creature?" Deacon added, pulling me into him.

"Ugh, you two are such homebodies," his little sister said with a laugh. "No fun."

"I'm sure Ivy will represent the film well enough for the both of us," Deacon assured.

"Damn straight I will," Ivy replied as she gave one more wave to the wall of cameras.

She looked back at Faith and beamed at her. She looped

her arm with Faith's, leaning into her side. The pair looked at each other with so much gushy affection, I swore cartoon love hearts were lifting all around them.

"We're not that bad, are we?" I whispered to Deacon.

"Oh please, you two are a million times worse," Faith replied with a guffaw. "You two are practically telepathic. You start laughing at each other's jokes before you've even said them aloud. Seriously. It's disgustingly adorable."

As Ivy leaned over and kissed Faith, a hundred camera bulbs flashed and cameras clicked, the shutters sounding like a swarm of chittering insects.

"I smudged your lipstick," Faith said, swiping her thumb across Ivy's cheek. The cameras all chorused again as the two of them laughed.

"I don't care," Ivy replied with a shrug, and Deacon and I exchanged glances.

*Yep, the two of them have it bad for each other*, I thought. I'd been seriously skeptical about Deacon matchmaking these two together, his sister and his costar, but they fit surprisingly well—both snarky, bold, brash, talented, and beautiful. They actually made a lot of sense. I'd even grown some fondness for Ivy while she'd been on tour with us—something I'd never thought would be possible three years ago.

On the way over the threshold, Deacon stopped to give Faith a hug. This was the first time she'd walked the red carpet with Ivy on her arm, the two making their relationship "red carpet official." And I knew what it meant to Ivy to have someone proudly stand in the spotlight with her, unafraid to love her even with a thousand eyes upon them.

"Photo of the four of you next to the poster," Deacon's new publicist, Ashley, called, corralling us like a group of school children to the poster outside the theater.

We posed, Deacon and I on one side, Ivy and Faith on the other.

"Now a funny one!" Ashley yelled, and we all made silly faces, pointing at the movie poster of Ivy and Deacon looking skeptically at each other from across a bamboo hedge, the movie title written in giant letters across their midsections: *Crocodile Tears.*

# Chapter Forty-Two

Deacon

Dove walked across the pebbly front garden with a towel around her shoulders, her ocean-wet hair curling at the ends. The water was still warm even as the leaves began to turn and the breeze carried an autumnal chill. Before we'd even gotten to the house, Dove had stripped off her sundress and run into the sea as if it were welcoming her home.

"I see now why you packed a towel in your carry-on," I said with a shake of my head as I rose from where I perched on the boardwalk.

She wandered up the rocky beach, her hips swaying in a distracting way that had my eyes glued to them. Her sundress clung to her wet skin, accentuating her curves.

"Look what I found on the beach," she said, holding up a silver coin in a currency I couldn't identify.

She closed the distance, offering out her palm for me to inspect the coin. "You are honestly a magpie for shiny treasure."

"I think it's an arcade token," she replied, turning it over and studying the markings. "I think there used to be an arcade on the boardwalk in the seventies, but it couldn't be that old. It's in too good condition."

"Another coin to add to the jar."

She grinned at me mischievously. "It's in my suitcase."

"Of course it is." I let out a surprised laugh. "Leave it to you to pack our coin jar for our vacation."

Within the old mason jar were dozens of coins that we'd found on our travels—the beaches of Malta, the hotel in Rio de Janeiro, the jungles of Indonesia. Each coin held a million memories—my European tour with Rusty Sky Reverie, the premiere of *Crocodile Tears*, and the beach cleanup during the first round of reintroductions of skinks to the Almadran Isles.

I mindlessly placed a comforting hand to the coin hanging against my chest, and Dove lifted her hand and covered mine with a smile. I sighed, spinning her back to my front and wrapping my arms around her as we stared at the Sea Pearl beach house. I dropped a kiss to her wet hair.

"Our home away from home." Dove sighed, looking at the house with the periwinkle painted door, the rocky garden, driftwood path, and giant hydrangea bushes growing from the white picket fence.

We rented the beach house whenever we came to visit. And now, after finishing the last leg of the tour, we were both looking forward to settling down in one spot for a while. There were still many corners of the world yet to explore, but we'd take our time. I was ready for my things to live in a dresser drawer for a while.

"I was thinking . . . ," I hedged. "This might be a good place to put down some roots when we're not traveling. Maybe nine months out of the year, this could be the place we call home?"

"I like that idea." Dove pursed her lips. "But you'd have to ask the owners."

I pulled the house key out of my pocket, a little red bow tied on the key chain. "We're the owners now."

Dove's mouth fell open as she looked between the key and the door. "This is *ours*?"

I brushed a kiss to her cheek. "Everywhere you are is home. The apartment in New York, the hotels, the tour bus . . . but I think here will be the best one of all. I love all of our travels, but after living on the road for the past few years, I think it's time for a long break."

She smiled. "Me too."

"Good," I said, giving her another quick kiss. "Because there's one more thing I think we need to make this house officially a home."

"Does that have something to do with why Heron is hiding in the bushes?" she asked, nodding to a suspiciously shaking hydrangea bush.

"You spotted that, huh?"

"I grew up with six siblings," Dove teased. "You've got to be sneakier than that, Harrow."

"Heron!" I called with a laugh. "You can come out now."

"What are they holding?" Dove spun around to see Heron standing from behind the hydrangeas and walking over with a tiny orange kitten. "Oh my god." Dove's voice jumped up an octave as she cooed at the kitten. She took it from Heron and held it to her chest. "How did you manage to keep this a secret?"

"Only I was looped in," Heron said. "None of our other siblings can be trusted."

"Very true," Dove agreed with a laugh. "Okay, fine, I redact my sneaky comment." She kissed the top of the kitten's head. "This is the best kind of sneakiness."

"Now that we're going to be in one place for a while, I

thought it was time," I said. "Think we can manage the responsibility?" Dove shot me a look, and I barked out a laugh. "Do you think being a zookeeper your entire life has prepared you for this little hellion?"

She weighed her head side to side in mock consideration. "I think we can manage."

"So . . ." I took another step into her side and kissed her temple. "What are you going to name him?"

"Rook Valestrider," she answered immediately as the kitten nibbled her finger. "A very strong name for a very fiery boy."

"Rook Valestrider-Hellfire," I insisted. "He needs both of his parents' last names."

"You two are seriously adorkable," Heron said, smiling as they shook their head. "Love the new digs by the way. Are you sure it's big enough for you two fancy pants?"

"Says someone who lives on a boat," Dove quipped.

"Hey, the two of us like boat living," they replied. "Especially so we can sail away from Crane whenever he gets too annoying." Dove laughed and gave Heron another hug before kissing Rook on the head again, as if she couldn't resist. "I'll leave you to it," Heron said. "My better half is cooking dinner."

I gave them a wink. "Thank you for your help."

They looked over their shoulder as they waved. "Happy to be your co-conspirator any time."

As they wandered off, Dove held Rook out and inspected him. "Valestrider-Hellfire might be a bit of a mouthful," she said. "Maybe I should just take the Valestrider name so we can all be Valestriders together."

My stomach flipped. "Are you... Do you mean our real last names too?"

She shrugged. "I'm saying I'm open to it."

I wrapped my arms around her and laughed. "This can't be our proposal story," I insisted. "I had a whole romantic thing in Venice planned for next year."

"Buying us a house and a kitten is pretty damn romantic," she countered. "I don't think Venice can beat this."

"But I wanted it to be perfect and—"

Dove shifted Rook into one arm and reached under my shirt with her free hand to grab the coin from my necklace. "We'll let the coin decide."

"You're going to let a coin decide whether or not I propose to you?" I asked incredulously.

"It's how we settle all our big life decisions, isn't it?" she retorted with a cheeky grin. "Heads you propose now, tails you do it in Venice. Agreed?"

I bit the corner of my lip as I considered her, trying to contain my smile. "Agreed."

She tossed the coin in the air and I caught it, dropping to one knee with it still clenched in my fist. "It was heads."

# Chapter Forty-Three

One year later . . .

Dove

A knock sounded on the door, followed by Deacon's voice. "Dove?"

"Yeah?"

"Don't open up yet," he said quickly. "I need you to hide in the corner so I can use the bathroom."

I folded my arms and arched a brow at the closed door. "You need me to hide in the corner so you can go pee?"

"I don't want to see you in your wedding dress before the ceremony. It's bad luck," he voiced through the door.

"It's just a plain, white sundress. You've seen me wear it

before," I chastised. I'd dolled up the outfit a little with jewelry and heels. Hannah had done my makeup and braided my hair off my face with delicate purple flowers, but still, at its heart, the dress was just a simple beach dress and I kind of loved that. "You don't get to see the fancy dress until we're in Lake Como," I added, my stomach flipping at the thought of donning a six-figure custom wedding gown.

Deacon and I had decided to have two weddings—a small, informal one in the backyard of the Sea Pearl and a massive, star-studded wedding in Lake Como. The Lake Como wedding had been my idea after *People* magazine had offered us $2 million for the exclusive, all of the proceeds of which would go to the Simon Lachlan Conservation Fund. We'd also asked all our guests to make donations in lieu of gifts, and the funds raised would support over a decade of future conservation efforts.

The spotlight didn't scare me the way it used to. Now we had over a dozen critically endangered breeding programs in the works and had successfully reintroduced five species that were extinct in the wild. If people were going to throw money at us for seeing my fiancé's ridiculously handsome face, then we'd take it and turn it into something amazing. And we would do so much more together, Deacon and I.

I was pulled from my conservation daydreams when I realized Deacon was still waiting for me to hide so he could use the toilet. "Why don't you use the bathroom downstairs?"

"Because between us, we have *four* nieces and nephews who are potty training and they seem to be in a constant rotating line for the bathroom," he replied.

I chuckled. "You can come in. I don't mind you seeing me in this dress. It's not the real dress."

"It *is* the real dress," Deacon countered, still not opening the door. "This is the *real* wedding."

"I know it is," I replied. "Just come in before you pee yourself."

The door opened and Deacon walked in with a hand over his eyes. His other one waved wildly in front of him, feeling his way around our bed toward the bathroom.

"You can't be serious." My shoulders shook with laughter. "And you call me stubborn."

Deacon hit his toe on the bedframe and, with a loud expletive, went tumbling headfirst into the carpet. Luckily, he had quick reflexes, and his hands shot out to catch him before he ended up with a carpet-burned face in all our wedding photos. He and I both exploded into laugher as I rushed over to him. He finally opened his eyes to look up at me, his hand lifting to cover his heart. "Hello, future wife."

"Hello, future husband," I replied as he adjusted the purple flowers woven into my hair.

"You look"—he shook his head, his eyes crinkling as he smiled—"so heartbreakingly beautiful."

"You don't look too bad yourself," I replied with a wink as I helped him to stand.

My eyes dropped to a patch of orange fur across the bottom of his jacket. "We're going to need a lint roller." I laughed, picking clumps of cat hair off him. "I thought we agreed no Rook cuddles in our wedding outfits?" I wasn't about to tell him I'd already broken that agreement twice today.

"He was purring so loudly. It's like he knew today was special. I couldn't say no to that little face!" Deacon exclaimed, like saying no to our fur baby was an impossible feat .... To be fair, Rook Valestrider did have the cutest cat face of any cat ever to exist in the history of the world, and I was definitely not in the least bit biased about it.

Despite all of the things that Cody had once told him, Deacon's fans actually loved that he was an absolute goofball of a cat dad. If anything, his fandom had grown since announcing our relationship. There were quite a few fan edits of him singing his new love songs to me in the VIP section and even more compilations of him talking about Rook and me in interviews. Apparently, Hollywood heartthrobs didn't have to be heartbreakers anymore. *Thank you, Gen Z.*

Deacon reached for his phone and started flicking through his photos. "Simon is carrying Rook around inside his shirt and Rook's making biscuits on him. It's so cute—"

"Sorry, Dove," Lark called, busting in through the door with her daughter, Lila, and a sheepish Finch in tow. The three of them stopped short when they saw us. "Oh."

"Are you two having a pre-wedding quickie? Frankie and I did the same thing—"

"Finch!" Lark snapped, covering Lila's ears.

"She's not even three. She doesn't know what we're saying," Finch said, waving Lark away.

"We were not having a quickie." I rolled my eyes and nudged Deacon toward the bathroom door. "Go pee before there's a line."

"Right," Deacon said, as if suddenly remembering he was busting, and dashed the rest of the way to the door.

I turned to my sisters. "*Why* are the three of you wet?"

Lark and Lila's floral summer dresses were caked in sand, the wet fabric clinging to their bodies. Meanwhile, Finch's gray linen button-down and slacks were similarly drenched.

"Lila wanted to go swimming," Finch said with a shrug, as if that were an excuse.

"And?" Lark added, folding her arms tightly across her chest.

Finch rolled her eyes. "And when Lars came to scold us, I pushed her in too."

I guffawed. "Hence the patent Lark Lachlan death stare."

Lark forced a tight smile at Finch. "I can't wait to repay the favor when Frankie pops."

I let out a low whistle. "You're in for it then, Finch."

Finch waved the comment away. "You'll be back in New Zealand by then."

Lark walked over and wrapped her arm around my shoulder. "I have accomplices everywhere."

"It's true," I replied with a laugh. "Do you want to borrow a dress?"

"Please," Lark said with relief. "Luckily, we packed about twenty changes of clothes for Lila so she's sorted. I just need to hose her down in your shower, if that's okay?"

"Of course." I waved to the bathroom.

We heard Hannah's voice calling up the stairs, "The guests are all getting seated in the backyard and the band's ready! You ready to get married or what?"

"One minute!" I called down.

Deacon emerged from the bathroom. "I'll go slow them down so the impromptu swimmers can change." He re-buttoned his blazer, getting one step to the door before making a quick U-turn and storming toward me. He grabbed me by the back of the neck and kissed me with a fervency that had heat flooding my veins. "I can't wait to marry you," he murmured across my lips before quickly sweeping out the door.

"Damn," Finch said, gaping at the open doorway. "I can see why he's a three-time Sexiest Man Alive winner."

"Keep it in your pants," Lark snarked.

"Keep it in your pants," Lila echoed, and Lark cringed, pointing at Finch. "I'm going to tell Logan that *you* taught her that."

"Okay, go shower quickly." I shooed Lark into the bathroom. "I'm kind of eager to marry the love of my life today."

"About time," Finch said with a laugh as Lark and Lila disappeared into the bathroom. Finch ambled over to the bed.

"Don't!" I warned before she sat her sandy, wet ass on my bed.

"Right, sorry. I actually have something for you," she said, fishing in her trouser pocket. "I found it in the back of our old dresser at Mom's house and I thought you might want it."

She fished out a folded photograph with thumb tack holes in the top corners and passed it to me. I opened it to reveal a photo of twelve-year-old Deacon and me sitting on an emergency room gurney, my hand wrapped in gauze. Dad sat with his arms wrapped around both of us, all three of us smiling and giving thumbs-ups to the camera.

Tears instantly welled in my eyes. "He made the nurse take the photo," I said, getting choked up. "He said I'd want to remember it one day."

"That sounds like him. He would've loved today," Finch murmured, her voice getting thick too. "He'd be so proud of you, for the person you've become, and since he's not here to say it, I'm saying it for him."

"Dammit, now I'm crying." I swept a finger under my eyes.

I reached out to hug her and Finch stepped back. "You don't want to ruin your wedding dress."

"Just hug me already," I demanded, and she closed the distance, wrapping me up in a tight hug. Lark emerged from the bathroom, and soon she and Lila were wrapped around us too.

"Your dress," Lark said with a laugh.

"It's perfect," I whispered, finally releasing them. I tucked the photograph into the pocket of my sundress and looked at my sisters. "Think he can manage being part of the Lachlan family?"

"He's been a part of the family for a long, long time," Lark said with a shrug. "Now you're just making it official."

"That doesn't mean we won't give him hell though," Finch added, and the three of us laughed.

I grinned. "I'd expect nothing less."

I led the way, dress wet and sandy and perfect as we navigated the narrow steps of the seaside house and out toward the backyard. Taking a deep breath of salty sea air, I put my hand in my pocket, closing my fingers around the photograph. I stepped out into the sunlight as Rusty Sky Reverie played me down the makeshift driftwood aisle. Our families gathered, only enough room to stand. As I took the first step, my eyes found Deacon's and hooked. He wore the biggest smile, his eyes misting with tears as he lifted his hand and placed it on the coin at the center of his chest.

# SIGN UP

# FOR ZOO NEWS

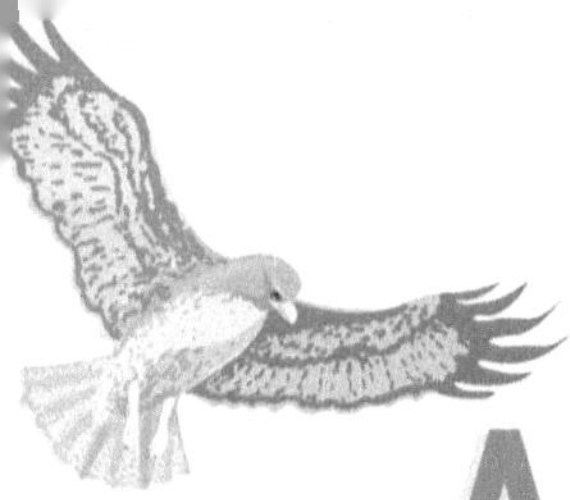

# ALSO BY

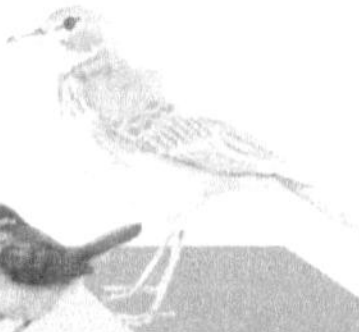

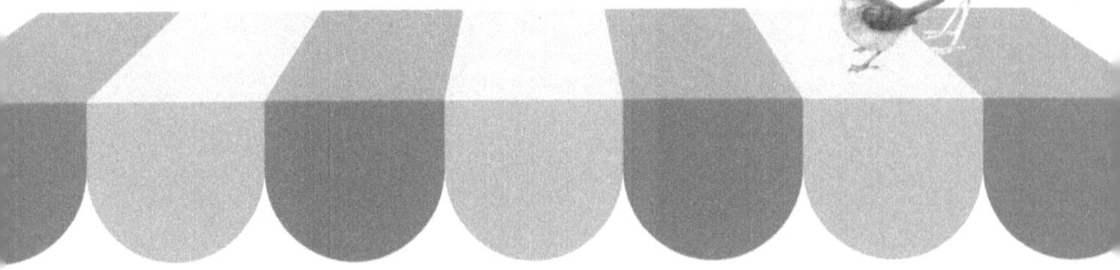

## Ali K. Mulford Books:

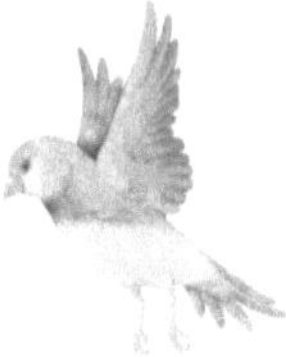

### The Prickle Island Zoo Series:

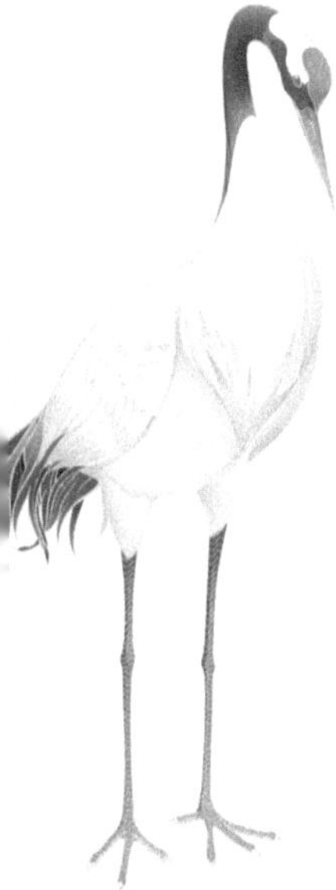

She's a Keeper

Easy Tiger

Party Animal

### Maple Hollow Series:

Pumpkin Spice & Poltergeist

## A.K. Mulford Series:

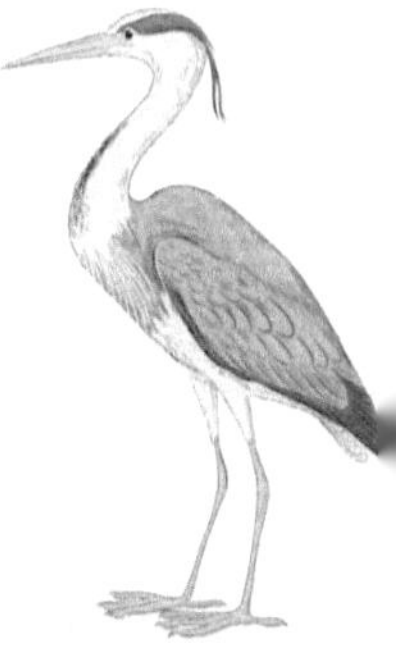

The Five Crowns of Okrith

The Okrith Novellas

The Golden Court Trilogy

Acknowledgments

Thank you to all of my amazing readers for coming on this new adventure with me. I am so humbled by your support and all the ways you champion my books out in the world!

Thank you so much to all of my Patrons! I love writing new stories, commissioning spicy art, and getting to connect with you on Patreon! A very special thank you to Cinya, A, Phoebe, Bethany, Aussie, Morgan, JC, Samantha, Bri, Kat, Stacy, Lauren, Latham, Jaime, Kelly, Marissa, Ciara, Linda, and Katie! Thank you for being on this bookish adventure with me!

Thank you to Norma from Norma's Nook Editing

Thank you to Enni from Yummy Book Covers for designing the gorgeous covers for this series

Thank you to Holly Dunn for designing the Zoo Map

Ali K. Mulford (also known by their bestselling fantasy pen name A.K. Mulford) is a rom-com author and former wildlife biologist who swapped rehabilitating monkeys for writing novels. A US and NZ citizen, Mulford now lives in Australia rearing two human primates, writing lovable characters, and making ridiculous TikToks (@akmulfordauthor).

**www.akmulford.com**